30 YEARS OF ADVENTURE:
A CELEBRATION OF DUNGEONS & DRAGONS

©2004 Wizards of the Coast, Inc.

Cover design by Matt Adelsperger
Interior design by Matt Adelsperger & Brian Fraley
Original Hardcover First Printing: October 2004
This Edition First Printing: February 2006
Library of Congress Catalog Card Number: 2005928131

9 8 7 6 5 4 3 2 1

ISBN-10: 0-7869-4078-6
ISBN-13: 978-0-7869-4078-3
620-96555740-001 EN

U.S., CANADA,
ASIA, PACIFIC, & LATIN AMERICA
Wizards of the Coast, Inc.
P.O. Box 707
Renton, WA 98057-0707
+1-800-324-6496

EUROPEAN HEADQUARTERS
Hasbro UK Ltd
Caswell Way
Newport, Gwent NP9 0YH
GREAT BRITAIN
Save this address for your records.

Visit our web site at www.wizards.com

30 Years of Adventure

A Celebration of Dungeons & Dragons

FOREWORD

BY VIN DIESEL

I was eleven when my twin brother returned home from a weekend sleepover at a friend's house with tales of a new mysterious game. My brother and I spent our early years delving into the mythological worlds of writers like J.R.R. Tolkien and C.S. Lewis. Therefore, his pitch was short and simple, "a game that allows you to be anyone you want to be, from an Elf to a Ogre or a Warrior to a Wizard . . . It's called DUNGEONS & DRAGONS!"

That Christmas, we took the train from our New York City apartment to our Grandmother's house in Hollis, Queens, where Christmas took on magical proportions. Like two Halflings standing before a treasure trove, searching for a gift of the right size and shape, we gently shook each present, hoping to hear the rattle of dice inside. At last we found the one that looked and sounded like the treasure we sought. And there it was, our first D&D set, the first in a long line of manuals, tomes, and handbooks that would eventually grow into a vast wealth of sacred knowledge. That Christmas present, given in love from my Grandmother, unknowing of its power and impact, would prove to be a portal into a never-ending world of imagination.

Ironically, my first campaign was DM'd by a childhood friend's mother, an artist, who collected comic books and lived with one foot in the world of fantasy. She hosted a Sunday evening D&D campaign for the kids that lived in the building. A group ranging in age from 10 to 15 would wait with bated breath for these infamous and highly anticipated campaigns. There we sat at her long, aged, dining table, eyes wide, palms sweating, our hearts pounding at the infinite possibilities of the unknown. The inexorable threat of a ravenous Orc War Party determined to enslave us. The slow whisper of mischievous footsteps creeping down the long dark corridor. We trembled at the sound of sulphured breath hissing from the chamber below. We became completely immersed in this new world of wonder.

During that first campaign, my character was killed when he sprang a poison arrow trap. Unfortunately, there were no characters of high enough level to cast slow poison or create an elixir. However, the DM showed leniency and allowed me to control an NPC magic user named Bale for the rest of the dungeon.

It wasn't long before we set out to play on our own, without adult supervision, in our tiny rooms, in stairwells or wherever we could find a quiet corner. This continued for a time until we piqued the interest of one kid's older brother. His room was the perfect gaming environment, not just because of the drawings of dragons, heroes and maps that covered his walls, but because we could play there indefinitely . . . or at least until we had given our best shot at gaining another level. We would set out from our apartments in the early evening, ferrying our book collections on our splintered skateboards. Sometimes we wouldn't return home from this journey into our imagination until "the nine to fivers" reclaimed the city

Initially my parents were concerned about the late hours that my brother and I were keeping, but they quickly realized that playing D&D at a neighbor's apartment was a safer alternative to running the city streets. Once they grasped the game's importance to me, it became the leverage they used to get me to finish my homework, take out the garbage, do my laundry, etc.

We graduated from the simple tunnels and standard treasures that enticed the novice. Our campaigns grew increasingly more political and military. In short, we went from creating dungeons to creating worlds where an advanced level of strategy was demanded. It was not enough to seek treasure in some rot-grub-infested dungeon, only to be rewarded with a '+I' long sword. We were now engaging in epic battles at sea and on land as we aspired to become great rulers.

There was an adjustment period of about an hour to get into the mood, the flow of the game and transition into the world. We didn't just roll dice and erase hit points, our games were animated, our voices changed as we took on our characters' personae. We jumped out of our seats at every opportunity to specifically act out our actions. Interruptions from the outside world were forbidden! Even the occasional loose conversation was met by a falling rock, a random monster encounter, or a plotting

NPC. Every DM had at one point or another, invoked the golden rule . . . "Every word spoken is in the dungeon."

Initially what attracted all of us to the game was the possibility of being something or someone different. When creating a character no alignment, class or race was too far fetched. We ranged from Chaotic Good to Lawful Evil. However, over the years we began to realize that certain characters ended up representing landmarks in our journey. A perfect example is when we were introduced to the Drow: our reverence for the Drow quickly took on mythic proportions.

The most important milestone, for me, was the birth of Melkor Tar Morloth. He was the Half-Drow that would become the most interesting and longest lasting of all my characters. He personified the feeling of being out of place and of enduring prejudice. Melkor leaned towards Neutrality with Chaotic tendencies. He was a loner who would travel many weeks without being seen or speaking a word. Because of Melkor's anti-social demeanor I often played him alone. The DM would have to play multiple parties on parallel adventures and was forced to handle the difficulties of timelines and possible player versus player encounters. Many tried to scry or hunt him down but Melkor, above all else, was a survivor . . . Some say he still lives to this day roaming the Northern Realms.

We were all drawn to the game because it allowed us to become these characters, vastly different in appearance and in actions, but what kept us hooked was the search for the character that represented our higher self. Playing D&D was a training ground for our identities. I imaginations and an opportunity to explore our own identities. I started acting when I was seven, and this game was a constant exercise in developing voices and characters. I believe now, but probably did not realize then, that I was attracted to the artistic outlet the game provided. My D&D journey paralleled my search for identity in those growing years.

INTRODUCTION

BY PETER ARCHER

The roots of DUNGEONS & DRAGONS lie in the small town of Lake Geneva, Wisconsin. There, in the mid-1960s, as a complacent America began to stir under the impact of the Civil Rights movement and the gradually escalating Vietnam War, a small group of wargamers led by Gary Gygax gathered to form the International Federation of Wargamers to promote the publishing of new wargames.

Wargames were played out on tabletops with plastic or metal figures, a tradition stretching back to the nineteenth century and beyond. Gygax and Jeff Perren developed a new set of rules for miniatures wargaming called CHAINMAIL. By 1971, Gygax had added supplemental rules to the game that allowed for the presence of elves, dwarves, and other fantastic creatures and races. It was a natural development at the onset of a decade that saw an explosion in the popularity of the fiction of an obscure British linguist and scholar named J.R.R. Tolkien. Across the United States, young people entered the enchanted world of *The Hobbit* and The Lord of the Rings to encounter strange and fearsome races such as orcs and goblins, dragons and balrogs.

In the fall of 1972, Dave Arneson, a Minnesota gamer, showed up in Lake Geneva with a new kind of game he was anxious to show to Gygax. Traditional wargames were played on the table or on carefully constructed miniature landscapes across which armies could be maneuvered. In Arneson's game, however, the players made up "characters," giving them features such as Strength and Wisdom. The make-believe characters existed not as figurines but as constructions in the players' heads. A storyteller unrolled a narrative in which the players were characters, free to choose their own course of action.

Another novel concept in Arneson's game was that each player had only one character, an idea that grew from the notion previously expressed in CHAINMAIL that some miniature units in this wargame would be designated as "heroes." Traditional wargames sometimes had "commander" units, but even they didn't have the mythic importance of Chainmail heroes.

Finally, in a remarkable feat of innovation, this game was played not competitively, with players going head to head against one another, but cooperatively. Players joined together to defeat foes, evade dangers, and win rewards. It was a change in play style that had immensely powerful implications. For traditional gamers, winning was everything. For players of Arneson's game, story was the centerpiece of the game, and what was essential was great storytelling.

Arneson sent the adventurers through the corridors of Castle Blackmoor. At each turn they were confronted with choices: Ahead or back? Down this corridor or through this door? Fight the monster or run? Arneson, himself a wargamer, had developed the game so that adventurers could sneak through the sewer system into a castle. The rules were scrawled on random sheets of paper stuffed into a bursting loose-leaf notebook.

Gygax and others who played the game were excited by it. It was a completely different style of gaming, combining the best of miniatures with the players' imaginations. Gygax and Arneson collaborated on a set of rules for what they called The Fantasy Game. However, when Gygax attempted to peddle The Fantasy Game to publishers, he found no takers.

By 1974, despairing of finding a publisher, Gygax formed a company in collaboration with two others, Don Kaye and Brian Blume. They wanted to publish, among other things, The Fantasy Game, now renamed DUNGEONS & DRAGONS. The company was named Tactical Studies Rules. It lasted a brief two years and was dissolved following the untimely death of Kaye. Gygax and Blume then formed a company, TSR Hobbies, which began publishing games, including two supplements to D&D: BLACKMOOR and GREYHAWK. BLACKMOOR was, of course, the original setting for Arneson's game, while GREYHAWK had been devised by Gygax. Other designers and artists joined the fledgling company, which,

in 1976, replaced its magazine *Strategic Review* with *The Dragon* (later, *DRAGON*) to bring news of D&D to its growing legion of fans.

In 1968, wargamers in Lake Geneva had begun an annual gathering, called Gen Con. The con rapidly grew in size and vigor. In 1976, in the con's eighth year of existence, for the first time TSR became the official host of Gen Con.

In 1977, the rules for D&D were rewritten for ease of play, and TSR published the first D&D Basic Set. Sales of the Basic Set were so good that there weren't enough dice to go around. Many customers received numbered counters or "chits" instead of the new-fangled polyhedral dice. That year also saw the first Monster Manual as well as new lists of treasure.

By this time, the game had become a phenomenon. Sales rose rapidly as across the country young people eagerly embraced a game that challenged their minds and stimulated the imagination. At the same time, the computer industry saw the faint stirrings of what would become the multi-billion-dollar computer fantasy gaming industry. Its earliest proponents were, not coincidentally, enthusiastic players of DUNGEONS & DRAGONS, often alternating long hours of writing code with marathon sessions of D&D.

In 1978 TSR released a new version of the game, ADVANCED DUNGEONS & DRAGONS. The basic compendium of the rules for this game was the Players Handbook. The company also began publishing adventure modules, including *Hall of the Fire Giant King* and others in the Giants series. The following year introduced *White Plume Mountain* a perennial fan favorite, as well as the first Dungeon Masters Guide.

The popularity of the game was so great that some backlash was, perhaps, inevitable. In 1979, a college student from Michigan, an enthusiastic D&D player, vanished. Though the student later turned up alive and healthy, a rumor spread that in fact he had died during a live-action D&D game. Other rumors quickly spread that the game was "dangerous" or even "Satanic," and many schools banned the game from their premises. Fortunately, members of the gaming industry banded together to explain the truth about the incident and rebut the malicious rumors about D&D.

Throughout the 1980s DUNGEONS & DRAGONS continued to grow in popularity. In 1980, TSR formed the ROLE PLAYING GAME ASSOCIATION (RPGA), which, in 1981, began publishing *Polyhedron*, its newsletter.

In 1983, Tracy Hickman and Margaret Weis, employees of TSR, began working with other company members to create a new kind of fantasy saga. Writing in their off-hours, they developed a world in which dragons soared through the skies with lance-wielding riders on their backs. The adventure modules for the game released the following year, and Weis and Hickman wrote the first novel based on the story of DRAGONLANCE. The story enlisted a new generation of fans, and during the next two decades Weis and Hickman would collaborate on ten more best-selling novels set in the world of DRAGONLANCE.

Despite this success, the company underwent a period of considerable financial hardship. Employees were laid off, and, after several unsuccessful ventures into other products, in 1987 TSR's founders sold their interest in the company to a new investor, Lorraine Williams. Williams revitalized the company's finances and launched it on a new phase of prosperity.

As well, in 1987 the company launched a new fantasy setting developed by a Canadian gamer Ed Greenwood. The setting, which Greenwood first started work on in 1967, was immense and offered unparalleled opportunities for storytelling. Among those who began writing novels for the FORGOTTEN REALMS setting was a then-unknown Massachusetts accountant, R.A. Salvatore. His novel, *The Crystal Shard*, first published in 1988, introduced to the world the character of the drow ranger Drizzt Do'Urden, soon to become one of the most popular figures in all fantasy literature.

In 1989, TSR released the long-awaited Second Edition of ADVANCED DUNGEONS & DRAGONS. The company, boosted by the momentum of this release, entered the last decade of the twentieth century with more settings: the gothic horror of RAVENLOFT, the mysterious sand-filled wastes of AL-QADIM, and the savage, magic-ravaged world of DARK SUN. Gen Con grew bigger than ever before, with 18,000 attendees in 1992.

By 1994 the gaming industry had been once again transformed. In the computer industry, the development of "first-person shooters" such as *Doom* and *Quake* had brought a new wave of attention. In more traditional gaming circles, fans were stunned by a new phenomenon that debuted in 1994: trading card games.

Introduced by Wizards of the Coast after its invention by Richard Garfield, MAGIC: THE GATHERING became an overnight sensation. Although many other companies— including TSR— tried to duplicate that success, none ever came close. Faced with this competition, the company once again began to struggle financially, and by winter of 1996, it had ceased publication of products. Several agonizing months passed until in June 1997 the company was purchased by Wizards of the Coast. The remaining staff moved to Seattle and began anew the task of DUNGEONS & DRAGONS.

Almost immediately, discussions began among the game's designers about the need for a third edition of D&D. As these discussions picked up speed, more and more ideas were tossed into the kitty, subject to the relentless scrutiny of those responsible for the game's direction.

In 2000, twenty-six years after the game first saw the light of day, Wizards of the Coast released DUNGEONS & DRAGONS in its third edition. Fan response was immediate and overwhelmingly positive. Wizards of the Coast then made a bold move that decisively influenced the gaming industry when it introduced the Open Gaming License and the d20 System. Under this license, any other publisher was free to publish material compatible with the D&D system, using the Players Handbook and Dungeon Masters Guide as their basic rules set.

In 2002, the company reviewed its campaign settings and determined to launch a new one. To gain maximum fan involvement, WotC announced that it would accept fan submissions for a new setting and that the author of the setting selected would receive a bonus payment of $100,000.00. Fan response was immediate and overwhelming, as more than 11,000 submissions were received in six weeks. From this massive outpouring, editors and managers slaved to whittle down the list to a small number of semifinalists. At last, after several months of intense reading, WotC announced that it had accepted the proposal sent by Keith Baker, a then-unknown designer from Colorado. The setting was named EBERRON.

The release of the EBERRON campaign setting in 2004, the thirtieth anniversary of the DUNGEONS & DRAGONS game, seems appropriate.

For three decades, D&D has challenged fans to use their imagination to create and explore new worlds. Now a fan-created world will become the home for millions of players in their campaigns over the next decade.

DUNGEONS & DRAGONS is no longer in the first flush of youth. But as it has aged, it has matured and become finer. The three editions of the game have each contributed something to its growth, and each has its crowd of loyal fans. Today, D&D is played by some four million people each month. Millions more know it from computer games such as Neverwinter Nights and Baldur's Gate. Others remember the old cartoon show that ran for several seasons. Still others have read novels set in FORGOTTEN REALMS, DRAGONLANCE, and other settings.

The book you hold in your hands is not a history of D&D. Nor is it a history of TSR or Wizards of the Coast, though some history of both companies is inevitable in a product such as this. It is a celebration—a celebration of something that has touched the lives of millions of people around the globe. Those millions have brought their hopes, their fears, and their passions to the game, and with each passing year they have made it richer. This celebration belongs to all of them.

Happy birthday, DUNGEONS & DRAGONS!

30 YEARS OF ADVENTURE

THE ADVENTURE BEGINS

BY HAROLD JOHNSON

WITH GARY GYGAX

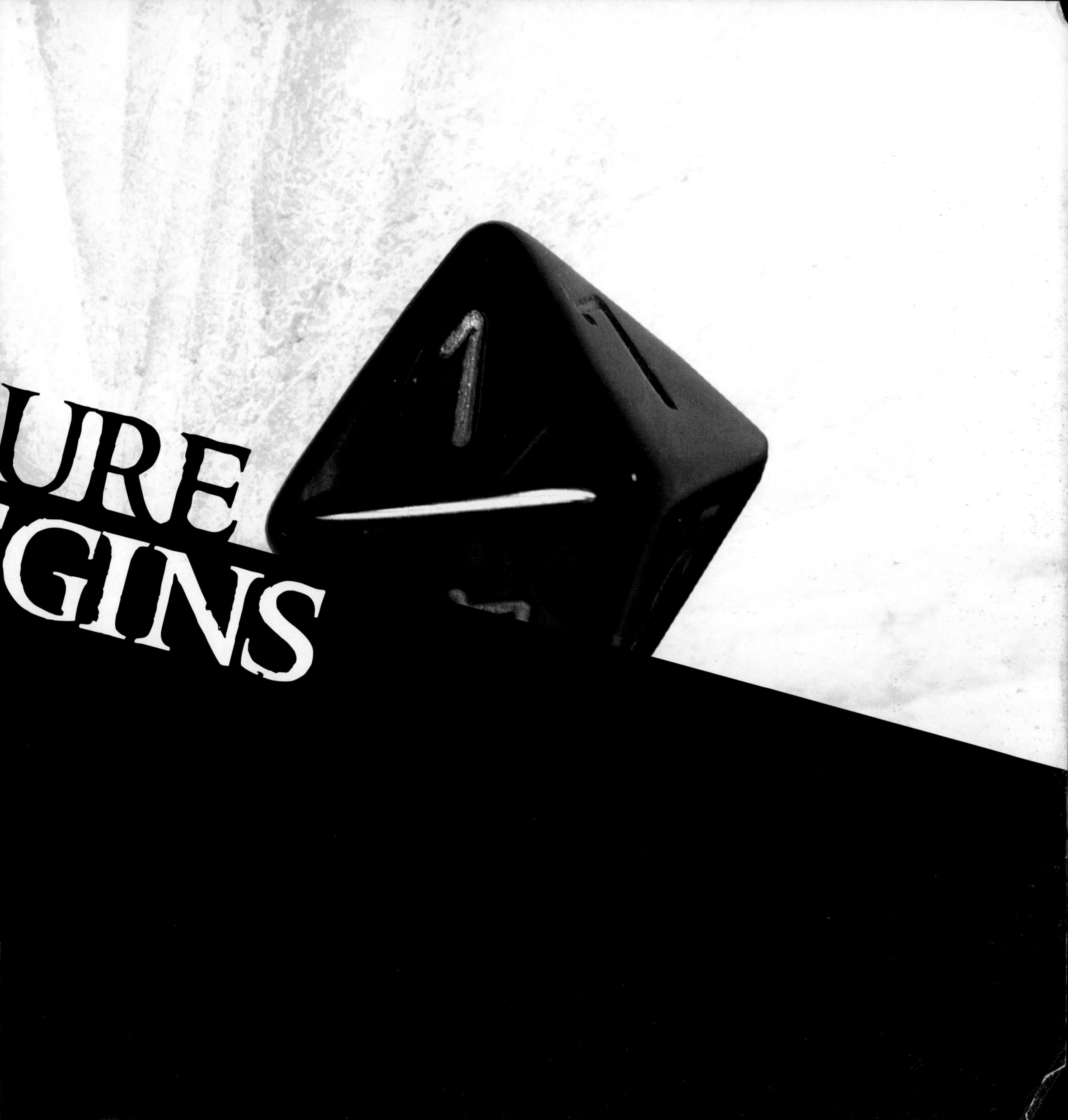
URE
GINS

THE ADVENTURE BEGINS

BY HAROLD JOHNSON

The darkness was warm and oppressive, the silence almost deafening. Things lived there in the dark, moved there in the dark, skittering along silently on dozens of legs or slithering through the dust on its belly. So it had been for years unnumbered. But that was about to change, the world was about to change.

The clang of metal striking stone tore the curtain of silence. Then, slowly, the sound of stone grinding on stone raised a groan and a block of darkness was set aside to let the outside light fill the cool breeze that blew in with swirling motes of dust. Shadows danced where before there had been only blackness.

"What do you see?" hissed the first voice.

"Just as the map tells," a hushed second voice answered. "There's a passage leading within. Come, bring the light. Let's go in."

Five figures, several bearing flickering torches, entered the dusty corridor— four as tall as men, the last with the stature of a child. Two were warriors as could be seen by their swords, the dwarven one sported a long beard and held a heavy warhammer. The other two were something of an oddity— the first wore long robes and carried a slender wand of white ash, his eyebrows were animated as he took in the scene. The other wore a loose fitting tunic and held a thin bladed dagger in one hand as his enigmatic gray eyes took in the setting. "There!" he said and pointed toward the far end of the hall.

"Pace it out," he said in a quiet tone as he studied a piece of parchment in his other hand.

All eyes watched as the blonde warrior in the lead counted his long steps down the dusty corridor, "Ten . . . twenty . . . thirty . . ."

"Stop! What do you see?" called the lad with the map.

START

"Just ahead there is a passage to the right and one to the left," came the response.

"Good! That's right. Now, move forward slowly. But stay to the left! There is something marked here in the middle of the way that I can't interpret. Count it out!"

The warrior moved forward again, this time more slowly, staying to the left side of the passage. "Ten . . ." his count echoed back from the dim reaches ahead, "twenty . . . thirty . . . forty . . . fifty . . . sixty"—there was a pause— "Hullo, what's this? It looked like the corridor ended, but it seems to be some sort of door, though I can't see how to open it. What should I do?"

"Hold up a moment," the leader pursed his lips, "I think it should be safe enough for us all to move forward, just stay to the left!" The rest of the party slid forward past the proscribed patch of floor.

"What do you think we'll find within?" the dwarf's black eyes glistened like opals in eager anticipation.

"A treasure beyond your wildest imaginings," whispered the berobed gentleman.

* * * * *

DUNGEONS

Such was my first foray into a dungeon with the DUNGEONS & DRAGONS role-playing game. But I was not the first. In the winter of 1974, a thousand brave gamers discovered the first adventure game of all time and were quick to enter and explore the challenges of a dungeon. Little did they realize that their lives and the world would never be the same for they had discovered the game that never ends and they had become true believers.

Despite the widespread public awareness of the existence of this game nowadays, in the early years the only way you learned about it was if a friend introduced it to you. Even today, despite greater channels of distribution and outstanding advertisement, many gamers still learn D&D from a friend.

As a child of the Midwest, my family was living in Lincoln,

Nebraska, where my father was a Professor of Industrial Engineering at Nebraska University and my mother was a high school math teacher. I, however, had returned to the land of my birth—Chicago—and was attending Northwestern University with a major in biology and a minor in history of religion. During the long summer break of 1975, I returned to Lincoln to attend my brother's wedding and for summer employment as a puppeteer with a professional troupe. My second greatest love however, next to acting was gaming. I had been a fan of chess and miniature wargames for nearly a decade, and all my friends knew I loved games. So that summer, one of my gaming buddies, Agris Taurins, sought me out to introduce me to a new game. And boy, was I filled with questions.

& DRAGONS

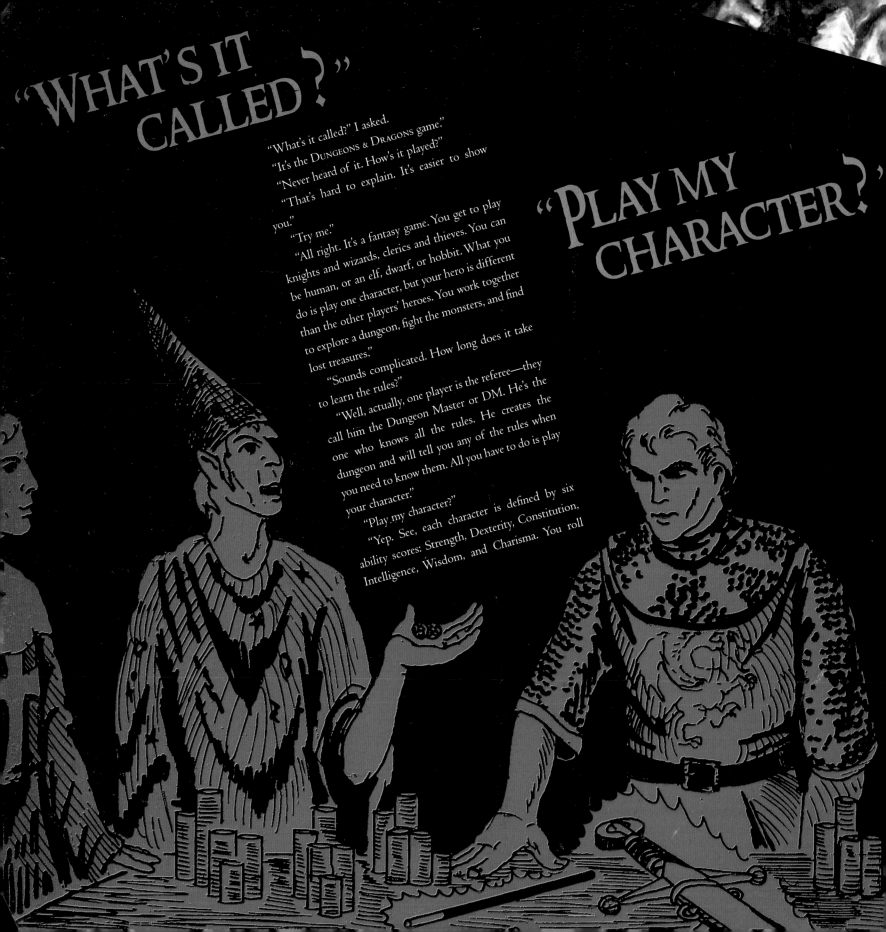

"WHAT'S IT CALLED?"

"PLAY MY CHARACTER?"

"What's it called?" I asked.

"It's the DUNGEONS & DRAGONS game."

"Never heard of it. How's it played?"

"That's hard to explain. It's easier to show you."

"Try me."

"All right. It's a fantasy game. You get to play knights and wizards, clerics and thieves. You can be human, or an elf, dwarf, or hobbit. What you do is play one character, but your hero is different than the other players' heroes. You work together to explore a dungeon, fight the monsters, and find lost treasures."

"Sounds complicated. How long does it take to learn the rules?"

"Well, actually, one player is the referee—they call him the Dungeon Master or DM. He's the one who knows all the rules. He creates the dungeon and will tell you any of the rules when you need to know them. All you have to do is play your character."

"Play my character?"

"Yep. See, each character is defined by six ability scores: Strength, Dexterity, Constitution, Intelligence, Wisdom, and Charisma. You roll

"HOW'S IT PLAYED?"

dice to determine your scores at the start of the game. Then you imagine what the character must be like with those scores, and you play your character to match those scores. For instance, if he's strong but dumb, then you play him like a lummox.

"You mean I pretend to be the character, making decisions the way he would and acting like he would. Great, I can do acting!"

"And the best part is that as you defeat more monsters and gather more treasure your character's chances to fight and survive improve."

"So how do you win?"

"Well, you don't really win or lose, you just keep playing, creating your own legend until your character dies. Then you can roll up a new character, or maybe your companions will discover some magic to bring your character back to life."

"It sounds hard."

"It's not that hard, really. All you need is some paper and pencils to take notes and create a map of the dungeon. Oh, yes . . . and you need imagination."

"SO HOW DO YOU WIN?"

NAME: BORG	CLASS: FIGHTER
STR 17	
INT 8	HIT POINTS: 6
WIS 10	
DEX 7	ARMOR CLASS: 3
CON 15	
CHR 6	ALIGNMENT: LAWFUL

LEVEL: 1   X. POINTS: 0   MONEY: 10 GP's
(NEED 2000)

SAVING THROWS
POISON		
MAGIC WAND	12	ATTACK ROLLS
PARALYSIS	13	AC 0: 17
DRAGON BREATH	14	AC 1: 16
SPELLS	15	AC 2: 15
	16	AC 3: 14
		AC 4: 13
EQUIPMENT		AC 5: 12
1 LONG SWORD		AC 6: 11
2 DAGGERS		AC 7: 10
1 SHIELD		AC 8: 9
1 SHORT BOW		
20 ARROWS		
50' ROPE		
1 BACKPACK		

My first experience with the game you already read at the start of this chapter though it didn't sound so dramatic when we played. It involved drawing a map as we explored the dungeon and sounded more like this:

DM: *You find the secret entrance to the dungeon and pry the capstone off.*

ME: What do we see?

DM: *An empty, dirty corridor running straight to the north. It's ten feet wide and covered with dust. It doesn't look like anyone has been here in a long time.*

ME: Maybe it's like the map we found. I'm going to look at the map as we explore.

DM: *Okay.*

ME: We enter the dungeon.

DM: *Fine. Ten . . . twenty . . . thirty feet. The passageway continues straight ahead, and there is a corridor to the left and right.*

ME: That's right. There appears to be something straight ahead on the map. Is there anything on the floor?

DM: *There doesn't appear to be anything. What do you want to do?*

And so it went. I remember that when it came time to speak with monsters or other characters my hero encountered during the adventure, the other players would say, "My hero says . . . ." Not me. When it was my turn to speak I chose a speech pattern and spoke directly to the character.

"I stride up to this fellow looking at my 'Men-At-Arms Wanted' posting. 'Ay, mate. Lookin' for a little adventure are you? Not much happenin' 'round this here burg.'"

My DM was delighted. I was having fun. And my fellow players began to follow my lead and act like their heroes.

That first month of gaming was fairly intense, and we played whenever we could. Then one night we planned to play all night. I wanted to spice the adventure up, make it more entertaining for all, and when you have access to a costume closet and prop storeroom, it was pretty easy. We wore hats to identify our characters for each other and used props to represent treasures and traps found. Vanilla wafers were used to keep track of gold, and hard candy represented any gems we

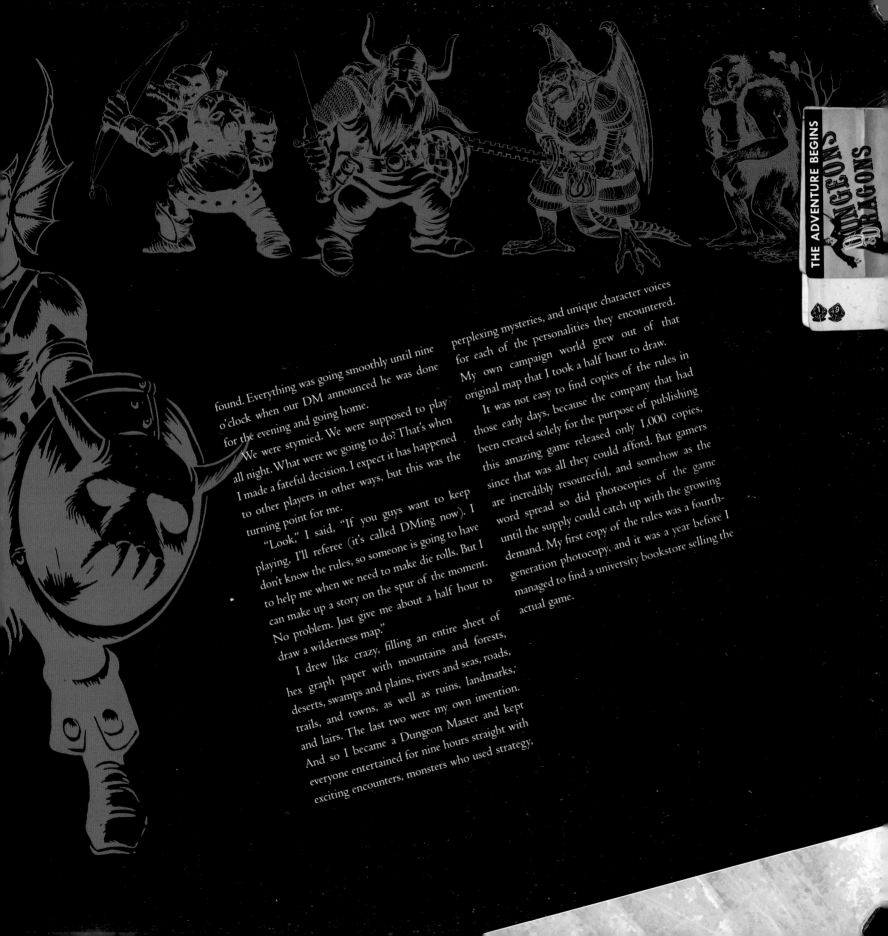

found. Everything was going smoothly until nine o'clock when our DM announced he was done for the evening and going home.

We were stymied. We were supposed to play all night. What were we going to do? That's when I made a fateful decision. I expect it has happened to other players in other ways, but this was the turning point for me.

"Look," I said, "If you guys want to keep playing, I'll referee (it's called DMing now). I don't know the rules, so someone is going to have to help me when we need to make die rolls. But I can make up a story on the spur of the moment. No problem. Just give me about a half hour to draw a wilderness map."

I drew like crazy, filling an entire sheet of hex graph paper with mountains and forests, deserts, swamps and plains, rivers and seas, roads, trails, and towns, as well as ruins, landmarks, and lairs. The last two were my own invention. And so I became a Dungeon Master and kept everyone entertained for nine hours straight with exciting encounters, monsters who used strategy,

perplexing mysteries, and unique character voices for each of the personalities they encountered. My own campaign world grew out of that original map that I took a half hour to draw.

It was not easy to find copies of the rules in those early days, because the company that had been created solely for the purpose of publishing this amazing game released only 1,000 copies, since that was all they could afford. But gamers are incredibly resourceful, and somehow as the word spread so did photocopies of the game until the supply could catch up with the growing demand. My first copy of the rules was a fourth-generation photocopy, and it was a year before I managed to find a university bookstore selling the actual game.

DUNGEONS & DRAGONS® CHARACTER RECORD SHEET

Player's Name

MORGAN IRONWOLF
Character's Name

LAWFUL
Alignment

Dungeon Master

Character Sketch or Symbol

FIGHTER
Class

1ST
Level

3
Armor Class

6
Hit Points

ABILITIES:

16	15 16 STRENGTH	+2 adjustment
7	7 INTELLIGENCE	— adjustment
9	+9 WISDOM	— adjustment -1 AC
13	13 DEXTERITY	+1 MISSILE & INITIATIVE adjustment
	14 CONSTITUTION	+1/HD adjustment

SAVING THROWS:

12	POISON or DEATH RAY
13	MAGIC WAND
14	TURN TO STONE or PARALYSIS
15	DRAGON BREATH
16	SPELLS or MAGIC STAFF

EQUIPMENT CARRIED

MAGIC ITEMS

NORMAL ITEMS

CHAIN MAIL ARMOR
SHIELD
SWORD
SHORT BOW
QUIVER OF 20 ARROWS
1 SILVER ARROW
50' ROPE
10' POLE
12 IRON SPIKES
6 TORCHES
1 WEEKS STANDARD RA...
LARGE SACK
1 QUART OF WINE
WINE SKIN

OTHER NOTES including places explored, people & m...

MONEY and TREASURE

2 G.P.

(+10

DUNGEONS & DRAGONS

Written by two young men from Lake Geneva, Wisconsin, and Minneapolis, Minnesota, the game was only available through Midwest regional hobby shops and via mail from the publisher, Tactical Studies Rules. However, once local college students became fascinated with the game, they carried copies back to their hometowns across the United States to share with their friends. These friends, who attended other colleges, continued disseminating the game to other states. Soon there were adventure gamers at all major campuses and college bookstores began to stock the game and dice for their student population.

The first edition of DUNGEONS & DRAGONS was not in a white box. It was in a brown, wood-tone box with hand-applied labels on the front and on one side. The white D&D Collectors Edition box followed several years later. Within this box were three half-sized books labeled: Men & Magic, Monsters & Treasures, and The Underworld & Wilderness Adventures. There were five sheets of key charts and tables used to play the game. But that wasn't everything you needed to play the game. A booklet in the box listed the following equipment on page 5 as necessary to play this new game:

DUNGEONS & DRAGONS (you have it)
Outdoor Survival (a game available from the Avalon Hill Company used
  to play travel across the wilderness)
Dice – the following different kinds of dice are available from TSR
1 pair 4-sided dice
1 pair 20-sided dice
1 pair 8-sided dice
1 pair 12-sided dice
4 to 20 pairs 6-sided dice
Chainmail miniature rules (available from TSR Hobbies)
Other Supplies
1 3-Ring Notebook (for the referee and each player)
Graph Paper (6 lines per inch is best)
Sheet Protectors (the heaviest possible)
3-Ring Lined Paper
Drafting Equipment and Colored Pencils
Scratch Paper and Pencils
Imagination
1 Patient Referee

Players

Summary:

1. Roll for ability scores.

2. Choose a class; note special abilities and spells.

3. Adjust scores as desired; note bonuses for high scores.

4. Roll hit points.

5. Roll for money; equip the character.

6. Find Armor Class, attack, and saving throw numbers.

7. Name the character.

PERIENCE   0
NED EXPERIENCE)

r next level: 2000

Chris Prynoski

Statistics and Attributes: Chris Prynoski is the founder and owner of West Hollywood's Titmouse, Inc. animation studio. He has worked on such shows as *Beavis and Butthead*, *The Osbournes*, *MTV Movie Awards*, and *Downtown*. Currently he is the Supervising Director of Cartoon Network's new show MEGAS XLR.

Description: "You're standing at the foot of an altar, built upon a rock embankment, overlooking a great valley. There is a dense forest to the west, a small cave opening in the mountainside to the east, and a stone citadel on the road ahead. What are you gonna do?"

"What do you mean, 'What are you gonna do'? Don't I have to roll these fucked-up-looking dice or something? What am I supposed to do?"

"You can do anything."

"What's anything? What are the rules?"

"The rules are you can make your guy do whatever you want."

"Are you sure you know how to play?"

"Yeah, dude. Just do something."

"Okay. My guy pulls down his pants and pisses on the altar."

"Are you sure you want to do that?"

"Yeah, yeah. Let's get on with it. . . What are you doing?"

"I'm rolling to see what happens to you."

"Shouldn't I be rolling to see what happens to me?"

"I'm the Dungeon Master, dude."

"What?"

"The clouds open up, and a giant bolt of blue lightning shoots down from the heavens, striking you and frying your ass to a shriveled-up, black piece of bacon. You're dead, dude."

"This game is great!"

In the fall of 1982, my good friend Andy German invited me over to his house after school. His older brother had introduced him to a game called "D&D" and we were going to try it out with a few of our fellow ten-year-old companions— Dave, Irv, and Michael. It was a life-changing experience. I put my STAR WARS action figures in a box and never looked back. For the next four

years we got together and played every single day. We couldn't conceive of doing anything else.

It may have been an imaginary, fantasy world, but it was real to us. We knew our characters better than ourselves and treated their situations as seriously as we would any in our own lives. Experience points were more important than grades. Magic weapons were more important than food. The death of a player character was a tragedy as terrible as losing a real brother.

DUNGEONS & DRAGONS opened our minds to the fact that life had no boundaries. It wasn't played out on a flat board with pieces that moved around a determined path — it was open to anything you could imagine. D&D was "thinking outside the box" decades before that stupid expression existed.

I believe that role-playing at an early age really hipped me to the fact that one could do anything in life. The only path available isn't the boring job in the boring suburbs. There are as many paths as you want to take. And if the path you want doesn't exist yet, you can go ahead and make your own – even if you have to kill some Bugbears to do it. ∎

Cardell Kerr

Statistics and Attributes: Cardell Kerr is the Senior Systems Designer for DUNGEONS & DRAGONS ONLINE™ at Turbine Entertainment Software

Description: "What do you think they mean when they say 20-sided dice? I thought they only went up to 6 sides?"

Ironically, when I was younger, we needed to search high and low for a place to even buy a 20-sided dice, since we had inherited our DUNGEONS & DRAGONS books from our elder siblings. Finally, after a while, we managed to find some at a local comic book shop. I can still remember how we all regarded the plastic containers with unmitigated glee, staring at the multicolored crystalline dice, being amazed by the varieties.

I remember buying two dice types that day, a d20 and a d8, because my character used a longsword, and I needed it to deal damage. I also remember getting back to my house and being quite annoyed that I didn't have a d12, since back in the day weapons did different damage to different sized opponents!

In retrospect, I think the only thing we looked for longer than dice was a person to actually run a game. Finding a Dungeon Master was hard work, especially in an age before gaming focal points, like MAGIC: THE GATHERING stores and Internet Cafés. After a few weeks, one of our friends finally decided he'd waited long enough, and was willing to run a game.

Looking back, it wasn't a cohesive game. We fought kobolds in a sewer. Did I mention they were riding dragons? Wow . . . thinking about it is almost embarrassing. I mean, kobolds would never ride dragons! It doesn't change the fact that we were hooked. We would gather together during recess and plan out our next adventures, allocating our party roles like other kids were allocating friendship bracelets. I would typically end up as the wizard, since most other people didn't want to learn the spells. But almost no one wanted to be the cleric. Oh how young we were!

When we all got to high school, the mood had changed a bit. Some friends stopped playing, but probably not as many as you would think. Meanwhile other people turned up, interested in "getting a game together." It was at this point that we could all carry a story well enough to actually make a good game. This was the period of time where stunning descriptions would drive the campaign and capture the players' imaginations. Ghost Mountains that were never in the same place twice (Krull), and amazing use of existing spells for stunning effects were the main focus this time. Lightning bolts used to bounce, so this was also the time when we learned the nomenclature of "Optimal spell placement." It is a mantra that will not – cannot – be forgotten.

Nowadays, I've been playing a bit with d20 modern. Guns and D&D? Who would have thought anyone could pull it off! But then again, looking at the current staff, along with the amazing revisions present in 3.5, I can't say I'm surprised!

ERE DID IT OME FROM?

BY HAROLD
JOHNSON

In the late 1960s, miniature wargaming was popular among students of history and warfare. Rules were published for battles of armies where each figure represented twenty men, and battles were played on boards made using railroad model terrain.

In 1968, two gamers, Gary Gygax and Jeff Perren, wrote CHAINMAIL, a set of rules for man-to-man medieval battles. Each figure represented only one man, and leaders or heroes could joust and fight individual duels. This was one of the first heroic battle games.

With the rebirth of fantasy literature in the seventies the authors, heavily influenced by J.R.R. Tolkien's Lord of the Rings, wrote a supplemental rules section to include the addition of magic and the use of elves, dwarves, giants, and monsters, using different scaled miniatures and plastic toys to represent the fantastic troops.

Between 1969 and 1972, a gamer from Minnesota, Dave Arneson, created his own rules for heroic fantasy battles, pitting heroes against monsters. One popular battle he ran involved a commando raid on a castle to open the gates. The heroes faced a dragon

DUNGEONS & DRAGONS

Rules for Fantastic Medieval Wargames Campaigns Playable with Paper and Pencil and Miniature Figures

GYGAX & ARNESON

Original Collector's Edition

3-VOLUME SET

PUBLISHED BY
TACTICAL STUDIES RULES

Chainmail
rules for medieval miniatures
by
Gary Gygax & Jeff Perren

3rd Edition

Fantasy
supplement

Most of the fantastic battles related in novels more closely resemble medieval warfare than they do earlier or later forms of combat. Because of this we are including a brief set of rules which will allow the medieval miniatures wargamer to add a new facet to his hobby. J.R.R. Tolkien, Robert E. Howard, and other fantasy writers; or you can conduct fantastic campaigns and conflict...

and other fantastic guards as obstacles to their goal.

In 1972, at a convention in Lake Geneva, Wisconsin, Arneson recreated this popular battle using the CHAINMAIL rules. Watching, Gary Gygax was inspired by the battle. He decided to codify the battle by writing a new set of rules, and in collaboration with Arneson he wrote a new game for running heroic fantasy battles, referred to as "The Fantasy Game."

In 1974, after Gygax struggled to get another game publisher to print their game, a business partnership, TSR, was formed for the express purpose of publishing the new DUNGEONS & DRAGONS game (a name suggested by Gary's wife). The first thousand copies were hand assembled in the Gygax home, with labels applied to brown boxes.

The original D&D rules set was written for college students and quickly became popular with them. However, as the years passed, high school and junior high students were also attracted to the game but found the original rules vague and confusing.

In 1977, J. Eric Holmes, a teacher and a fan of the game offered to rewrite the rules to create an introductory set for younger players. D&D continued to attract younger gamers, and TSR recognized the need for a more polished version of the game. As well, a second step was needed once players grew beyond novice level. The company revamped the D&D Basic Set and introduced the D&D Expert Set in 1981.

D&D became a favorite among the military forces because it was never the same game twice, and the game was introduced to many countries as a result of servicemen abroad. Recognizing the need for foreign translations,

FANTASTIC CHARACTERISTICS (See also Appendix D)

HALFLINGS: These little chaps have small place in the wargame, but you may ... them for recreation of certain battles. Remember that they are able to blend ... background and so make excellent scouts. They can fire a stone as far as an ... hoots, and because of their well known accuracy, for every two Halflings ... unt three on the Missile Fire table.
...e Rating -- 5   Point Value -- (-)

...S (and Pixies): These are also small creatures who have the power to ... visible -- and remain so in battle ! When Sprites attack they suffer no ... uring the first round of melee; thereafter, surprise wears off and the ... e able to note the minor shadows and air distortions caused by the ... es can fly for three turns (maximum) before landing.
...ting -- 3   Point Value -- 4

...nd Gnomes): Because their natural habitat is deep under the ... ut folk operate equally well day or night. Although they are no ... r creatures, Trolls, Ogres, and Giants find them hard to catch ... mall size, so count only one-half normal kills when Dwarves or ... with them, for either attacks upon the Dwarves and Gnomes or ... Dwarves be the attacker. Goblins and Kobolds are their nat- ...) enemies, and Dwarves (Gnomes) will attack Goblins ... other enemies in sight, regardless of orders to the contrary. ... d Gnomes will not have to roll an "obedience die" (or ... rs, i.e., they will not automatically attack. ... Kobolds) are within charging dis- ... mation to the exclusi-

TSR tackled the task of translating the game into the French language.

Three separate translations were completed, one by a computer company, a second by a French exchange student, and the third by a French gamer. Finally an amalgam of all three translations was released in 1982, heralding the start of the translation of D&D into more than fourteen different languages.

D&D gained public acclaim and now was demanded by the non-hobby gaming public who found even the revised rules too convoluted. So a new edition of the D&D Basic Set and Experts set was published in 1983 in a new step-by-step instructional form. D&D Expert rules allowed play through the 14th level of experience, and as interest in the game continued additional sets were introduced from 1984 to 1986, including the D&D Companion, Master, and Immortal sets.

While the original D&D game required gamers to create their own adventures, TSR recognized the potential for another category of product and in 1978 began publishing written adventures. In the late eighties TSR organized its collection of adventures by publishing a series of accessories detailing the countries of a fantasy world where all D&D adventures could be set. This series was called the Gazetteers. Then in 1990, in order to introduce alternate societies to host adventures, TSR produced the HOLLOW WORLD line of products, which dealt with ancient societies.

In order to introduce even younger gamers to the D&D Game, a new version of the Basic Set was released in 1991. It featured a board and playing pieces and pre-created adventures so that new gamers could get a taste of the excitement without having to struggle with the creation of their own game.

Further, in order to simplify D&D, all of the rules introduced in the Basic, Expert, Companion, Master, and Immortal sets were gathered together into one Cyclopedia book.

A Gathering of Gamers

by Harold Johnson

As TSR, Inc. and its customer base grew, so too did the gaming convention that is most associated with roleplaying. What began as a small gathering of friends to play wargames has grown into a major annual event where more than 25,000 gaming enthusiasts gather to play games of all sorts, from wargames to roleplaying, board games to computer games. It remains a time to make friends and to renew old friendships.

In 1968, a local Wisconsin gaming club, the Lake Geneva Tactical Studies Association and the International Federation of Wargames decided to host a convention devoted entirely to playing wargames, and the first Gen Con Game Fair was formed. Held at the Horticulture Hall in town, it drew almost 100 gamers from all parts of the country. The Gen Con Game Fair would prove to be what drew the various founders of Tactical Studies Rules together.

Over the next few years the convention continued to be hosted in Lake Geneva at the Horticulture Hall but made brief sojourns to the American Legion Hall and the George Williams Campus in Williams Bay. It remained a wargaming convention but also evolved into a yearly gathering of friends.

In 1972 Dave Arneson ran his fantasy game, using CHAINMAIL, which featured dragons and monsters in a dungeon setting. His audience included Gary Gygax. Thus, Gen Con was itself part of the birth of DUNGEONS & DRAGONS.

In 1976 TSR Hobbies became the new owner and organizer of Gen Con. This year more than 300 attendees packed both Horticulture Hall and the American Legion Hall. It was time to move the fair.

1976 was a year of beginnings as the Ral Partha miniatures company appeared on the scene. Ral Partha's metal miniatures would become many roleplayers' standard D&D miniatures until the release of pre-painted plastic miniatures more than twenty-five years later. Also in 1976, TSR licensed another company, Judges Guild, to produce the first official accessories for the DUNGEONS & DRAGONS game.

In 1977 the convention moved to the Playboy Club convention center in Lake

GEN CON

AMERICA'S PREMIER GAME CONVENTION & TRADE SHOW

If you're a gamer of any type, there's an annual event you should know about no matter what your particular area of interest is. The event is the Gen Con® Game Convention and Trade Show. This premier event is sponsored by TSR Hobbies, Inc., and held in August of every year at a location in southern Wisconsin. Well over two thousand enthusiasts gather annually for this gaming extravaganza, which runs events and features dealing with all facets of the hobby: tournaments, general gaming exhibits, auctions, seminars, movies, boardgames, role playing events — plus special celebrity guests, prizes, and trophies. It all adds up to four days of gaming that you won't want to miss, so make your plans now to attend!

Inquiries regarding the Gen Con® Game Convention for any particular year (including dates, general information, accommodations, et. al.) should be made between February 1st and July 1st by writing to:

Gen Con® Game Convention
POB 756
Lake Geneva, WI 53147

Gen Con® and the Gen Con® logo are registered service marks of TSR Hobbies, Inc.

Geneva, with additional activities being hosted at Horticulture Hall and the church next door. Attendance topped 1,000, and again it was obvious that the show must move.

Gen Con now throve on a combination of wargames and roleplaying adventures.

In 1978 the convention relocated to the University of Wisconsin-Parkside Campus, a series of buildings connected by a skywalk. Games and dealers vied for space in the hallways, while tournaments were hidden away in myriad classrooms. Attendance figures grew rapidly, keeping pace with the growth of the gaming industry. By 1984 attendance was over 3,500. Parkside had become too small for the convention, despite the fact that the dealers were moved to an un-air conditioned gymnasium a block away and additional events were run at Gateway Technical Institute two and a half miles away. Another move was necessary.

1984 also marked the appearance of the first art show at Gen Con, featuring works of TSR's artist staff members. Later this show was to grow into a premier showcase for fantasy artists across the country.

In 1985 Gen Con moved to Milwaukee at the Milwaukee Exposition Center and Convention Arena ("MECCA"). Beginning only in two side halls, Gen Con began to grow again to fill the new space available.

By 1986 Gen Con attracted well over 5,000 gamers. The number of game tournaments and seminars became so overwhelming that scheduling had to be managed by a computer, much like a college curriculum. By 1987 over 1,000 events were hosted by the convention.

In 1988 Gen Con combined for the first time with the Origins Game Fair, its major competitor. Attendance broke the 10,000 mark, and more than 1,200 events were hosted. For the first time there was a waiting list of exhibitors for the dealers hall.

Thereafter, Gen Con never fell below the 10,000 attendance mark.

In 1992 the twenty-fifth anniversary of Gen Con, the convention once again partnered with the Origins Game Fair and broke all previous records. More than 18,000 people attended, cramming the halls and gaming booths. For the first time dealers had to be turned away, and more than 1,500 events entertained the attendees.

The growth of the convention now began to show signs, once more, of bursting out of its space. Hotel rooms in the Milwaukee area were filled to the bursting point at convention time, and some unfortunate guests had to settle for making the trip daily from such outlying places as Kenosha and Racine.

In 1997, amid financial troubles for TSR, there was some concern by the gaming community that Gen Con might not be held. Fortunately, Wizards of the Coast, which purchased TSR that year, made Gen Con a priority. Attendance was up, and the convention was filled now with wargamers, roleplayers, boardgamers, and devotees of trading card games.

In 2002 Gen Con was sold by Wizards of the Coast to Gen Con LLC, a company founded by Peter Adkison, who had left Wizards the previous year. Under his firm direction, the convention in Milwaukee that year was a resounding success, but it was obvious that the resources of the city had reached their limits in hosting the convention. It was time, once again, to move.

Beginning in 2003, Gen Con moved to Indianapolis, Indiana. In its new home, it shows every sign of flourishing and growing. It's now been joined by a sister convention, Gen Con So Cal, held in Los Angeles every winter.

Gen Con is only the largest of hundreds of gaming cons that are held around the country and around the world. Some draw only a small number of participants, while others are massive events. But at each one, the passion and creativity of the gaming community is on display.

Stephen Colbert

Statistics and Attributes: Stephen Colbert is a correspondent and writer on the Emmy Award-winning show *The Daily Show with Jon Stewart*. His career began at the Second City improv troupe in Chicago. There he met Amy Sedaris and Paul Dinello, with whom he later created television series *Exit 57* and *Strangers With Candy* and wrote the book *Wigfield*. He has recently completed filming the full-length feature, *Strangers with Candy: The Movie*, and will perform in the upcoming film *Bewitched*, starring Will Farrell and Nicole Kidman.

Description: In the spring of 1976 I was in seventh grade. I had been reading science fiction for two years and had just started bleeding over into fantasy.

One day at lunch I overheard my friend Keith saying, "I listened at the door, and I didn't hear anything, so I went inside and got attacked by a giant rat!"

I said, "What do you mean, you listened at the door? What are you talking about?"

They said, "Well, it's kind of hard to explain but in this game called DUNGEONS & DRAGONS there's a probability that you'll hear something through a door, and my character's a thief so he can hear better. The game just came out. Come over Friday and we'll play."

I did and was instantly hooked. A whole new kind of game. No board – just dice, just probabilities. It allowed me to enter the world of the books I was reading.

I put more effort into that game than I ever did into my schoolwork.

We were all complete outcasts in school — beyond the fringe, beyond nerds. We were our own subdimensional bubble of the school. I'm not even sure we were on the rolls of any of the classes; that's how outcast we were.

D&D made quite a little explosion when it first came out. We were close to the Bible belt, and ministers were preaching on TV against it, saying that it was a cult, telling stories about kids going too far, playing in the sewers and getting swept away when it rained or getting carried away and believing that the games were real and hurting each other with swords or trying to do incantations, demon worship. I remember thinking, "Who'd be stupid enough to believe this was real?" And while I certainly wished it was real at times, I was sure these were boogymen stories made up by preachers who didn't like the implications of stories like Tolkien's and by what they believed to be dabbling in the occult.

We would do huge campaigns where we had multiple characters and would take them through dungeons, one person running multiple characters. I created characters based on the personalities of my eleven brothers and sisters. I included myself and my mother and my father.

I took them through an old Judge's Guild module called *The Thieves of Fortress Badabaskor*. They were all killed, except my sister, whose name is Lulu. She was a witch, a variant of a magic user that was described in DRAGON magazine. She had powers like a dance of seduction and love potions and stuff like that. She survived quite well, and she ended up being my favorite character for years. All my friends bugged me that my favorite character was female, but I thought it was kind of cool that it didn't matter what sex your character was.

When she was twenty-third level one of the Dungeon Masters that I played with all the time just, I guess, got tired of her, and he killed her. She was riding on her dragon's back above the clouds, and he made it rain acid upwards.

Those old Giants modules, those were tremendous. Those are some of my favorite memories: working my way through Fire Giant, Frost Giant, and Storm Giant castles. But the best campaign to me was *Expedition to the Barrier Peaks*, a Sci-Fi/Fantasy mix.

I had an eleventh-level paladin (it took me years to advance those levels) whom I took on *Expedition*, and he got the Power Armor, which was *the* big thing to get in that module. But he also went a little power mad. On the next campaign we saw a merchant caravan crossing the desert, and my character flew down and landed next to a merchant and tore off the guy's head.

The DM informed me that I was not a paladin anymore.

I said, "Oh, shit, I forgot. I'm lawful good!"

DM: "Yeah, and the gods are angry. So you're not a paladin anymore. You can start again as anything you want, but that character's done."

Eventually we started to judge each other based on how our characters behaved. One DM seemed to believe we were our characters too much. We wanted our characters too greedy. We wanted too much. We wanted them to be too strong. But, you know, within the culture of high school we were the weak puppies and were looking for power, albeit imagined. Well this one DM, Haskell, started using his dungeon mastering as a critique of that. He would tempt us with ways to get seemingly unlimited power (say, a poison with no saving throw) and then throw huge roadblocks in with ways to keep us from achieving it. I may be remembering the way wrong, but I think by the end we were using the game to express how we felt about each other.

Ben Kweller

Statistics and Attributes: Ben Kweller's second album, *On My Way*, released in April 2004.

Description: I grew up in a small town north of Dallas called Greenville, Texas. The first time I heard about D&D was from a neighborhood friend. There was a kid in the neighborhood two or three years older than me – his name was Casey – and he always talked about DUNGEONS & DRAGONS.

I was eight or nine when I first learned about it. We would go to the bookstores and sit there for hours reading the books because we didn't have the money to buy them. We were fascinated by this fantasy world set in medieval times, with heroes and sorcerers. We weren't able to buy the books and actually play, but we dreamed about being in that world. We would go home and draw pictures of our characters. We didn't know all the rules, but I remember I had a trampoline in the backyard and we'd act out our games and play out our characters.

That was the first time I really got bit by the bug. It took me many years to actually get my first game. But I always dreamed about playing.

There were about four of us who would get together and play, but in my town there wasn't a huge outlet for gaming. There was one comic book store, but it was a lot of older people that would always play and I was not in their group. I would hang out there and watch people play. I wished I could play too, but they thought I was too young.

One year I was at summer camp – I was about thirteen – and I played my first game. We had a free day and there was this really cool kid with jet black hair. I'll never forget him. He had a backpack full of every book: the ranger book, the rogue book. They looked like bibles with the page markers. I just thought he was the coolest kid because he had this backpack full of these amazing books. He was the Dungeon Master, and I played my first game and loved it.

About two years ago I finally got myself a lot of the books and started playing games with some friends.

I'm a half-elf ranger. I love rangers, especially with the new 3.5 rules. I love the stealthiness – it's not quite a fighter, and you have a few spells you can cast. It's just a good . . . it reminds me of a Navy SEAL. You can almost do everything.

I like to create characters that are like me, that are small and fast. I've never really wanted to play a dwarf or a big barbarian or anything.

When I was young, I read a ton of the DUNGEONS & DRAGONS Choose Your Own Adventure books. Music's always been my one passion in life. I had piano lessons when I was growing up, but I never wanted to practice the piano lessons I was given. I would take a few chords that I could get and make up my own songs. I think for me early on when I was younger, reading wasn't as much fun if it was something already created. I could really relate to the Choose Your Own Adventure books because I was able to be a part of it and make a decision. Otherwise I'd get distracted or bored. So I was really into Choose Your Own Adventure, because I had a say in it.

That's what I love about DUNGEONS & DRAGONS: You're creating reality.

When I was a kid, it was hard because I always wanted to play but couldn't. Now, on tour after the concerts in the hotel rooms or on the tour bus, we play on the road during our down time. My sound engineer is our Dungeon Master, my guitar player is a cleric, my tour manager is a fighter, and I'm a ranger. As a matter of fact, the name of my publishing company is Twelve-Sided Die Music

Brian, the DM, had played for years. I've really been the ringleader. I was, like, "We gotta do this!"

My tour manager especially has taken to the game. I mean, we're so into it! It's really just now ten years later that I'm playing it for real. I've just had my first three consecutive sessions.

But most of all, I remember back to that summer camp. I remember lying on the carpeted floor of the clubhouse, and this guy with his backpack full of stacks of books. I was in awe of him.

THE BIRTH OF D

The name DUNGEONS & DRAGONS is something to conjure with today. Such is its power that it is likely to be recognized nearly anywhere in the world when spoken. That power comes from the fact that it was not merely the first fantasy roleplaying game, but it was the first RPG, period. When the D&D game was published, it was the advent of a new form of game, and its coming gave birth to a whole industry. But you know all about that. Only a few years ago, though, things were different . . .

In 1972 the name did not exist. Imagine yourself sitting before a small Royal portable typewriter. It is winter. A newly written manuscript of only 50-page length is there. The pages explain how to create a "character," a wholly imaginary game persona whose calling will be that of a "cleric," "fighter," "magic-user," or "thief." How will this be done? By rolling dice, three normal dice, what we now call in the shorthand that has since developed, 3d6. Each roll made is to indicate the relative capacity of the character in six heretofore unheard of "statistics"—Strength, Intelligence, Wisdom, Dexterity, Constitution, and Charisma.

These are "old standards" now, but in 1972 this was a breakthrough. This was a quantum jump from tabletop games with miniatures. Not only was the action of the game to be centered on such characters, but they would grow in power as they successfully progressed through "adventures."

More astonishing, the play was mostly imagined, not depicted on a table. The impartial and disinterested role of the "judge" or "referee" typical for a military miniatures tabletop game now expanded considerably. That individual, destined to become known as the "Dungeon Master," had the critical part in the new game. He it was who had to devise the nature of the adventure, impart all of the imaginary details of the environment, and then assume the roles of all active entities that the players' characters encountered therein. Astonishing stuff! But the rules lacked a name.

Pondering this problem, I created a list of words, writing them in two columns. Having had some considerable experience in naming games by that time, thinking of potentially "good" names for the new design was not difficult. You can see for yourself some of the "rejected"

DUNGEONS & DRAGONS

Rules for Fantastic Medieval Wargames
Campaigns Playable with Paper and Pencil
and Miniature Figures

GYGAX & ARNESON

Original Collector's Edition

3-VOLUME SET

PUBLISHED BY
TACTICAL STUDIES RULES

BY GARY GYGAX
Dungeon Module S3
by Gary Gygax
SPECIAL ILLUSTRATION BOOKLET INCLUDED
ADVANCED DUNGEONS & DRAGONS
T1
FIRST OF 2 MODULES
Dungeon Module T1
The Village of Hommlet
by Gary Gygax
9072
EX1
Adventure Module For Character Levels 9-12
Advanced Dungeons & Dragons
Fantasy Adventure Module
Dungeonland
by E. Gary Gygax
You may have adventured in strange places before, but when your party suddenly fi
Dungeonland, you will have to employ all your wits and skill!
WG6
Approved for use with ADVANCED D&D Game rules
9153
Advanced Dungeons & Dragons
WORLD of GREYHAWK
Fantasy World Adventure
Isle of the Ape
by Gary Gygax

“ . . . COPIES OF THE COPIES OF THE FIRST

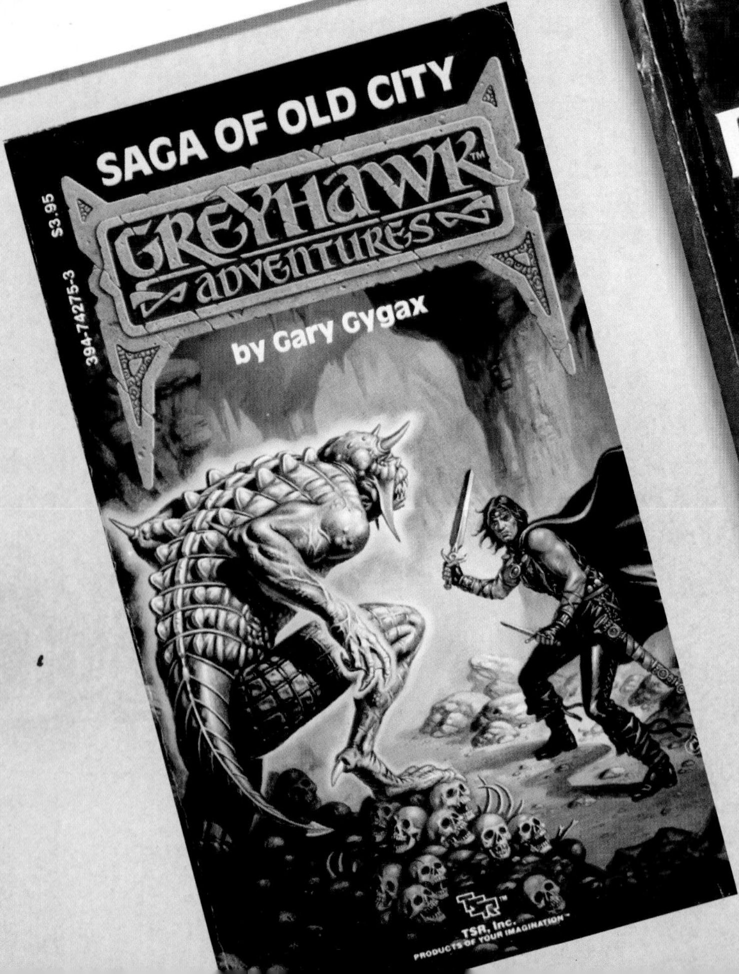

SAGA OF OLD CITY
GREYHAWK™ ADVENTURES
by Gary Gygax
394-74275-3 $3.95
TSR, Inc.
PRODUCTS OF YOUR IMAGINATION™

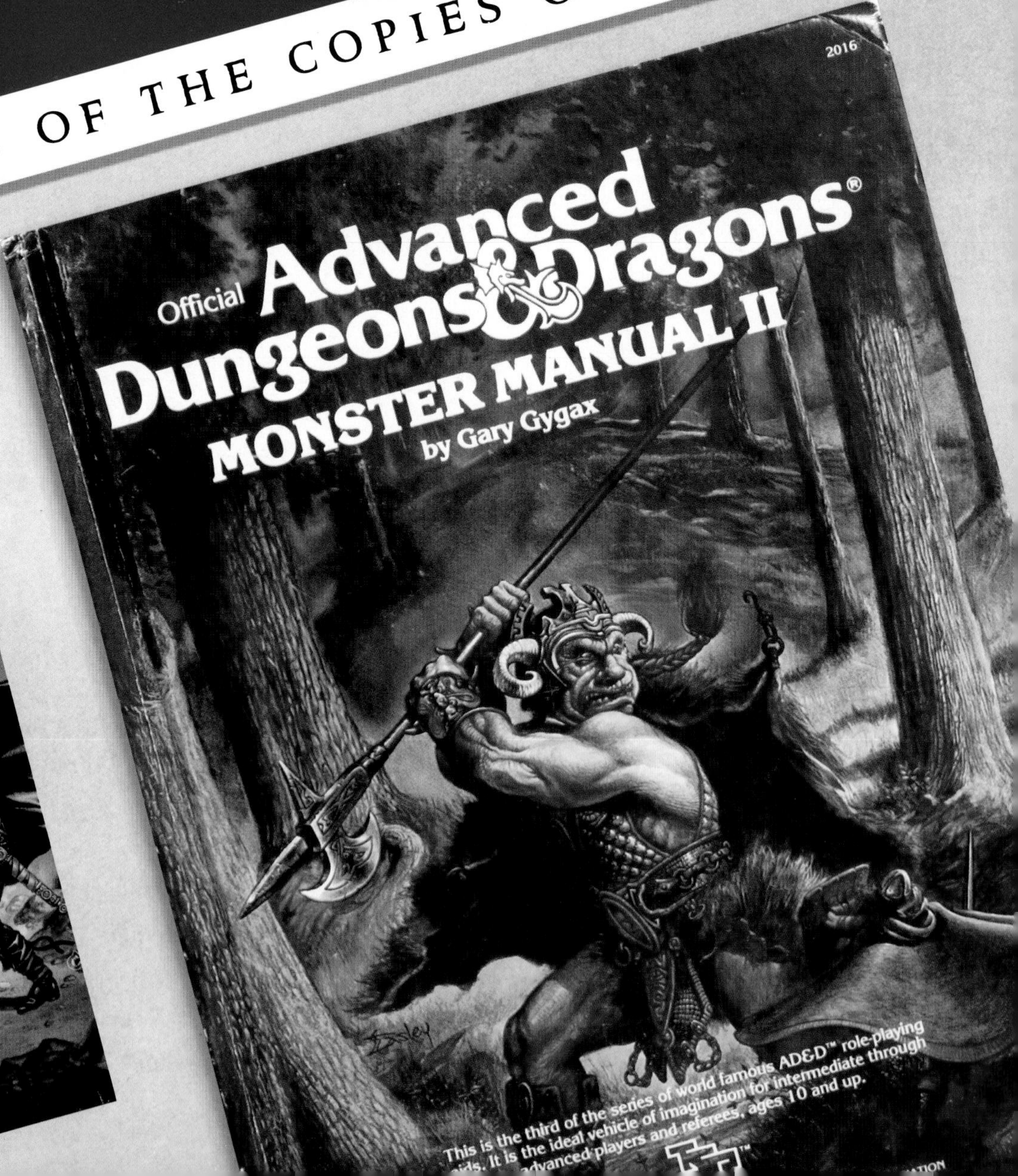

2016
Official Advanced Dungeons & Dragons®
MONSTER MANUAL II
by Gary Gygax
This is the third of the series of world famous AD&D™ role-playing
It is the ideal vehicle of imagination for intermediate through
advanced players and referees, ages 10 and up.

choices on the covers of the three booklets that eventually came to comprise the finished product, the first edition of the DUNGEONS & DRAGONS game. That's right—men, magic(al), monsters, treasure, underworld, and wilderness were on the list. So were castles, dragons, dungeons, giants, labyrinths, mazes, sorcery, spells, swords, trolls, and so forth. I cannot recall all the choices, but there were about 15 words in each column. I took a poll of my players (two of whom were my children Ernie and Elise). After reading aloud from the list, there was no doubt. Youngest daughter Cindy's delight at the alliterative pair chosen confirmed my own personal favorite. After all, I had before that time created the "Castle & Crusade" society as a special interest group for the International Federation of Wargaming. It followed that a medieval-based new game should have a similar name, one evocative of its nature.

When the scant manuscript was copied and mailed off to some two dozen or so gaming comrades, mostly IFW members, of course, a few days later, it bore the title, "Dungeons & Dragons." When 1973 was welcomed in, it is likely that some 200 people had heard of the new game. By the spring of that year I had expanded the manuscript to three times its former size and divided it into three portions. By then it was, in fact, just about the same as the three booklets that were soon to be published. My own experience from intensive Dungeon Mastering, and much feedback from the wildly enthused recipients of the initial draft of the game rules, made creation of the enlarged version a matter of delight, no effort at all.

By then, of course, copies of the copies of the first manuscript were proliferating. I sent out only some 50 copies of the expanded new version of the DUNGEONS & DRAGONS game manuscript because of time and costs. Letters and even telephone calls requesting that I "please, please mail me the new stuff," and so on were coming in daily by then. It

was apparent to me that the game was destined to be a hit. I was sure most wargamers and even a lot of fantasy and science fiction literature fans would love the new D&D game. (OK, I was pathetically underestimating the appeal, but nobody is perfect.) One copy was even sent off to what was then the leading game publisher, a company I had long admired, for whom I had written articles and done game design work. They laughed hysterically, I was later informed, then when I telephoned to see if there was interest, they declined.

When through the auspices of the Lake Geneva Tactical Studies Association I staged Gen Con in August 1973, one of my D&D game campaign group came to the event for the first time. Don Kaye saw the turnout, noted the interest in the fans there, and after the event was over asked, "Do you really think you can make a success of a game publishing company?" No need to detail my response. In October Tactical Studies Rules was born, and in December of 1973 the 150-page manuscript went

"THE FACT IS, THIS GAME IS UNIQUE."

off to Graphic Printing in Lake Geneva. We were in a great hurry to get it done, and I was concerned about editing. The printer assured us that the work would be corrected as it was typeset—the retyping on an IBM typewriter of my draft—for burning of printing plates. Hah! The work was copied faithfully, so the errors were and are all there, just as they appeared in my original draft. Ah, well. At least it was finally in print!

The first sale of a DUNGEONS & DRAGONS game was made late in January 1974. Thus, 1999 is the Silver Anniversary, the 25th year after the publication of the game. By the summer of 1974 we had sold some 500 copies. Amazing! Counting all of the illicit photocopies that were floating around, and the players who didn't own their own set, it is a safe bet that no fewer than 10,000 persons then knew of and were enthralled by the D&D game. Before the end of the year we had to reprint, and this time we ordered 2,000 copies. There was no doubt anywhere now. The game was

a success. Little did we know how great a success it was to be.

Before publication, in 1972 and 1973, people looked blank, or perhaps a little askance, when hearing about the D&D game. Its name was odd-sounding to most, and the concept of a game without player opponents, one that had no winner, lacking a conclusion, was so new, literally unheard of, that many simply could not comprehend it. Imagine, if you will, attempting to find new "converts"—then, as now, the true enthusiast is always seeking to add fellows to the "ranks"—and having to explain roleplaying from the most basic concepts on up. Even with thousands and thousands of dedicated players actively out doing just that, and by 1975 that was the case, it was daunting. Still, we managed. My own gaming group was but a handful in 1972. In 1973 it had grown to a dozen. When the D&D game was actually published, the number of people showing up for one of the several weekly sessions in the

basement of my house was often in excess of 20. To accommodate all those eager RPGers, I made Rob Kuntz co-DM of my "Castle Greyhawk" campaign. We merged our dungeons and worked both as a team to manage huge groups of player characters adventuring simultaneously and also ran several separate sessions each week with "only" a dozen or so players in each.

Through the power of the game, the burning enthusiasm it engendered, this sort of thing occurred all over the U.S., Canada, and then beyond. England and other English-speaking places discovered the D&D game; then those able to manage the language even though it was not their native tongue were playing. Just two years after its release, when only about 10,000 copies had been sold, the DUNGEONS & DRAGONS game had a following on at least three continents. In due course it went on to gain a million or more fans, as the game was translated into many languages.

The fact is, this game is unique. It is the first roleplaying game, the original fantasy RPG, and more. The D&D game has the "nuts & bolts" from which all roleplaying games coming after drew in some measure to develop different approaches to the new game form. Beyond that, it is in and of itself special. This little game is a marvel in that it touches some primal chord in so many persons. It resonates with the mythic, strikes deep into the subconscious where the heroic dwells. This is a basic and uncomplicated roleplaying game. It has little structure, few rules, but unlimited horizons. It offers such vistas of fantasy as were never beheld before it came into being. Welcome to the "new" multiverse that the DUNGEONS & DRAGONS game offers.

Is it still viable? Of course! Despite being around for a quarter of a century and more, it is new. Considering that much of the stuff upon which it is actually based is older than mankind's recorded history, that being the hero and the mythic quest, this "old" game is barely an infant. Indeed, it has such power that despite it being in competition with more detailed, complex, and better supported fantasy RPGs published by its own company and those from competing game publishers too, there is still a considerable following who play the D&D game in its largely original form. That this is the case after all these years, and seeing that this set has not been available for so many years, it is remarkable in the extreme.

Time marches on. The DUNGEONS & DRAGONS game does not stand still, it moves ahead as well. The game form and the genre are so absolutely compelling as to demand change as well as honoring tradition. Without placing a value judgment, consider that the advent of the ADVANCED DUNGEONS & DRAGONS game brought vast numbers of new roleplaying enthusiasts onto the gaming hobby. "Advanced" is an apt term, for the new game did further many of the base concepts of the D&D game while adding much and detailing a vast amount of new information so as to expand the realms of fantasy yet further. What innovations lie in the future? I cannot say, but as with all lovers of this game, I am certainly looking forward to them with eager anticipation. So many possibilities, so much to explore, endless adventures ahead. . . .

Meantime, I think I will step back a moment. Even though it seems like yesterday, the blink of an eye, it has been a long time since I played a real D&D game. It is so easy to roll up a few characters, my players won't mind, and what DM worthy of the name can't "wing" an adventure as he was meant to by these rules? So, I leave you to your own devices. Pardon me, but I think I need to get in some gaming.

Gary Gygax
Lake Geneva, Wisconsin
March 1999

Wil Wheaton

Statistics and Attributes: Film audiences first met Wil Wheaton in the classic film *Stand By Me*, while television audiences followed his journeys on the starship Enterprise in *Star Trek: The Next Generation*. Wheaton, 32, recently opened the Second Act of his life with two books: *Dancing Barefoot*, and *Just A Geek*. His personal website at www.wilwheaton.net is one of the most popular weblog sites on the Internet, and was recently named *Best Celebrity Weblog* by Forbes.com.

Wil is a life-long gamer.

Description: At Christmas 1979 my great aunt gave me the red box set of D&D that had the basic rules, the stapled Dungeon Masters Guide, and the *Keep on the Borderlands* module. It had the old dice that you had to color in the numbers.

She said, "I hear this is a game that the kids really like to play, and I think you'd really like it because you get to use your imagination."

When I sat down and started reading, my head immediately filled with images of dragons and orcs. I'd never heard of those things before — I was a little young for Tolkien and I didn't know what an orc or a bugbear was. But I thought it was the coolest thing!

Fifth and sixth grade was when I really began to play extensively because a lot of kids in my school were really into it. One friend had a ton of little lead figures and pieces of Styrofoam that he had cut to look like bricks and then painted gray. We used to build dungeons all over my bedroom floor.

I always liked being a wizard, because I thought they were super-cool. Nowadays with 3rd Edition I play monks and rangers, but when I was a kid I loved to play wizards. In real life, I've always been slight and not especially strong or big. Instead I've been really cerebral. Unlike some players who wanted to portray characters very unlike themselves, I wanted to play a wizard who was my idealized version of myself. Wizards are based on Intelligence and Wisdom rather than being based on Charisma, like sorcerers are in 3rd Edition. I always wanted to be a wise, intelligent person, so I was drawn to wizards.

I think the Forgotten Realms setting is fantastic. It reminds me so much of Middle Earth. My friends gave me the campaign sourcebook for my birthday a couple of years ago. I find that D&D manuals, especially the 3rd Edition manuals, can be read kind of like the appendices in *Return of the King*.

I stopped playing during 2nd Edition but started up again with 3rd Edition. I went to my local Wizards of the Coast store every day for a week ahead of time, trying to cajole the manager into letting me see the stuff before it came out. When the first set of core rulebooks finally all came out I stuck them in my backpack and carried them around everywhere.

Nowadays I DM a lot. I'm teaching my stepchildren, who are twelve and fourteen, to play. It's so great for me to sit down with them and describe a dungeon. I was doing a hack-and-slash dungeon one afternoon, and I put them in a really big empty cavern. I'm describing this big empty cavern to them, and they can hear water dripping somewhere, and there's this breath of wind across their faces. A really awful smell comes from the back of the cave. They both looked at each other, and I could see they were putting two and two together.

My older stepson said, "Stop! I know what it is!"

I'd made a bunch of bugbears standing over goblin corpses, and that was what they smelled.

Roleplaying games are incredibly interactive. I tell my kids all the time that when you have free time it's fine to watch a TV show, but try to strike a balance between using your time in a way that's entertaining but also enriching. And roleplaying games are incredibly enriching. ∎

Sherman Alexie

Statistics and Attributes: Sherman Alexie is a poet, novelist, author of the screenplay for *Smoke Signals*, and one of the most dynamic forces in modern American literature. He lives in the Seattle area.

Description: I first learned about DUNGEONS & DRAGONS when I was eight or nine years old. Maybe older, maybe younger. *The Spokesman-Review*, the only paper in Spokane, Washington, sixty miles from my reservation, published a story about a local hobby store that was home to a dedicated group of men who were conducting a months-long DUNGEONS & DRAGONS campaign. The story was accompanied by a four-color photograph of a chubby man leaning over a table decorated with tiny plastic trees, boulders, and castles. He looked like a Twinkie-addicted giant as he stared at the two-inch-tall lead miniature figure of a medieval warrior. That little warrior was muscular and fierce and heroic, completely unlike his owner. That hero was the fantasy doppelganger for a chubby gamer who probably couldn't have run a mile without serious heart damage. Other readers might have laughed at the story and photograph. Heck, ninety-nine percent of other readers probably made fun of that guy. But I was in love. Well, not in love with the guy, but in love with the slightly crazed look in his eyes. There was a mysterious passion in his eyes. Something mystical. Yes, I said it. It was mystical.

Maybe mystical is not the right word. Maybe there are no words to explain why the story and photograph appealed so strongly to me. But I'm a writer, so I have to try to find the words, enit? So listen: I knew instantly that I wanted to play the game. Moreover, I knew I would love the game and play it and love it forever. Can you fall in love with a game? Heck, can you fall in love with the idea of a game? I don't know, but I instantly wanted to become a weird obsessive-compulsive geek-boy gamer. Other kids wanted to be U.S. President or quarterback for the Dallas Cowboys, but I wanted to be a twentieth-level warrior with triple-digit Strength and Dexterity. I wanted to be heroic.

So I bought used copies of the Dungeons & Dragons' books and played the game mostly by myself. It's hard to find sympathetic gamers anywhere in the world and pretty dang impossible on the Spokane Indian Reservation. I created campaigns and dungeons and heroes and villains and played all of the roles. I was the Dungeon Master and the courageous and hapless adventurers. I was the wizard and the warrior and the elf and the dragon and the orc and the troll. I created entire worlds and tribes that I could control. I was a small version of God.

My family is troubled and has nearly been destroyed by poverty and alcoholism. My tribe is even more troubled and has nearly been destroyed by more poverty and alcoholism than my family has. I was a little boy growing up in a dangerous world where nobody gave me the chance to make a saving roll. And yet, while playing D&D, I pretended so often to have courage and strength that I learned how to display courage and strength in my real life. I love D&D, the game, because I never thought it was a game. ∎

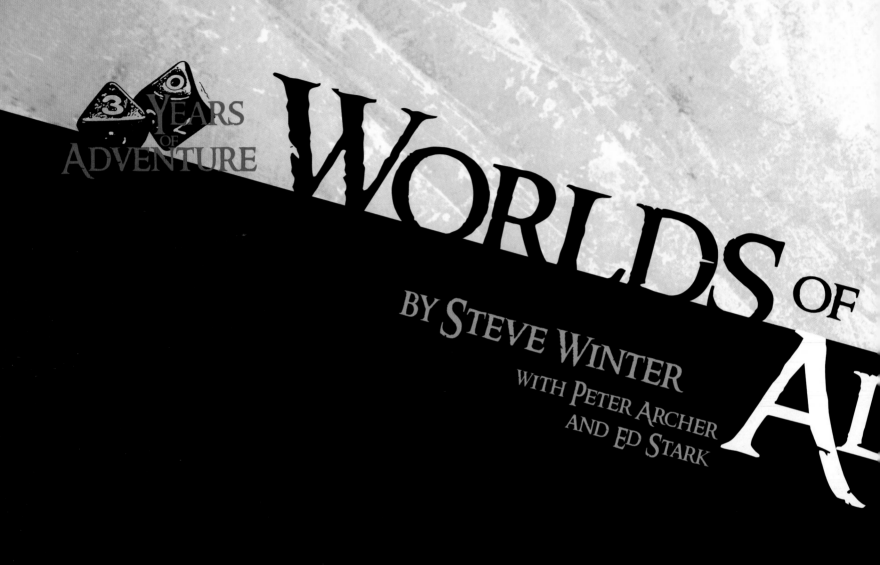

30 Years
OF
Adventure

WORLDS OF

BY STEVE WINTER
WITH PETER ARCHER
AND ED STARK

AD

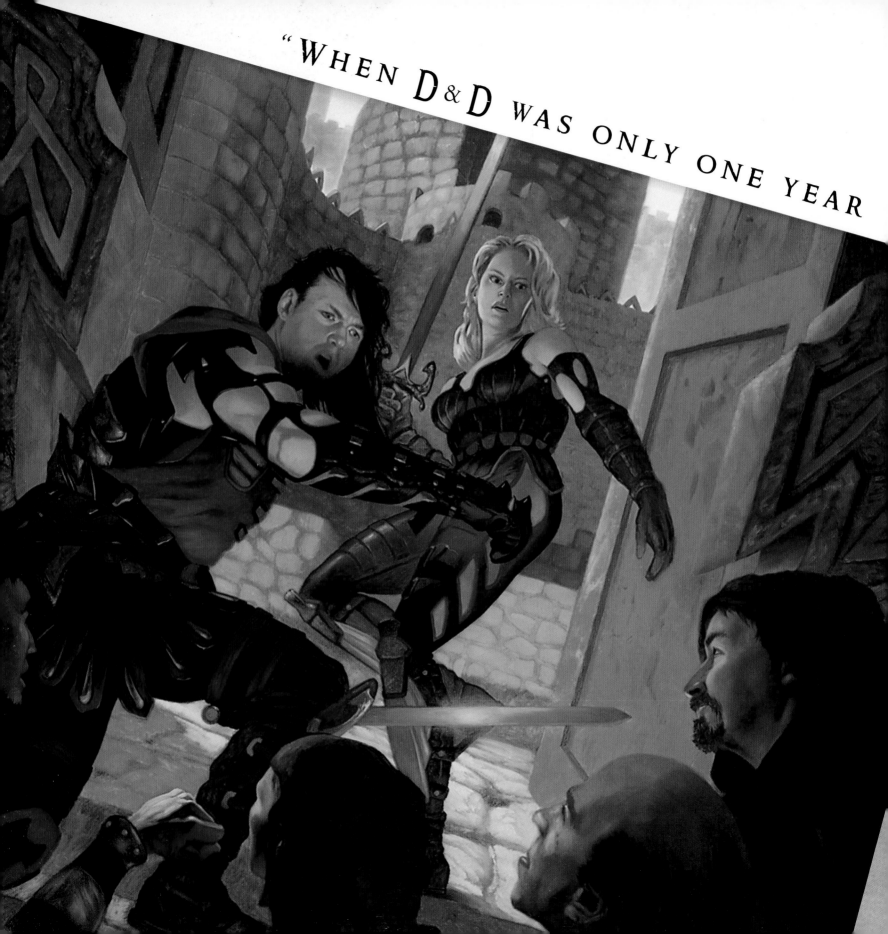

GREYHAWK

BY ED STARK

To many, the phrase "world of GREYHAWK" is synonymous with the "world of DUNGEONS & DRAGONS." Until TSR published Gary Gygax's home campaign setting back in 1975, D&D was a fantasy game without a fantasy setting. Supplement I: *Greyhawk* took Gary's notes from his home campaign, organized them, mapped them, and threw them out into the world for D&D fans to enjoy.

How important was this to DUNGEONS & DRAGONS? In today's roleplaying game community, one campaign setting more or less probably wouldn't cause even a ripple among players. Dungeon Masters today are used to picking and choosing from a multitude of fantasy worlds or even creating their own. But "back in the day," when D&D was only one year old, this was a monumental first step.

As you've read in other parts of this book, D&D grew out of a wargame background. The world of the wargame is the battlefield. Even those set in the real world don't need back-story or characters

or myths to be adequate game experiences. But D&D was, and is, something different. The world of GREYHAWK gave D&D a home and a place to live and grow. It also set a standard easily forgotten in later years.

The GREYHAWK setting comprised the world surrounding the City of Greyhawk, which lies in the Flaness, on Oerik, on the world of Oerth. It included such organizations as the Scarlet Brotherhood and villains such as Vecna and Iuz.

When Gygax & Co. laid out Supplement I, however, they remembered that the world of GREYHAWK was home to a game, not just someone's fantasy stories. The original GREYHAWK supplement introduced a brand new character class to the game—the thief—new spells, new magic items, and a host of new monsters. Gary Gygax's world could easily have been just another setting (as many of today's RPG campaign settings are), but he chose to use the much-needed developed fantasy world to build upon the rules of the infant D&D game.

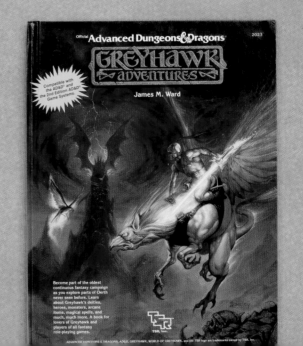

The history of D&D's first game setting is much like D&D itself. The GREYHAWK setting started small and grew. From Supplement I it became a campaign setting, with a full-color map and a book. It became a boxed set, a larger book, and even a living campaign. To say that everyone who has ever played D&D has played GREYHAWK might be an overstatement, but not by much. The setting has included such iconic and well-loved adventures as *White Plume Mountain*, *Against the Giants*, and *The Tomb of Horrors* ("No one got out of the Tomb of Horrors alive!" some old-time gamers will still tell you.) The world of GREYHAWK has permeated D&D's own core rules so thoroughly that to extract all the GREYHAWK elements from D&D would strip it of the core fantasy surrounding the game.

Between 1978 and 1980, TSR published a series of adventures set in the world of GREYHAWK. In 1980 *The World of Greyhawk* appeared, expanded to a boxed set in 1983. The first GREYHAWK novel, *Saga of the Old City* by Gary Gygax, appeared in 1985. The setting was revived at various times, most recently in 1998.

Currently, the GREYHAWK setting remains a place where die-hard roleplayers, old-time fans (often called "grognards"), and members of the ROLEPLAYING GAMERS ASSOCIATION (RPGA) have adventures and pass their D&D time. It was the "default, implied" campaign setting for the 3rd Edition of DUNGEONS & DRAGONS, partly because it holds so much of D&D within itself already but also because the number one grognard of them all, Peter Adkison, wanted it that way. So from one of the original creators of DUNGEONS & DRAGONS to the man who revitalized an industry, GREYHAWK still has its fans, and it still survives.

WORLDS OF IMAGINATION

GREYHAWK ADVENTURES

Ralph Sanchez

Statistics and Attributes: Ralph Sanchez is a former production executive for MTV Networks.

Description: I remember the moment as if it was only yesterday. But it was really twenty-six years ago almost to the day.

It was a chilly day in early February. Second semester was about to start.

I stood at the doorway. I listened. Somebody said the words, "roll for initiative." I was about to step into a new world.

It was 1978, and I was halfway through my sophomore year at the University of Southern California. Still living at the dorms, one Friday night I wandered past an open door near the end of the hallway. Even over the Aerosmith blaring from two doors down, I could hear the strange conversation that was taking place in Dan's room. Phrases like, "what's your armor class," "I'm checking for secret doors," and "conjuring hold portal" were being bandied about enthusiastically, as if the guys in Dan's room were participating in some sporting event . . . yet, they were as static as three guys sitting on top of dorm bunks.

"What's this?" I asked, poking my head in.

Dan simply said, "DUNGEONS & DRAGONS."

I don't know if it was the fact I was on my third beer, or that my girlfriend was studying for a final and was half a campus away, or that I was just plain curious – I ventured into the room with a "Say what?" and a sudden desire to join.

DUNGEONS & DRAGONS soon became part of my life. At USC, it was mostly every Friday night that at least five of us would gather for an adventure. Dan started running a campaign. He was our DM. I was the initiate. So was another buddy of mine – fresh fodder for the Dungeon Master to torture. It was a perfect time for me, too, to be getting into a game that demanded so much imagination from its players. I was on my second screenwriting class at SC, and the interactive storytelling that is, in my opinion, the basis for D&D helped my developing skills as a writer tremendously.

Of course, it was also a heckuva good time.

One of my first characters was a Paladin-wannabe fighter whom I uninspiredly called "Arthur." Our DM thought I could do better. Well, I quickly changed his name to GoForIt. Okay, so maybe I was breaking a little bit of the mood since the others were calling their characters Alagorth and Blortok the Great, but I thought it might be fun to have a noble warrior with a blue collar name and personality.

GoForIt turned out to be one of the great heroes of the campaign we ran that year. He was also a huge pain in the butt. You see, GoForIt was completely committed to stamping out evil. All evil. Anything that he ran into that even smelled of evil, he would lunge after, raising sword high over his head, and exclaiming in no small voice, "In the name of God!" He would charge into the fray almost without thinking. If it was orc, kobold, or goblin, he would dash and slash. He was a berserker paladin. Even when faced with a foe that those with reason would recommend a hasty retreat from, GoForIt just charged with his all-too-familiar war cry. He charged a Beholder once. The outcome was not pretty. It's a good thing there was a high-level cleric in the party that day.

GoForIt learned a little about restraint when one time, he was hit by an arrow in his left shoulder blade. The arrow came from one of the party members. GoForIt was trying to charge a Balrog that time (yes, Dan ran Balrogs in his dungeon!). His party dragged him into retreat. From that day on, GoForIt learned to play a little nicer with his friends.

The thing that kept GoForIt valuable to the group was his uncanny ability to always hit. He would roll more hits than the

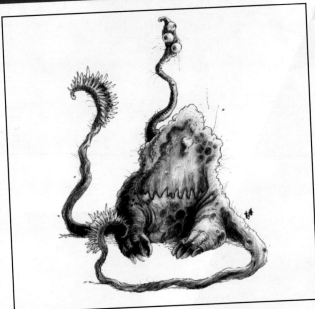

laws of chance would supposedly allow. He rose quickly in experience and rank, and was soon one of the leaders in the Quest for the White Sword – the campaign that lasted the rest of the school year. There was a final confrontation that took place over Memorial Day Weekend. Three straight days of D&D. The party confronted the elusive but legendary "Death Dealer," a sort of medieval Darth Vader, who had stolen the powerful White Sword (this artifact could open portals between dimensions, aside from being a really good weapon). We won. We took the sword back. Our Memorial Day Weekend was a celebration of our love for the game.

After college, life happens. The opportunities to play D&D seem less and less. But the fond memories of the games shared with friends keep tugging you back to an occasional dabbling into the arena. For me, as I tilted at the giant windmills of the entertainment industry in order to get a job in television, D&D found me again and was instrumental in helping me get my first "real" job.

In the fall of 1983, CBS was airing the animated children's series *Dungeons & Dragons* on Saturday mornings. I just so happened to be working at CBS at the time, as an assistant to one of the directors of prime time programming. I eagerly watched the show. I liked it, despite the obligatory funny unicorn that was inserted for comic relief and to push plush merchandise, no doubt. Still, this was D&D. On TV! Suddenly, I was sparked to write a treatment for an episode. I showed the treatment to the executive overseeing the production of the show, and he liked it. Before I knew it, I had an interview with the head of Children's Programs at CBS, because they thought I had captured the sensibilities of the show, and because, more importantly, there was an opening in their department.

I was hired a week later all thanks to D&D.

By the way, the episode I wrote – it was about how the heroes encountered this Death Dealer. Sound familiar? Well, they say you write best about what you experience. And for me, the experience of DUNGEONS & DRAGONS will be part of who I am forever. It is a fun and influential part of my life. It is a small part of my current life, as I have DM'ed once or twice for my own kids. The legend just keeps going, and going. . . . ∎

Mark Tremonti

Statistics and Attributes: Mark Tremonti along with Scott Phillips, Myles Kennedy, and Brian Marshall, is a member of the band Alter Bridge.

Description: I started playing DUNGEONS & DRAGONS when I was about eight years old and played for years. My brother was the Dungeon Master, and we'd play all day long. Our parents would have to yell at us to come to dinner.

We'd take the manuals and go through and list all the monsters. We'd shuffle up the monsters in a hat and take every monster and do battle with our characters, all kinds of fun stuff.

My favorite character was probably my barbarian. He had an 18 Strength, but he wasn't the smartest guy. His name was Conan — naturally. I remember my brother got mad at me once and purposely poisoned him to death. I had a fit and wouldn't play with him anymore unless he revived Conan, so we had to work something out.

I played until I was a freshman in high school, then my brother stayed in Detroit while I moved down to Florida, so I didn't have anybody to play with. Otherwise, I'd probably still be playing today.

Things happen all the time that remind me of D&D. Just recently I bought a Trivial Pursuit DVD. One of the questions had a picture that you had to identify, and it was a twenty-sided die.

Today my most prized possessions are the original cover art for The Players Handbook, The Dungeon Masters Guide, Monster Manual, *Keep on the Borderlands,* Manual of the Planes, and other D&D books. How it happened was, I have a signature model with Paul Reed Smith guitars, and they do a guitar called a dragon model. They commissioned Jeff Easley to paint the dragon. I saw the painting in Paul Reed Smith's office and asked him what it was about.

He told me it was the painting for the guitar and asked if I wanted it. Of course, I said yes.

He said, "It's by the guy who did all the DUNGEONS & DRAGONS stuff."

I said, "Jeff Easley?"

He sent the painting to Jeff, and Jeff signed my name on it and sent it back. I called Jeff and asked him, "Do you happen to have any of your old paintings sitting around?"

He said, "Sure, I've got tons of them."

I said, "You wouldn't happen to have the Monster Manual one?"

"Yes."

"Players Handbook?"

"Yes."

"Dungeon Masters Guide?"

"Yeah, I've got that too."

It was like hitting a gold mine. Today they're my most prized possessions. It's amazing. Whenever I look at them, I see a piece of my childhood. It blows my mind. ∎

DRAGONLANCE
BY PETER ARCHER

In the fall of 1980, TSR was looking closely at the DUNGEONS & DRAGONS property and at ways to expand and develop it. D&D was rising in popularity, and the company, which now employed more than 200 people, was bursting at the seams.

Meanwhile, in Provo, Utah, a young man was looking for a job.

Tracy Hickman, a Mormon, had returned from his mission abroad in Indonesia in March 1980. He married his sweetheart, Laura Curtis, in June, and the young couple struggled to make ends meet. Laura Curtis had introduced Tracy to D&D in 1997 before he went abroad. Hickman became fascinated with the game, working with his wife to design their own modules, covering page after page of graph paper with detailed diagrams of dungeons. (Later when several of their modules had circulated around gaming circles, a myth arose of "the Hickman sisters," Tracy and Laura.) Hickman self published one module, and in 1980 Mike Gray from TSR picked up a copy. Gray was impressed enough to set up an interview for Hickman in Lake Geneva. The upshot was that the Hickmans set out

by car for Wisconsin in March 1981, with a job awaiting Tracy at TSR.

On their way across the country, husband and wife discussed ideas that had been percolating for several years. What about a world dominated by dragons? What about an entire world to support a storyline?

The idea fell on receptive ears at TSR. The company's marketing department had concluded that TSR's products had plenty of dungeons but needed more dragons. Hickman suggested a series of twelve modules, each featuring a dragon. Harold Johnson proposed to Tracy that they get additional support from other departments for the project.

Thus DRAGONLANCE was born as a kind of underground movement within TSR. Hickman went from department to department, gathering support for the project. He and Johnson pitched the idea to the art staff at an evening meeting held in artist Larry Elmore's basement. Week after week, month after month, a group that included Johnson, Hickman, Jeff Grubb, Larry Elmore, Roger Moore, Doug Niles, Michael Williams,

WORLDS OF IMAGINATION

"JUST WHO ARE MARGARET WEIS AND TRACY HICKMAN,

and others met in various combinations to discuss ideas and try out themes.

Meanwhile . . .

By 1983 Margaret Weis was ready to leave Independence, Missouri. She had just finalized a divorce and had two young children. Since she'd had extensive experience working as an editor in Missouri and since she wanted to move, it was only natural that when she heard about an open position for a book editor with a company called TSR, she should apply for it. She was hired and prepared to relocate.

She arrived in Fontana, Wisconsin, ahead of the movers with two children and three cats, and had to wait a week for her belongings to arrive. In the meantime, she began her new job in Lake Geneva.

The Book Department that had hired her had begun as the "Education Department" of the company. Its first publications were Endless Quest books in which readers chose between various alternative passages to make their way through the story. The wrong choice could end in disaster.

Weis wrote several of these books, as well as books based on the DUNGEONS & DRAGONS cartoon show. She worked on the Endless Quest books as an editor, as well as editing books in a series aimed at young girls, Heartquest. As an experienced editor, it was only a matter of time before she was drafted into the DRAGONLANCE project.

The notion that evolved from the DRAGONLANCE designers was that in addition to the game modules, there should be novels, books that would tell the story of the world. The company agreed — albeit somewhat reluctantly — and after much debate a writer was hired to produce the books.

ANYWAY?"

James Merendino

Statistics and Attributes: James Merendino is the acclaimed writer/director of the Sundance Film Festival classic, *SLC Punk*, which is soon to become an animated series for MTV. Merendino has written and directed a number of independent films, among which are *Magicians*, starring Alan Arkin and Claire Forlani; *Terrified*, starring Heather Graham; and his latest, *Trespassing*, starring Estella Warren. James was born in New Jersey and was raised in Salt Lake City.

Description: When I became aware of DUNGEONS & DRAGONS, I must have been nine years old.

I read Lord of the Rings when I was eight years old, and I wrote a book that was a rip off of Lord of the Rings. It was, like, 800 pages. Somebody gave me *Deities and Demigods* so I could come up with gods for my book. For Christmas I got the Dungeon Masters Guide, the Players Handbook, and the Creatures guide. So I had all these great books I could refer to. I used the books to help structure my story. At some point I realized this book needed some history so I started writing a history to go with it, and that's when I started using these books.

I got my first adventure … I don't remember what it was called. The next-door neighbors and I played it immediately.

I was the Dungeon Master. When I wasn't, I played a chaotic good elf. My favorite character was Zenta, a magic user, who became a fourteenth-level magic user.

I still play with some actors I know, and I still have all the stuff. But back in high school we played every weekend or after school or all summer long.

We got to a point where we started making up our own dungeons. It was more fun that way. We played all the old adventures—*White Plume Mountain, Expedition to the Barrier Peaks*—but then we made up our own adventures. I think that's the best part of it.

I lived in Utah, and there was a lot of scandal about D&D back in the eighties. In the midst of all that, there was a competition, and we won the competition. We won $1000, but we won it by accident. The DM had made the dungeon with a back door, where there was a secondary way to win and find the treasure. We found this trapdoor that no one would ever look for in a tunnel. Then when we crossed a certain lake, we found the treasure and won the game. It was supposed to be a six-month tournament, and it ended in two hours. Everyone was mad at me.

My interest in filmmaking was totally driven by DUNGEONS & DRAGONS. We used to do live action gaming and film it. We'd play part of adventures, and I'd film what happened. I lived right against a mountain, and there was nothing on it, so it could look like a D&D world if you wanted to. That's when I started directing.

I'd love to make a fantasy movie. To me it would be interesting to make one of the adventures—or have a competition and see how the script would play out. Of course you'd have to brush it up, but it would make a great movie.

I shot my movie at this place called the Old Mill, where they had live role playing. I like the live stuff. But it's lots of fun to sit down at the table and play the game. We start in town and buy your stuff. Some people skip that stuff—how far you can go in a day and so on—but I like that. ∎

John Rogers

Statistics and Attributes: John Rogers created the hit WB Kids show *Jackie Chan Adventures*, has written over ten feature films, and is currently executive-producing the TV show *Global Frequency* for the Warner Bros. Network.

Description: "We don't want to go into the cave."

I stared at my sister and my friends. But the graph-paper maps were all done. The monster stats. The random treasure tables! How could they not understand?

"You said there were ruins near the village. We want to go there."

I slid the graph-paper maps away, stuck a thumb in the Monster Manual, and started, well ... winging it. The mad king, the bargain with the monsters, the betrayal by his daughter—I was just telling a story. My first story. I had no idea I'd be "just telling stories" for the rest of my life.

Obstacle, conflict, resolution, complication—people spend years at college learning to master these crucial writing tools. I learned them through the tiny arrows leading from room ("obstacle") to room ("complication") in the Vault of the Drow. I learned about good characterization, cliffhangers, and reversals. All good TV shows and movies create their own internal, consistent worlds. So do all good Dungeon Masters.

And most important, when I came to Hollywood, the DM's greatest tool was mine: the ability to lie quickly and enthusiastically. It doesn't matter how off the rails a story meeting goes, what insane question a producer asks, or how vast a rewrite we need in an hour, I can always convince people that whatever I'm spewing out was my clever plan all along. You think an angry director is tough? Nothing compared to a PC arguing over his beloved paladin's death, my friend. Nothing.

It may be my mid-thirties talking, but I pity kids now, playing alone in video simulations of someone else's worlds. Worlds where if you don't do the "right" thing, you don't "win." I played with a group of friends. There were no limits, and the world was ours. (And we had to walk to our games in the snow, uphill both ways, but that's another rant....) The rules were often impenetrable on the first, third, and fourteenth read-through, forcing us to teach the game from generation of gamer to generation of gamer. Fact is—although it may have been an accidental by-product of some very bad copywriting (you know who you are)—DUNGEONS & DRAGONS is one of the few remaining oral traditions in our high-tech world.

Thirty years of D&D has also produced an entire generation of players who are out there now, in all walks of life. They're particularly heavy on the ground in the entertainment world, using all those same lessons I picked up along the way. I recently started playing again, something I'm not shy about telling people. I expected a bit of mocking from my fellow writers, but almost to a one the eyes go wide, the jaw drops, and I get a whispered "No ... way."

How ingrained is D&D in Hollywood? I once walked out of a meeting with a studio president during which one of his less-important execs had interrupted with an idiotic pitch. In the hallway, one producer turned to another and asked, "Who was the dude with four hit points?"

My friend Andrew Cosby (creator of the TV show *Haunted*) was recently in a meeting with an Oscar-winning writer-producer. The writer, discussing a character in a $60 million script, said "He's like, you know, a multi-classed fighter/thief." After an awkward pause, the writer chortled "Come on, I knew you'd get that reference." Andrew nodded and picked up the phone.

There, in the middle of an insanely important meeting, he took time out to dial his mother back in Georgia. As soon as she picked up the phone, Andrew yelled into the receiver: "I TOLD YOU IT WASN'T THE DEVIL'S GAME!" and hung up.

Sweet victory at last.

So next time you're in LA, give a yell. Bring 4d6 and come with me.... ∎

"...THE WORLD OF DRAGONLANCE WAS

More and more, the design group found themselves disillusioned by his work. Mike Gray, a strong supporter of the project, suggested several times that "Margaret and Tracy really ought to write the books." Finally, over a weekend, Weis and Hickman sat down together and wrote five chapters of material.

This being a DUNGEONS & DRAGONS-based world, they began the story — naturally — with an inn.

Shadows were dwindling as noon approached. The Inn of the Last Home would soon be open for business. Tika looked around and smiled in satisfaction. The tables were clean and polished. All she had left to do was sweep the floor. She began to shove aside the heavy wooden benches, as Otik emerged from the kitchen, enveloped in fragrant steam.

The story, as it evolved, was not only one with plenty of action and high adventure. It was also about friendship, about choices, and about the tragedy of loss and the joy of discovery.

The following Monday Weis and Hickman took the manuscript tremulously to Jean Black, head of the Book Department. Black took it into her office and shut the door. After an interminable time, she opened her door, looked at Weis and Hickman sitting in Weis's cubicle across the hallway, and said, "Wow!"

Matters were not, of course, quite so simple. Black fired the previously contracted writer and hired Weis and Hickman to write the books,

but there were still other people to convince of the value of the project. Random House, TSR's distributor at this time in the book trade, wanted to know, "Just who are Margaret Weis and Tracy Hickman, anyway?" The company settled for the lowest possible printing of the first book, titled *Dragons of Autumn Twilight*, which appeared in April 1984.

Weis and Hickman were still concerned with how the book was being publicized. To help, they organized the Weis and Hickman Traveling Road Show to give dramatic readings from the book. They enlisted the help of some friends, including Terry Phillips, whose whispery, raspy version of Raistlin Majere inspired the authors'

portrait of the mage. Gary Pack played Tanis, Doug Niles was Flint, Tracy was Fizban the Fabulous, Laura Curtis played Bupu and Tika, and Harold Johnson portrayed Sturm Brightblade. Janet Pack was drawn in to play Tasslehoff, and other people were grabbed as they became available. The shows were a resounding success and helped build buzz about the novel.

At the following year's Gen Con, Weis's daughter, Lizz Baldwin, was recruited to go through the convention hall handing out fliers inviting participants to the road show. The show was a success, the second novel, *Dragons of Winter Night*, was a runaway hit, and the world of DRAGONLANCE was on its way to immortality.

Weis and Hickman left TSR a few years later to pursue careers in writing. The fruits of their collaboration included the DRAGONLANCE Legends trilogy; *The Second Generation*, which recounted the fate of the children of the Heroes of the Lance; and in 1995, *Dragons of Summer Flame*, the epic story of the Chaos War that swept across Krynn and left devastation in its wake.

Following the publication of this book, Weis and Hickman felt they were done with the world of DRAGONLANCE. TSR continued issuing game material, this time in a new non-D&D system called SAGA. The system had only limited success with players (not helped by the fact that its first products were released just before the onset of

TSR's serious financial troubles and eventual sale to Wizards of the Coast), and the setting seemed destined to be retired.

In the spring of 1997, just after the sale of TSR to WotC, Weis and Hickman came to TSR's headquarters in Lake Geneva with a new proposal. They wanted, they said, to tell another story set in the world of DRAGONLANCE.

"It begins," Hickman told a meeting of the DRAGONLANCE creative team, "with a kender and a time-traveling device."

The story became the War of Souls Trilogy. The saga revived DRAGONLANCE's sagging fortunes and revitalized it as a D&D world. All three novels in the trilogy hit the *New York Times* best-seller list, drawing a new generation of fans into the on-going story of Krynn.

In 2002, Wizards of the Coast agreed to license the DRAGONLANCE campaign setting to Weis's Sovereign Press. Wizards produced a core DRAGONLANCE book in 2003 updating the setting for 3rd Edition rules, while Sovereign Press began work on supplementary materials. Meanwhile Weis and Hickman have continued their writing careers —Weis with novels for both Tor Books and Wizards of the Coast and Tracy and Laura Hickman with a trilogy of novels for Warner Books.

It's been a long, long journey from Provo, Utah, and Independence, Missouri. And it's not over yet.

WORLDS OF IMAGINATION

DRAGONLANCE

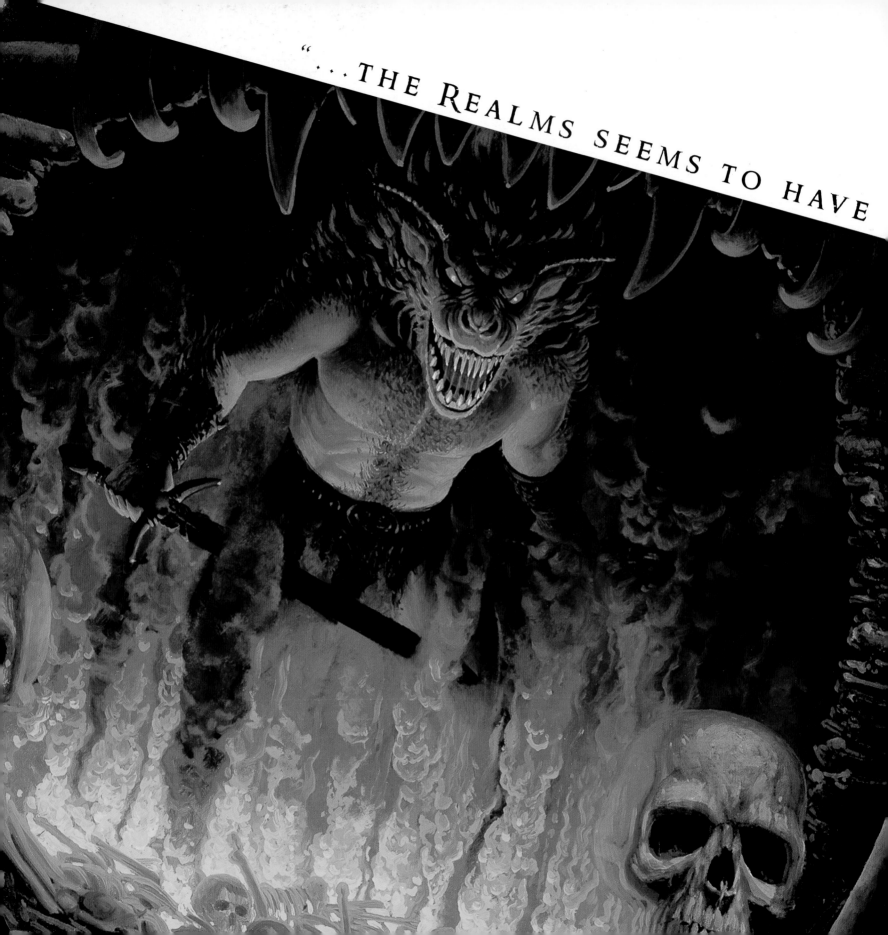

THE FORGOTTEN REALMS
BY STEVE WINTER

EXISTED BEYOND THE D&D GAME."

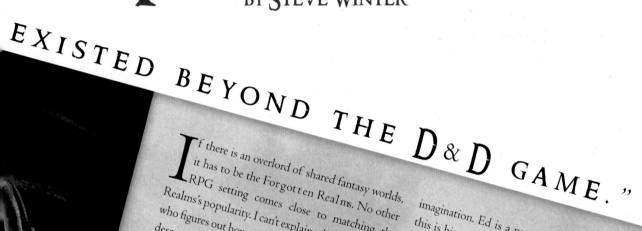

I f there is an overlord of shared fantasy worlds, it has to be the Forgotten Realms. No other RPG setting comes close to matching the Realms's popularity. I can't explain why – the person who figures out how to quantify lightning in a bottle deserves to become a bajillionaire. I doubt that it's a case of "right place, right time." That gets your foot in the door but it doesn't create a favorite that lasts for decades. Maybe it's because the Realms are at once both familiar and exotic. Maybe it's because the place seems to have that most elusive of all capacities, the ability to offer something for everyone.

I tend to believe that it's related to two factors: the Realms's authenticity and the enduring popularity of its leading spokesman, Elminster.

By authenticity, I mean that the Realms seems to have an existence beyond the D&D game. It's almost as if D&D exists to quantify the Realms rather than the other way round.

In fact, the lands of Faerûn predate the D&D game by several years. They were created by Ed Greenwood, a Canadian with a nonstop imagination. Ed is a natural storyteller, and since this is his story, let's let him tell it.

The Realms . . . was my "dream space" for swords and sorcery stories that I wrote from early childhood. I was one of those prodigies who devoured my father's den full of books and always wanted to know what happened next to the characters I liked. If I couldn't find sequels, I wrote them. I started spinning Realms tales around 1967.

When I discovered the first incarnation of the D&D game, I considered it a great storytelling idea but holes and flaws in the rules could cause huge arguments during play. Then the Advanced Dungeons & Dragons game appeared, with the nice presentation of the Monster Manual (every monster of mythology quantified and compared, dragons to vampires to zombies!) and the Players Handbook (specific limits and details for spells! Wheee!). I was hooked and quietly converted everything about the Realms into AD&D terms. Once regular AD&D play sessions started in the Realms, I felt it was fairest to my players if I

GLORIOUS, COLORED MAPS OF THE REALMS PRINTED."

got the new monsters and magic items I threw at them published, so I started writing articles for THE DRAGON [as it was called then]. I thought (and still do) that it's incredibly awkward and arrogant to write something like: "Hi, I'm Ed, and I've thought up this great new way of rolling dice that none of you have, so read this." I also believe it hurts roleplaying to state things definitively ("There are six orcs in this room in the ruins" instead of "The innkeeper tells you some folk in town say they've seen orcs near the old castle"). For those two reasons, I started dressing up the articles with an old storyteller character who was clearly an unreliable narrator (Elminster, of course).

The first published Realms piece was a monster, the Curst, which appeared in issue number 30 of THE DRAGON. That only encouraged me, and I

started pouring stuff onto THE DRAGON's pages. Apparently, folks noticed the Realms references I was sneaking into my articles in order to make them seem more real.

Some of the people who noticed were TSR designers, who took more than a passing interest in Ed's work. The one who would become most closely involved with the Realms and ultimately a twin father to this 800-pound baby was Jeff Grubb. As Jeff explains,

In 1986, there was concern about DRAGONLANCE fading (yeah, it sounds silly now, but it was a concern at the time), and we were looking for the "next world" to replace it. I did not know Ed personally at the time but I did know that he wrapped his articles for THE DRAGON in descriptions of his home campaign. I suggested to my boss, Michael Dobson, that we check into whether Ed had more background for that

world. I made the initial contact with Ed, and for my troubles I became the in-house half of the team.

Soon thick packages of typewritten notes wrapped in heavy, industrial Canadian plastic arrived on my desk, and I was supposed to untangle everything.

Ed recalls that first phone conversation.

Jeff phoned me and asked (more or less): "These DRAGON articles; do you really have a complete, detailed fantasy world at home, or do you just make it up as you go along?" To which I replied: "Yes, and yes."

Whereupon Jeff said, "Great! Send it!" and we both laughed. Then he explained that TSR might really be interested in publishing books and modules and boxed games about my world. First I would have to telephone Mike Dobson to see "if we could

Ed Greenwood, creator of the Forgotten Realms campaign setting, is the author of more than a hundred novels, articles, and roleplaying products set in the continent of Faerûn. His latest novel is Elminster's Daughter.

I didn't really fall in love with Dungeons & Dragons until an unforgettable moment in a sun-dappled ravine when a beautiful young woman in armor extended her hand (the one that wasn't holding a drawn sword) for three gamers to kiss-one of them me-and softly bade us to "Come, play with me."

Now, that's a Dungeon Master to dream about!

I first set eyes on the game a little earlier, at the much-loved Toronto sf bookstore Bakka (which recently celebrated its thirtieth anniversary, albeit in a new location and several owners later). The Bakka of "then" (1975) was a treasure-trove of shining dreams, with fantasy and science fiction books jostling with pulp magazines, decaying used paperbacks, and glorious fantasy art books. It was dingy and crammed, with homemade bookshelves built around magnificent old glass-topped drugstore cabinets, to use every inch of space.

Movie posters and Middle Earth figurines, maps, and tarot decks were stuffed in around the books. One windowsill was home to the "won't fit" or "not really sure why it's here" stuff.

Which is where I found three little pamphlets-chapbooks, really. A single set of the precious first edition of D&D, not very impressive to look at and obviously shoved onto the sill because someone else thought so too.

Madly-in-love-with-fantasy dreamer that I was, I seized them, glanced through them, and thought, Great idea! But how will this Dungeon Master and the players keep their storytelling from degenerating into arguments? (Almost every

wargame session or discussion of fantasy books I'd ever participated in, up until then, seemed to plunge straight into disputes.) Regarding them as a fascinating but flawed experiment, I bought them on the spot.

Why? Well, I'm both a gamer and the sort of fan who always buys "companion" and "concordance" books, guides to faeries and little people, tomes that map and chart Sherlock Holmes's adventures or the life cycles of dragons, and so on.

I showed the rulebooks to my friends because they seemed to offer a secret passage to the glory of the Holy Grail of our fandom: When an author dies or stops writing about favorite characters or an imaginary world that you really love, what happens to the characters next?

We ached to know, we had to know. Oh, we could write our own stories about the characters, but we knew as we were doing so that we were, well, guessing blindly. Making things up. Only the author knew what happened to that world or those characters "for real." (Roger Zelazny's first cycle of Amber novels was coming out then, and we spent hours eagerly speculating about which family member was behind this or that attack on Corwin or plot against Amber.)

So we tried D&D, and ended up with arguments.

Then came the a booklet, and The Dragon magazine, and the Monster Manual . . . and piece by piece, TSR put the Holy Grail into our hands.

Thank you.

To tell the truth, I was hungry to somehow, anyhow, get glorious, colored maps of the Realms printed that didn't show my pencil-crayon strokes all over the seas and forests. I phoned Mike and told him (to his astonishment and no doubt delight) that money didn't matter — I'd agree to anything! Then I started pounding out the packages full of maps that Jeff couldn't read and text that drove him nuts because the "t" on my typewriter was broken. I had to draw in every "t" and "T" by hand, making the pages look, in Jeff's words, "like so many graveyards, with little crosses sprouting all over them."

I never had enough time to find all of my faint pencil notes and type them up. And yes, I was typing — I had no computer. Cut-and-paste with real scissors and glue was the only way to revise or expand. Plus I had a real, long-hours day job with a hellish 100-mile-each-way commute and a busy family life. It was like riding a runaway steam locomotive while frantically shoveling coal into the firebox, nonstop, for the first few years.

I kept sending weekly packages on whatever topics Jeff requested until he called a frantic halt. His telephone calls were full of tales about taping

WORLDS OF IMAGINATION

ORGOTTEN RE

"AND HE PRODUCED MAPS UPON MAPS."

together the world map pages, and then those of the Waterdeep map.

Those maps, once assembled, were so big that the only place they could be laid out as a whole was on the floor. The only stretch of floor that was sufficiently large was the approach to the restrooms. Needless to say, the presence of huge, paper maps blocking off the restrooms attracted attention to the project. Most of it was enthusiastic bordering on amazement, in spite of the inconvenience. Jeff recalled that:

Ed is a wonderful mapmaker, and he produced maps upon maps. We thought we could just "bring them across" [with little modification]. Well, we couldn't because of TSR's code of standards. There were a lot of brothels in the city map keys. The choice was either to redo the map key (risking all the errors that might creep in) or find something to replace "brothel." I came up with "festhalls" and

we did a universal change in all the keys. It has since become a part of fantasy lore. Whenever I see a "festhall" in another campaign world, I just laugh, because I know its origin.

Also on the maps, we had temples to Tyche. I checked with our editor at the time, Karen Boomgarden, about making sure we did not use recognized deities, and she confirmed that people still venerated Tyche. We changed the name to Tymora but didn't catch it in all the first draft maps, so temples to Tyche got out there in the first editions. Later came the story that Beshaba and Tymora were the split parts of the early Tyche.

The final map problem was just getting them together. When I got the map packet for the big Realms map, it consisted of thirty-two eight-and-a-half by eleven pieces of paper that I had to fit together. It was hand-written, and that caused some confusion, too. The Great Dungeon of Cavenauth

was actually on the original maps as "Cave mouth" but I couldn't read it.

Those original maps still exist. When Jeff Grubb left TSR (the first time) to pursue writing full time, he passed the original, black-and-white-then-hand-colored maps to the line's editor—at that time, Julia Martin, who as of this writing still has them (rolled up) in her office at Wizards of the Coast.

Eventually, TSR bought a computer for Ed and shipped it, with much difficulty, through Customs to Canada. That simplified everyone's job tremendously and probably saved the price of the computer in postage.

Given the overwhelming size of the Realms, it didn't take long before other people got involved in detailing and just keeping track of everything. You might think that Ed would have been sad to lose complete control over his creation, but it had definite advantages from his perspective.

"THE REALMS ARE NOTHING IF NOT VIVID."

The one thing the Realms couldn't do as long as it was just "my world" was surprise me, and both game and fiction writers (like Jeff and Kate Grubb, Elaine Cunningham, and Bob Salvatore) gave me pleasant surprises and added new Realms characters that I wanted to meet. Steve Schend and Eric Boyd led the way in writing Realmslore to fill in the gaps, explain away apparent inconsistencies, and weave history to make everything hang together better.

My greatest delight in the unfolding Realms was watching other creators race off madly in all directions across the misty gaps in the landscape I'd handed to Jeff. It was like one of those old Disney animated films where drab landscapes come alive in an instant as colorful splashes of paint race everywhere.

All of which explains where the Realms comes from, but what about its huge popularity? What

made Forgotten Realms the standard against which all other fantasy settings are measured? As stated earlier, I think that the Realms's origin does play a role. The setting wasn't created to fill a market niche but to fulfill a human need for legend, mythology, and discovery. If you place any weight in the writings of Joseph Campbell — and it's hard to imagine a D&D player who wouldn't be affected by *The Power of Myth, The Hero With a Thousand Faces,* or *Myths to Live By* — then it's easy to understand why someone else's sincere attempts to create a personally fulfilling world of powerful myth would resonate with many people.

Robert E. Howard, the author who created Conan the Barbarian (the greatest fantasy hero ever, in this humble writer's opinion), claimed that the spirit of the brooding Cimmerian often peered over his shoulder as Howard was penning

the hulking warrior's tales. While Ed and Jeff never claimed to actually converse with any natives of Faerûn, both found that idea useful when they were writing for the setting.

"In writing," said Jeff, "I always treated the Realms as if the place had always existed, and we were just reporting on it."

"Me too!" agreed Ed. "That approach has been the key to making this vast, imaginary place seem real and has helped make our depictions of it work."

Another factor in the success of Forgotten Realms was the level of detail in the descriptions. A hallmark of Ed's early articles in The Dragon and a key element in the decision to approach him in the first place was his "make it seem real" approach. That meant details. Ask any detective what makes a suspect's story believable and he'll

tell you, "It's the details." Maybe it's neither God nor the Devil who lives in the details, but Waterdhavians and Dalelanders. The Realms are nothing if not vivid.

They're also extensive. Hundreds of game accessories and adventures have been published about the Realms and almost as many novels have been written. Taken together, these writings account for many millions of words of text. That's millions. The lands of Faerûn are probably better documented than some small, real countries.

Like an actor who's portrayed the same character in a soap opera for fifteen years, it's not surprising that Ed sometimes gets confused for his most recognizable creation, Elminster the mage. The misapprehension isn't deterred by Ed's obvious enjoyment over showing up at conventions dressed as the amiable, enigmatic wizard. Some might say that he does an uncanny Elminster impersonation – a little too uncanny, perhaps. Ed has never claimed to be Elminster. His

involvement with the Realms has, however, led to some interesting encounters with devoted fans.

I've often been asked for life guidance because of my supposed wisdom or understanding or sensitivity, as a result of someone liking my Realms writings.

I've been asked to perform weddings or send Elminster's (or Storm's, or Azoun's) congratulations to nuptials.

I've been trusted by strangers who believe they know me through the Realms. Once, in a country far from home, a policeman with too many people to deal with in a problem situation asked me to chaperone two very good-looking and inebriated young ladies. He told me later that "anyone who cares about people as much as you must, to write what I read in those books, is someone I can trust."

For years I was asked to name babies and even father babies. No kidding.

Then there was the year that the Midwest

Express Convention Center opened, with GenCon as its first official event. I arrived in Milwaukee a few days early, and I wanted to walk around the new place, or at least get a map of it before the show, so I'd know where the washrooms and some of my events were. We didn't know that a hush-hush governors' convention, with President Clinton attending, was being held there in the days immediately before Gen Con set up. I found the place ringed with cops. They sent me around to the security checkpoint at the back, where Secret Service guys in shades and suits didn't like my bearded good looks. Then the exasperated, older security guard whom they'd been pushing around all day informed them tartly that they'd better be polite to me because I'd been coming to Gen Con for years and was a wizard with magic enough to turn them and their guns to frogs if they didn't smarten up. One of them sneered, "Right" … and then added quickly, to me (just in case, I guess), "Sir."

Don Daglow

Statistics and Attributes: Don Daglow is president of Stormfront Studios, producers of such video games as Lord of the Rings: The Two Towers, Lord of the Rings: Return of the King, and Forgotten Realms: Demonstone.

Description: Sitting down to write this piece, I was shocked to realize that I've been playing DUNGEONS & DRAGONS for most of its thirty years. What started as a weekend passion for a group of grad school friends ended up as a centerpiece of my career in video games.

It's good that we'd completed college before D&D exploded into our lives in 1975 — otherwise we might never have graduated. As it is, we were fanning out to grad schools and careers, armed with theatre arts degrees. On weekends we'd come together to play a campaign that someone had worked all week to expand in time for our next session.

I'd been writing computer games on the underground college circuit since 1971. Some ran on just one college's room-sized mainframe computer, while others were copied and shared across the country. We could only print text — no graphics — and users played by watching their progress printed out on ancient teletypes at the breakneck speed of one page a minute. I'd written Baseball and Star Trek games, and in late 1975 I started work on a computer tribute to D&D.

The game was called DNGEON, since only six letter names were allowed. It followed 1st Edition rules, printing the script that the computer DM "spoke." Players chose an action for every character on each regular or melee round as they explored, faced random monsters, and faced each of the game's encounters. Although DNGEON had historical significance as the first computer RPG, it was grueling to play. If the computer's terminals were crowded, a random orc encounter could take forty-five minutes to resolve. At a whopping 32K of computer memory, it was too large for many college systems.

When we got black-and-white monitors instead of teletypes in the computer center, I added an option to display a map of the party's location. Allowing for infravision and line-of-sight, the map used asterisks, dashes and the capital letter "I" to create its lines and markings. Refreshing the screen as the party moved still meant a wait of twenty seconds as it unfurled one row of symbols at a time.

It was seven years later, in 1982, when I again had the chance to work on D&D, when Mattel acquired the rights to do the first electronic D&D game. I'd joined Mattel as one of the five original in-house programmers for Intellivision, written the strategy title Utopia, and by 1982 led the Intellivision design group. I couldn't believe our good luck at getting the rights to D&D, and our team created DUNGEONS & DRAGONS: Treasures of Tarmin, with a simulated 3D point-of-view display. Unique in a video game world dominated by sports and arcade titles, Treasures of Tarmin was a success even as many other video game genres began to fade.

Seven years passed again before my next chance to create a D&D game. I had founded an independent development company called Stormfront Studios, and we were working with game publisher SSI on a series of D&D FORGOTTEN REALMS games in their famous "Gold Box" series. Until then all multiplayer roleplaying games used text, not graphics, to display the action — getting pictures on the screen seemed like an unattainable holy grail. I had worked with Steve Case in the early days of AOL, and knew that we could create an

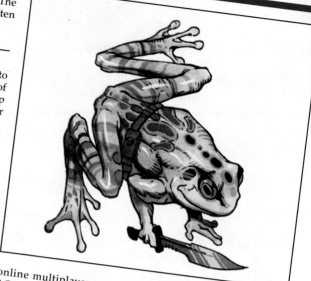

online multiplayer version of the SSI D&D games on the AOL system.

After a series of discussions, we scheduled a fateful meeting at a 1989 trade show in Las Vegas — in a medieval-themed restaurant at the castle-like Excalibur Hotel. Four companies were represented: AOL (then called Quantum) had the online network; TSR held the rights to D&D; SSI owned the computer game rights to D&D; and Stormfront had the online experience to design the game. By the time Neverwinter Nights went live on AOL in the spring of 1991, each company had played a critical role in the technical and creative process that made the first graphic online RPG possible.

Neverwinter Nights ran for seven years, paving the way for later hits like Ultima Online and Everquest. The title then passed to Bioware and Atari, who developed an innovative and original Neverwinter Nights RPG system that has become a perennial best seller.

As this is written in 2004, our team at Stormfront is working on a new D&D console action adventure with Atari, building on the technology from our game The Lord of the Rings: The Two Towers (published by EA). After DNGEON at 32,000 bytes and Treasures of Tarmin at 8,000, today's video games count their sizes in billions of bytes. Where the old games were created by a single designer-programmer, teams of fifty or more people collaborate today.

In the end, however, it isn't important that in the 1970s a D&D game was played with text printing slowly on an old teletype. It isn't important that thirty years later a D&D game has the cinematic graphics, soaring music, and realistic sound effects of today's blockbusters.

After all is said and done, DUNGEONS & DRAGONS is an enduring game in any form. It is a landmark in our culture that has affected not just my life but the lives of generations of people around the world. Whether it is played by a group of friends at a kitchen table or by millions of players linked to massive fictional worlds, it is the same game of DUNGEONS & DRAGONS that captivates, fascinates, and ultimately fulfills us.

I am intensely proud to have been involved in the first thirty years of D&D. I cannot wait to see what the next thirty years of the game will bring.

MYSTARA
BY STEVE WINTER

"IT WAS PULP SWORDS-AND-SORCERY ADV

Although it seldom gets the press or the respect of the other D&D settings, Mystara (a.k.a. The Known World) is one of the oldest campaign settings published by TSR. The Known World made its first appearance in 1981 in the D&D adventure XI, *Isle of Dread* by Tom Moldvay and Dave Cook. It was very loosely based on the film *King Kong*, with the adventurers exploring a distant island inhabited by dinosaurs and mysterious people and creatures. The island could be placed anywhere in a campaign by the DM, but XI was the first adventure published for the (then) new D&D Expert rules. As such, it was designed not only as an adventure but also as an example of how a wilderness campaign should be structured. For that reason, a sample game world was outlined at the beginning of the module. The setting, created by Dave Cook and Tom Moldvay, was generically labeled "The Known World" on the assumption that individual DMs would add their own names. It showed the setting in broad strokes, from the land of the Atruaghin Clans in the southwest to the Nordic Kingdom of Ostland in the northeast and from the sorcerous Principalities of Glantri in the northwest to the colonies of the Empire of Thyatis in the southeast. In between lay the Ethengar Khanate, Republic of Darokin, Broken Lands, Alfheim, Emirate of Ylaruam, Five Shires, and the key Grand Duchy of Karameikos. All these kingdoms, duchies, and empires, along with mountains, deserts, great forests, jungles, swamps, plains, and barren lands, were packed into a relatively small space (by FORGOTTEN REALMS standards, anyway) of about 800 by 1,200 miles.

One page of descriptive text for the whole continent provided only the barest hint of what lay within these lands. Fleshing it out was a job for the Dungeon Master. The entire framework for what would eventually become MYSTARA was contained in that first map. From time to time another D&D expansion or adventure would mention a locale somewhere on the continent in

...ENTURE AT ITS VERY BEST."

WORLDS OF IMAGINATION

MYSTARA

"IT TURNED OUT THAT THE KNOWN WORLD WAS HOLLOW, AND THE INSIDE WAS JUST AS BUSY A PLACE AS THE OUTSIDE."

general terms, but very little was done to fill in the blanks.

That was the situation until 1987, when the first of the Known World gazetteers appeared. The gazetteers came about largely through the effort and devotion of Bruce Heard. Bruce was a transplant from France. His job was managing the freelance writers and editors who worked for TSR's creative division. Bruce was also a big fan of the Known World, and he stepped into the role of its champion.

The first gazetteer was published in 1987 the same year that the FORGOTTEN REALMS debuted. The gazetteer format was a very different approach from that taken with the Realms, which presented the entire world to the DM in one massive, detailed, heavy, extensive, and expensive set. The gazetteers offered the world in bite-size pieces. Generally, they included a sixty-four-page world book for the DM, a thirty-two-page players' book, and a poster map. The maps were designed to be attractive but with the main emphasis on ease of use. They were simple and clean, printed in muted primary colors, and gridded with 8-mile hexes. They reminded me of the maps that hung on classroom walls in grade school, and most of them hung in my office at one time or another, purely as decorations.

Gaz 1, written by Aaron Allston, covered the Grand Duchy of Karameikos. The Duchy was always considered to be the central locale in the Known World and the best place for starting characters to begin their adventures, mainly because of its familiar, western European flavor.

Karameikos was followed by three more gazetteers in 1987: The Emirates of Ylaruam (by Ken Rolston), Principalities of Glantri (by Bruce Heard himself), and Kingdom of Ierendi (by TSR editor Anne Gray). These would be followed by ten more gazetteers in a run that lasted until 1991.

The Known World didn't end with the gazetteers, however. Like a popular TV series, it spawned several spinoffs. The best of these (and my personal favorite) was The Hollow World. Yes, it turned out that the Known World was hollow, and the inside was just as busy a place as the outside.

"MYSTARA NEVER TOOK ITSELF TERRIBLY SERIOUSLY."

It was populated by pseudo Aztecs, Greeks, and Egyptians, along with the usual array of beastmen and other fantastic creatures.

Not only was the world itself hollow but even the solid portions of it were honeycombed with passages and caverns where numerous subterranean races thrived and plotted their eventual takeover of the outer and inner surfaces. Intrepid adventurers could travel from the surface, through the labyrinthine crust, and emerge in the interior of the world. How cool is that? It was pulp swords-and-sorcery adventure at its very best.

Aside from its completely different marketing approach, other features set MYSTARA apart from the FORGOTTEN REALMS. First was its scale. Where the Realms was huge, MYSTARA was positively cozy. The next kingdom or adventure site was seldom more than a few days' travel away. In the Known World, every hex was a potential adventure because there weren't that many hexes between here and there.

Second was MYSTARA's everything-goes attitude. Vikings, desert nomads, dwarves, elves, orcs, medieval knights, pirates, and renaissance condottiere coexisted within a week or two's travel of each other. You could find yourself in a very different sort of setting and game just by crossing the mountains or passing through the swamp. Every staple of fantasy/swords & sorcery fiction could

WORLDS OF IMAGINATION

MYSTARA

"In the Known World, every hex was a

find a comfortable home in the Known World. Third was the lighthearted tone. Mystara never took itself terribly seriously. That's not to say the setting was a fantasy parody, but occasional parody and good-natured lampooning of fantasy stereotypes wasn't out of place. Bruce Heard's long-running feature in Dragon magazine, "Voyages of the Princess Ark," is a perfect example of this. Mystara was a fun place to be.

Sadly, I never got to be involved in creating gazetteers for the Known World in any more than an auxiliary role. It spent most of its life as a D&D accessory and I was part of the AD&D team. While I would have loved to contribute more directly to the world, the separation had a nice payoff of its own. Even though I was surrounded at TSR by incredible imagination and never-ending creativity, new installments in the Known World saga could still hold surprises when they arrived in the office. I could tear off the shrinkwrap, unfold the map, and thumb through the books knowing that I would find plenty of new ideas and exciting adventure seeds. However jaded I might become from time to time through overexposure to AD&D, the Known World was always fresh. Of all the many campaign setting published by TSR, Mystara is still my favorite.

POTENTIAL ADVENTURE."

Nik Davidson

Statistics and Attributes: Nik Davidson is Community Relationship Manager for DUNGEONS & DRAGONS ONLINE with Turbine Entertainment Software

Description: I've always been a gamer. I think I was taught the basics of chess at six or seven, and I was inventing complicated rules to resolve disputes between warring Lego tribes by ten. I first encountered DUNGEONS & DRAGONS (basic red book; elves were both a race and a class) in the sixth grade. It didn't exactly do wonders for my social status, but all of a sudden I had a creative and social outlet: interactive storytelling.

My gaming friends were always considered a step above my other friends. Friends helped you move furniture. Real friends used their last teleport to get the rest of the party out of the keep before they broke their staff of the magi.

My memory is awful, but while phone numbers, addresses, names, birthdays and the like move cleanly between my ears without leaving a trace of their passage, I can recall obscure details about rules, game systems, and gaming sessions of years long ago. RPGs can be more than a pastime; they can become the sort of oral history that you don't find often in modern society. For friends with whom I've gamed with for years, the RPG has become our shared mythology, the anecdotes have worked their way into our language (to "Nandor," for example, as a verb, is bad) and the characters we've played are unlikely to ever be forgotten.

I think I was around fourteen when I started getting more into computer gaming: Bard's Tale, Wizardry, Moria, some of the classics. My friends and I were becoming vaguely aware that at some

point in the nebulous, distant future, we would likely stop being able to have our weekend gaming sessions that lasted until the wee hours. Between reading *Neuromancer* and becoming dimly aware of the potential of dial-up BBSes, I remember sitting in my friend's attic (not the basement, we weren't quite that stereotypical) talking with my gaming group about how cool it would be to have some way of playing D&D in some sort of "cyberspace."

Fast forward to today, and an idle geek dream is fast becoming a reality.

I expected my old friends to be excited beyond belief when they heard what project I was working on. Their reaction (positive, but not exuberant) was a shock to me at first, but it quickly became clear. DUNGEONS & DRAGONS ONLINE would be a great thing, but they had more pressing questions to ask – like how long was I going to be in town, and did I bring my dice?

Ken Troop

Statistics and Attributes: Ken Troop is the lead designer for the DUNGEONS & DRAGONS ONLINE game, coming from Atari and designed by Turbine Entertainment Software.

Description: I am a game designer. More importantly, a "Massively Multiplayer Online Role-playing Game" designer. We build virtual 3D worlds where thousands of people across the world can create an online persona and play and adventure together. We need to continually fill these worlds with content for players to experience: new quests, new items, new foes, new stories.

That's what I do — content design. It is quite possibly the best job in the world. I owe it all to Raistlin.

In a basic sense, the fact that MMORPGs exist at all is due to DUNGEONS & DRAGONS. Almost everything that the first generation of these games and their MUD (Multi-User Dungeon) ancestors did was based on the D&D ruleset. And since I'm working on DUNGEONS & DRAGONS ONLINE, I owe a very direct debt to D&D for my current job.

But the reason why I'm a content designer at all is because of a short story I read in DRAGON magazine when I was eleven years old. "The Test of the Twins," by Margaret Weis, was my first exposure to the world of DRAGONLANCE. It told the story of the twins, Raistlin and Caramon, and of Raistlin's test within the Tower of High Sorcery. In order to complete the test, Raistlin kills his brother, who is revealed to be an illusion by the end of the test. You don't know whether Raistlin knew this during the Test. I was immediately hooked. This story and its characters seemed more real, more interesting, than any D&D campaign my friends and I had put together (which were really just exercises in advancing the abilities of our characters and getting phat loot — as I said, D&D really was the precursor of MMORPGs).

I knew that I wanted all my D&D experiences to have the same resonance, the same sense — an other-place in which power is tangible, good and evil exist, and individuals can help save or destroy a world. "The Test of the Twins," and the two DRAGONLANCE trilogies that followed, were the catalyst for me to move away from D&D as an excuse to raise arbitrary numbers (although I still enjoy that part), and towards using the mechanics of D&D to set up the frame of a story, a story in which you matter.

And that is what I do today — create interesting stories in the frame of an interactive game. Create interesting game-play in the frame of an interactive story. Story and game working together to provide the ultimate fantasy that either one alone can't quite achieve. The story giving you a sense of why what you're doing matters. The game giving you a sense of how it matters. Crafting these synergies is an art form, one in which I still have so much to learn . . . but that I'm on the path at all is because of Raistlin. ∎

SPELLJAMMER
BY STEVE WINTER

"HAD BEEN KICKING AROUND FOR A WHILE."

ADVANCED DUNGEONS & DRAGONS launched into space (albeit a very different kind of space) in 1989. (In an odd coincidence, this was the same year that the gaming company GDW launched its game of Victorian science fiction and space travel, Space: 1889.) SPELLJAMMER broke new ground in numerous ways.

The idea for a spacefaring AD&D campaign had been kicking around for a while below the radar so it's difficult to say who was the "originator." Such arguments don't hold a lot of weight in a creative hothouse like TSR, anyway. Ideas would be tossed around so much and undergo such extensive cross-fertilization before reaching fruition that it usually became nonsensical to talk about an idea being the product of one particular person.

Suffice it to say, sometime in 1988 the two managers of R&D, Jim Ward and Warren Spector (who liked to say they were so completely in sync that they jokingly dubbed themselves "the two managers with one brain"), took the designers to a local bar for an afternoon of brainstorming. Two

ideas came out of that marathon drinking session with a solid go-ahead: Taladas (a major expansion to DRAGONLANCE) and SPELLJAMMER. Zeb Cook, fresh off over two years working on AD&D 2nd edition and eager to work his way back into polite society, was assigned to write Taladas. SPELLJAMMER fell to the man who'd championed it, Jeff Grubb.

If the idea was untraceable, the form and presentation it took was all Jeff's. Several different approaches were considered, from "traditional" ships like winged chariots drawn by swans to Baron Munchhausen-style constructs to Jules Verne capsules blasted into space with exploding fireballs. Instead of those, Jeff adopted the spelljamming helm, a device for channeling mystic energy into propulsion.

More important than the power source, however, was the physics behind the universe. Real physics were no good. Their very reality got in the way of suspending disbelief. Instead, Jeff, a former engineer, derived his laws of "Grubbian physics." The basic concepts were that gravity was ever-present and,

like water, it would seek its own level so that every space-going vessel was accompanied by a convenient gravity plane; and that oxygen would naturally clump around anything with a gravity plane, forming a bubble of breathable air even in deepest space.

Space itself was not empty, either, but was filled with a swirling, highly unstable gas called phlogiston. Interestingly, phlogiston had its origins not in Jeff's fertile imagination but in eighteen-century science. Jeff explains that . . .

Phlogiston was a "real" substance back in the day – the British scientific community believed it was the substance that made things burn. The French believed instead that burning was a very rapid form of oxidation. The British mocked the French but they turned out to be right, and phlogiston went away. Phlogiston was like Aether or Dark Matter—it existed only to make a particular theory work.

To keep all that explosive phlogiston away from the hotly burning suns of planetary systems, the planets had to be encased in something protective. Each system, therefore, was sealed inside its own crystal sphere. The stars of the night sky were glowing spots on the inside surface of a sphere. Individual spheres could have their own physical laws, their own magical rules, even their own gods.

The ships themselves were some of the most imaginative fantasy vessels ever conceived. Jeff gives much of the credit for their distinctiveness to illustrator Jim Holloway.

He was key to the way the ships looked. I'd give Jim a vague description ("Something that looks like a nautilus") and he would come up with the look (the mind flayer nautiloid). Then Diesel [cartographer Dave LaForce] and I would figure out how it worked and what the decks were like.

That wasn't always an easy task, given the strangeness of some of the designs. With Grubbian physics to guide them, however, even the most outlandish vessels could be rationalized somehow.

In a few cases, Jim's ship designs affected the phlogiston-spanning societies Jeff created.

Jim drew about a half-dozen beholder ships, and I liked them all so much that the beholders became a nation of genetic xenophobes, each type believing they were the 'true beholders' (which also worked because every artist drew beholders differently).

The mind flayers, however, were the true stars of the spelljamming races. Gary Gygax revealed in S3 *Expedition to the Barrier Peaks* (1980) that mind flayers were not native to the world of GREYHAWK but had arrived from space. With their sleek and devastating nautilus ships, slave economy, and brain-based cuisine, the illithids quickly became SPELLJAMMER's poster villains. This identification was so strong, in fact, that we would sometimes hear objections from the marketing department when we wanted to use mind flayers in any other product line. They were SPELLJAMMER's iconic monsters. The RAVENLOFT team, for example, had to build a strong case for why illithids should be allowed into the realm of mists.

Besides the nefarious mind flayers, Jeff created several other memorably menacing societies: the multi-limbed, slave-dealing neogi, the enigmatic arcane, and his unique twists on the beholders and drow.

The other iconic creature to emerge from SPELLJAMMER was the dreaded giant space hamster. These beasts were written up in AD&D terms by DRAGON magazine editor Roger Moore. For years, Jeff publicly denied any responsibility for their existence. The true story, however, is that Roger got his inspiration directly from Jeff.

I had nothing to do with giant space hamsters.

Well, very little.

Okay, I started it.

Jim [Holloway] came up with the Gnomish Sidewheeler ship which had these two, huge paddlewheels on the sides. There was nothing in space for the wheels to churn, so I said (a little too loudly), "They must be giant hamster wheels." Roger Moore heard that, inferred the giant space hamster, and things went downhill from there.

SPELLJAMMER also spawned a line of comic books from DC, only one of which was written by Jeff (he was busy writing all of the FORGOTTEN REALMS comics) and drawn by Joe Quesada.

Between 1989 and 1993, the SPELLJAMMER line produced four boxed sets, two monstrous compendiums, fourteen accessories and adventures, and six novels. It wasn't to everyone's taste, but those who liked it loved it, and many still love it. SPELLJAMMER resurfaced in 2002 in the POLYHEDRON supplement to DUNGEON magazine number 92. SPELLJAMMER: *Shadow of the Spider Moon* was a d20 adaptation of the setting written by Wizards of the Coast designer Andy Collins.

Jeff's only regret about SPELLJAMMER is the way in which it raised the bar for future products.

Whatever we did at TSR would be considered "standard fantasy." We were setting the level for what "standard fantasy" was, and if we did something wild like SPELLJAMMER, it just stretched the definition that much further. It was hard to get "outside the box" when every new idea just made the box bigger.

SPELLJAMMER did indeed make the box much, much larger. The box wouldn't be stretched to that extent again until SPELLJAMMER's replacement appeared: PLANESCAPE.

Dan T. Trethaway III

Statistics and Attributes: Dan T. Trethaway III is a Senior Level Designer for DUNGEONS & DRAGONS ONLINE at Turbine Entertainment Software.

Description: My parents always encouraged me to play DUNGEONS & DRAGONS despite all of the negative press it was getting at the time. To them D&D was getting me to read, and the game had become a passion of mine. I got my start in D&D at the young age of ten, and I would save my allowance for weeks to buy the AD&D hardback books. I had them all: Dungeon Masters Guide, Players Handbook, Monster Manual, Fiend Folio, etc. The side effect to owning all the books and my never-ending imagination was that I was always elected to be the Dungeon Master. I would spend all my time drawing up my latest dungeon on my pads of graph paper for my friends to thread their way through.

It was in my early and mid teens that I was able to start stocking up on the AD&D modules. I loved each and every one of them, but my all-time favorites were the S and C series of modules. The absolute king of the crop for me was S3, *The Tomb of Horrors*. That dungeon was the most evil, devious, and enjoyable I ever had the pleasure of torturing my friends with. Whenever I broke out the module with my friends, they knew that it was time to retire the characters and start fresh. No one ever made it through, but they never complained and always enjoyed the challenge.

When I entered the video game industry I always gave credit to D&D for sparking my passion for gaming. While most of the games I worked on were in a modern day or sci-fi setting, I always spent my spare time building gothic and medieval levels for people to play. Now here I am, so many years later doing what is the combination of all my passions. I am playing Dungeon Master in what could be considered the biggest D&D campaign of all time. ■

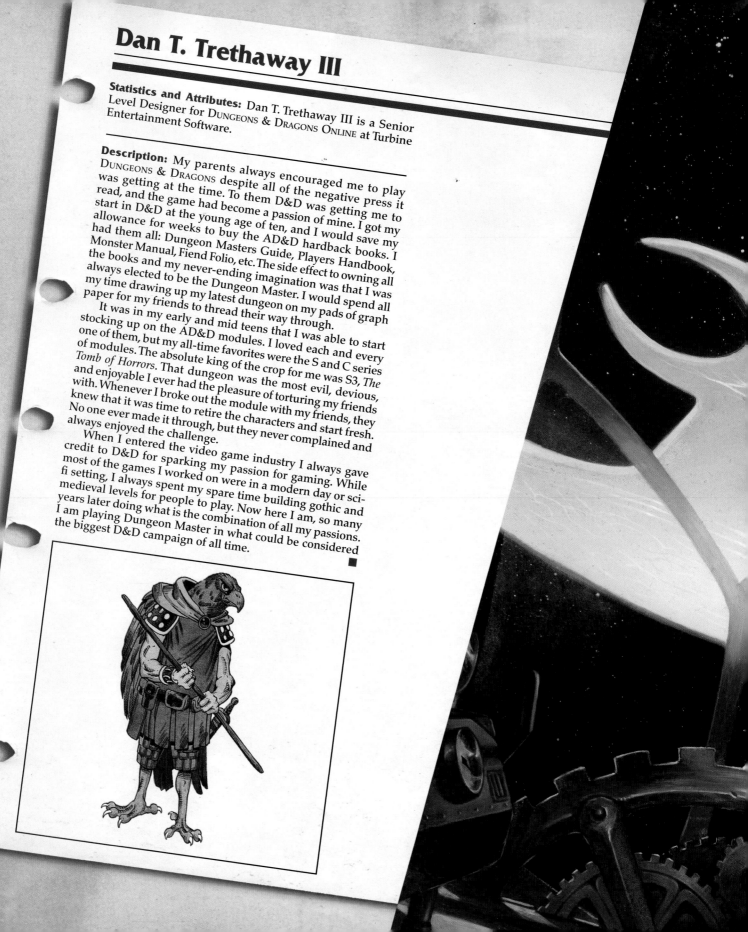

WORLDS OF IMAGINATION

SPELLJAMMER

John Frank Rosenblum

Statistics and Attributes: John Frank Rosenblum is a writer and producer who has worked on such projects as *Doctor Who*, *Trailer Park*, *Mimic*, and *Impostor*.

Description: When I was a kid there were two things I couldn't get enough of: DUNGEONS & DRAGONS and *Doctor Who*. I went to visit the set of *Doctor Who* when I was ten, and I knew right then that I never wanted to work a day in my life—I wanted to be a producer! When I went to work on *Doctor Who*, I was awestruck. It was my chance to work with so many people I had admired, adored, and idolized. I was sure that all my dreams had come true and that the excitement would never wear off.

Since then, I have had the pleasure of working on many television shows, documentaries, and feature films, allowing me to experience things I never would have dreamed of twenty years ago. I have had my film at Sundance, sat next to Brad Pitt at the Oscars, and waited with Michelle Pfeiffer at the Emmys. I have met the President, been to Buckingham Palace, and eaten with Steven Spielberg. I have sat in the captain's chair on the bridge of the starship *Enterprise*, spent the night at the Big Brother House, and stood under the English Channel on the dividing line between England and France. I have partied backstage with Phish in Amsterdam, Madness in London, and They Might Be Giants in Athens. I have hoisted a famous actor's Ferrari out of a swimming pool, had an Oscar-winning director throw a coffee mug at my head (he missed), and once I almost ran over Harrison Ford. And yet, these things no longer give me that golden glow they once did. I worried that I had become too jaded and that I would never again feel that sense of exhilaration.

Luckily, even though the reality of living in the movie/television business has made me immune to the excitement of standing behind Jim Carrey at the buffet, I still get goose bumps when I think about the first time I opened the D&D box. And even though I had played D&D on many a production set (with everyone from grips to stars), I had never met anyone who actually worked on it. So imagine my surprise when I discovered in the middle of a meeting that the people I was dealing with were previously from TSR. In front of the studio executive, the rights holder, and the development people, I blurted out, "You worked on DUNGEONS & DRAGONS?" I was struck with awe.

Now that I have subsequently met Cindi Rice, Ed Stark, Peter Adkison, Ed Greenwood, Dave Arneson, and Gary Gygax, I find that the glow of excitement has not slipped away after all. When I pick up the phone to call Ed Stark and ask him whether I should have Improved Initiative or Combat Casting as my first feat, I hear in the back of my head those fan voices which used to always ask us at *Doctor Who*, "If the TARDIS is supposed to be infinite, how can you jettison twenty-five percent of it? What is twenty-five percent of infinity?"

It just so happens that Ed likes *Doctor Who*, so Ed and I enjoy a special relationship—I am a fan of his work, and he is a fan of mine. Whenever we get together, it is very much like the old spy movies where they trade hostages over the bridge: "You tell me a good D&D story, and I'll tell you a good *Doctor Who* story."

After twenty-five years, the majesty of D&D is still able to bring out that fanboy hidden inside me, just as it ignites that little spark of excitement in each and every one of us. ∎

RAVENLOFT

BY STEVE WINTER

"THE BROODING CASTLE, THE MISTY MOORS, THE SHADOWY
HERE WAS A THEME THAT NO ONE

In 1983, a small adventure written by Tracy Hickman caught everyone by surprise. That adventure was I6, *Ravenloft*.

The idea was simple: take a classic monster, one that's been so overused that it has become trite and mundane, and make it frightening again. The monster chosen was the vampire.

It was a good choice. Decades of cheesy monster films turned this once-frightening creature into something more like a joke. To counter that pathetic reputation, Tracy did two things. First, he created a vampire that was more than a simple monster. Strahd von Zarovich was a complex, intriguing villain. Second, he re-examined the stock of vampire powers listed in the Monster Manual and found ways to combine them with one another and with a carefully constructed environment so that Strahd would be tremendously dangerous and difficult to kill.

The resulting adventure, a mere thirty-two pages long, turned out to be one of the most popular adventures TSR ever published.

Over the years, as adventures fell out of favor in the business plan and were replaced by campaign settings, the astounding, continuing popularity of RAVENLOFT was always there, chewing away at the back of everyone's mind. The result was predictable—turn the adventure into a campaign setting.

In 1989 this job was assigned to Bruce Nesmith and Andria Hayday. One of the first problems they confronted was that Strahd's realm of Barovia was not suited for becoming a campaign setting. It didn't have the inherent flexibility, size, or variety to be a long-term setting.

Furthermore, the basic idea behind the adventure—reviving the reputation of a worn-out monster in new and surprising ways—wasn't sufficient to build a campaign around, either.

The hook that could work was the adventure's atmosphere. The brooding castle, the misty moors, the shadowy streets dripped gothic horror. Here was a theme that no one had ever explored in AD&D. Horror roleplaying games weren't new. Call of Cthulhu broke that ground in 1981 and was a

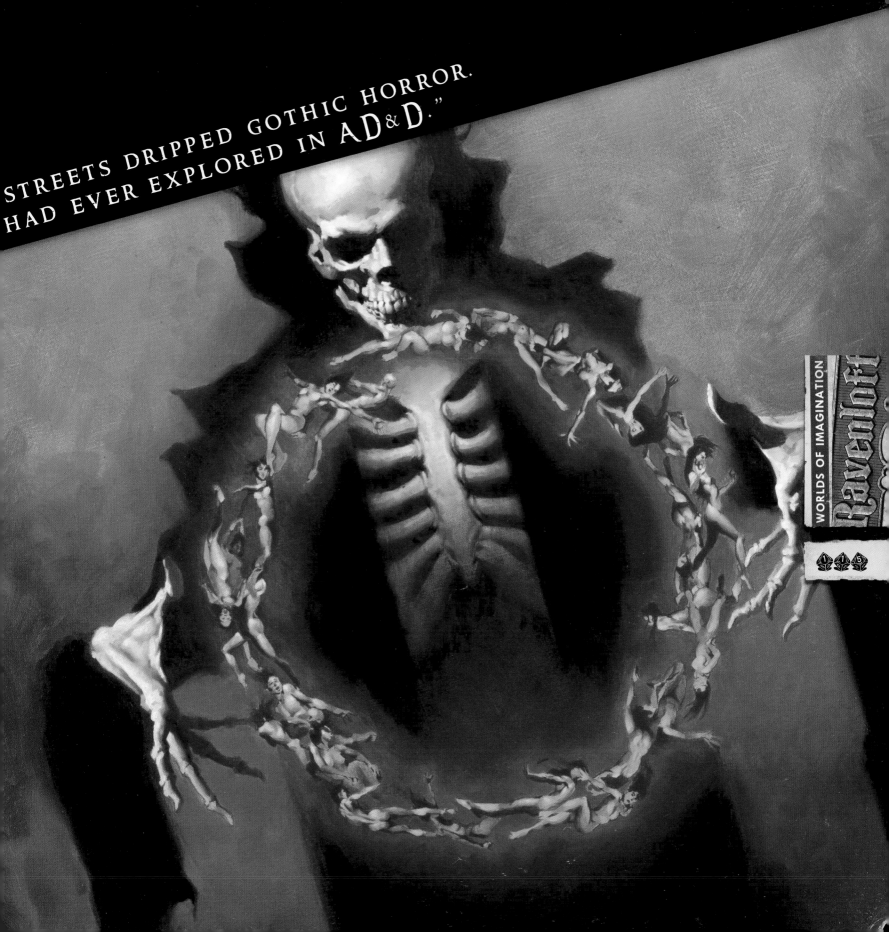

WORLDS OF IMAGINATION

Ravenloft

revelation in the industry. Here was a milieu wherein the heroes weren't meant to confront and defeat the forces of supernatural terror but to be obsessed, seduced, and ultimately consumed by them. The more you could prolong your character's inevitable decline into madness, the longer you could keep him or her functioning at the fringes of sanity, the better the game became. It was a delicate balancing act between horror and absurd comedy, but the game was so well built that competent game masters could keep it from sliding into dark humor and frequently scared the pants off their players.

The second well-known and successful horror RPG was Chill, published by Pacesetter in 1984. Chill adopted a more traditionally heroic approach to roleplaying in which the heroes were meant to survive their confrontations with unearthly powers and actually defeat the forces of darkness. The atmosphere and approach owed less to H. P. Lovecraft's nihilistic stories than to the best of Roger Corman's horror films.

Both of those games were greatly admired, and they set a high bar for any other horror RPGs. Many imitators and competitors came along to challenge those two groundbreakers but few achieved their level of innovation, acclaim, or commercial success.

That was the market RAVENLOFT had to break into.

In shaping their world, Bruce and Andria faced hurdles that none of the previous games had to leap. First and foremost was that RAVENLOFT was a setting for the AD&D game. Unlike characters from the Victorian period or the roaring twenties, typical AD&D characters have a substantial arsenal of magical powers to draw on when confronting supernatural forces. Death itself holds little terror when you can buy your way back to life with accumulated treasures looted from enemies. Second, the question of the underlying geography of the setting was a big problem. How could you posit a believable world where horror reigned? Would anyone believe in a setting in which mummies and vampires ruled neighboring baronies? The whole thing could too easily melt down into a tabletop version of a cheesy horror parody of the "Dracula Meets the Wolfman" variety. Unintentional humor was the worst possible outcome.

WHERE HORROR REIGNED?"

The solution they arrived at seems obvious in hindsight, but it was a tough call at the time. Traditional gothic horror includes many of the atmospheric trappings that were already common to any AD&D game—decaying castles, dripping catacombs, dusty tombs, haunted mansions, bleak and shadowy forests. Dozens of AD&D monsters were inspired directly or influenced indirectly by the great, gothic horror films of the 1930s, 1940s, and 1950s.

The problem was that gothic horror was distinctly out of fashion in the late 1980s. In movie theaters, you couldn't find a horror film that wasn't a blood-drenched shocker featuring a deranged, inbred murderer armed with a chainsaw, an axe, a machete, or a kitchen knife that might as well be a machete. Close-up, blood-drenched, gut-wrenching violence was the main emphasis. Lest that sound too negative, some of these movies from the seventies and eighties are groundbreaking films that are genuinely terrifying, but they are almost the complete antithesis of gothic horror. That's why the decision to emphasize gothic horror in RAVENLOFT was both courageous and novel. It would have been hard to buck the trend more completely.

The team wisely decided to make the Domains of Dread a pocket dimension that existed outside all campaign worlds but that could, when the conditions were right, impinge upon any of them. Your characters couldn't reach Barovia or Darkon simply by turning left at the crossroads on any sunny day. If you turned left at the crossroads on just the wrong moonless, foggy night, however, you could find yourself in a place very different from where you were headed.

Aside from its classically gothic locales and meticulously detailed, often tragic villains, RAVENLOFT was really notable for the way in which it blended horror into the power structure of the AD&D game.

Despite all of its supernatural elements, standard AD&D is not conducive to horror. Death and the supernatural are such common foes in AD&D adventures that they quickly lose their ability to frighten. A good adventure could get your heart racing the way a roller coaster does but that sort of excitement is a long way from a real scare. Bruce and Andria were after scares.

To get them, they turned to the traditional ingredients of gothic horror. They analyzed and dissected the genre and boiled it down to a few, key maxims that could be applied in a roleplaying game to frightening effect.

1. Make it believable. Much about any AD&D game is inherently unbelievable. The trick is to introduce the credulity-stretching elements slowly. Taken singly, each item is only slightly odd. Once you accept the first piece, you're ready to encounter the next odd bit, and it won't seem so odd or out of place in a setting where you've already accepted one strange idea. This way, the threat develops so gradually that players are unprepared for it when they finally grasp the danger.

2. Everything is more frightening when you're alone. AD&D characters are seldom alone. "Never split the party" is one of the first things they learn. The group itself can be isolated, however, cut off in an unfamiliar, menacing place.

3. There's a reason why the villain is called "Master." The force of evil controls the situation. That control may be subtle or overt, but the heroes are not the ones calling the shots.

4. Bad luck trumps good plans. Almost anything the heroes do to ensure their victory can be undone through bad luck, unfortunate circumstance, and ill omen. Enough small incidents of bad luck add up to a significant sense of dread and paranoia.

5. It's a trap! Being trapped creates a sense of helplessness. Even the strongest heroes may lose

Feargus Urquart

Statistics and Attributes: Feargus Urquart is president of Obsidian Entertainment, an electronic entertainment studio.

Description: It's interesting to think about how D&D has influenced my life. If I answered this question when I was sixteen, I would probably have said that it made me a lot more resistant to the ridicule of people who thought of me as a geek, nerd, or dork. I pretty much dreaded the weekly announcement in homeroom that the Tustin High gaming club was meeting that afternoon, as it did every Wednesday. But I lived through the smirks and strange looks and went and had fun every week. We didn't always play D&D, but it's what originally drew us all to the club and what we returned to after short forays into other game systems like Bushido and Paranoia.

Now, as I look back, I can see that playing D&D fed my ability to imagine the fantastic and that sitting around and telling stories is still something that really can happen in our day and age. Interestingly enough, the friends that I met in that club are still my friends to this day. Even now after being out of high school for over fifteen years, we still get together from time to time for a game day and the occasional convention. Like years past, we have to plan our game time around other things in our lives, but it's baby sitters instead of calculus homework now.

Professionally, I've been extremely lucky to work on twelve D&D computer and video game products. If anyone had told me when I was sixteen that I would have been in charge of that many, or even a single, D&D game, I would probably have thought they were absolutely insane. I was the guy playing the computer games, not making them. But as it has turned out, I've gotten to do both. It's great to look forward to going to work everyday, and it may sound corny, but it's D&D which has given me that opportunity. ■

Laurell K. Hamilton

Statistics and Attributes: *New York Times* best-selling author Laurell K. Hamilton is the author of the Anita Blake, Vampire Hunter series from Ace Books, the latest of which, *Incubus Dreams*, appears in October 2004. Hamilton's new series: Merry Gentry- Fey Princess and Private Eye, from Ballantine, began with *Kiss of Shadows* and most recently continues with *Seduced by Moonlight*. She lives in St. Louis, MO.

Description: I became aware of D&D in junior year of high school and played with a group of guys from school. Most of us were in the Drama Department. I played old style D&D. At one point I was a bard the hard way, before they had all the rules that made it easier. When I found out years later that they'd made the rules easier, I resented it because of how much work I'd put into that character.

Over the years, I've had four different gaming groups: one in high school, one in college briefly, and then when my first husband and I went out to California after college, we had a group out there. When we moved back to the Midwest we had another gaming group.

I went to a small Christian college, and the fact that I played D&D at all was something some people equated with Satan worship. You had to be careful whom you even told about it. It was hard to find people. Nobody wanted to fess up. One of the things that led me and my first husband to date was that we found out we both gamed.

I was the only girl in my high school group through most of high school. We got one girl who played the second year we were together. We had another girl who came briefly. She insulted me terribly by rolling up a guy character. I thought she was a traitor, because there were so few women. I've spent most of my life being in hobbies or occupations where I'm one of the few girls—everything from martial arts to the weight room when I was in college to what I do now for a living. Fantasy and science fiction is still generally a boys' club.

I was raised to be a boy. No gentleman with a strong back popped out of the woodwork when heavy things had to be lifted and work had to be done, so I was raised to be the boy and think much more like a traditional male in our society. The result is that I don't game like a girl.

We had two women in the last group I was in, besides me. It was the most women I'd ever had in a gaming group for the longest time. These were the people who threw a surprise party for me when I sold my first novel

Early in my career I approached my agent and said, "You know, my husband and I want to get into a house and we need a down payment. Can you find me some work playing in somebody else's playground?" She knew the head of TSR's Book Department, Brian Thomsen. We talked to him about it. He wanted me to write Ravenloft because I write the Anita Blake, Vampire Hunter series. He was looking up people who had done vampire/horror and trying to get them to write Ravenloft novels. So I wrote *Death of a Darklord*.

I gamed in FORGOTTEN REALMS but not in DRAGONLANCE. I read the books when they were coming out and everything. So many of us of that time had gamed since junior high or high school that many of the Dungeon Masters wound up writing their own adventures.

At one time we were in the Tomb of Horrors, and everyone died—except for me, because my longest running character was Sadan the Cautious. She earned her name because even though she didn't get good treasure, she didn't scramble after it. She always wanted to see if it was trapped or cursed. Other characters got wonderful things but they died sooner. She was the only person to survive the Tomb of Horrors. She actually risked her life to recover one body. Everyone else was yelling, "Help!"

Gamers who first played it when it came out talk in hushed tones about the Tomb of Horrors. I have yet to meet any group that didn't cheat. Sadan the Cautious was Chaotic Good, which was probably the worst alignment for me because I didn't understand Chaotic. She retired at eleventh or twelfth level. The campaign turned evil, and the evil characters started assassinating everybody. Again, she was one of the only people who survived that campaign.

The characters didn't have a big influence on Anita Blake, Vampire Hunter, but my very first novel, *Nightseer*, was something that I DM'ed in high school and early college. I started out with something that people could game in then got frustrated with everybody because these high school and college-age guys would goof off and wouldn't behave. I said, "I'll take it away from you, and I'll write my own damn book!"

It was interesting to watch people go through something I had created. It showed flaws I hadn't seen; it showed pitfalls and things that worked. That was very interesting, to allow live people to go through part of my made-up world.

It was also very enlightening. A decade or so later I find that my imaginary characters are just about as uncooperative and sometimes as the players were. When people are alive and can talk to you and tell you what they want, they don't always want what you want. When your characters are alive enough to look up from the page sometimes they say, "I don't think so!" So having real people going through an imaginary world probably did have an influence on me and made me more open to listening to my imaginary characters as well. ∎

heart when caught with no clear path out and no way to call for or receive help.

6. Attack the body and the mind. No one likes watching himself or his character get whittled away a bit at a time. Don't inflict massive damage. Attack the characters with a thousand small cuts so their demise is drawn out. Make them doubt their own senses. Make them doubt their sanity and their companions' loyalty or even humanity.

The result of this work was a game that was clearly still AD&D but was also distinctly different from standard AD&D. A good DM could genuinely frighten players who were in no danger themselves. Strahd von Zarovich and Lord Azalin, the lich, became two of the most recognized villains ever created for AD&D. Ravenloft went through two editions, dozens of adventures and expansions, and several novel series. It was quite a heritage for a simple, 32-page adventure.

A year after RAVENLOFT was published, White Wolf brought out its groundbreaking game Vampire: The Masquerade. You can argue whether Vampire was really a horror RPG. If it was, it represented

a completely different type of horror. There's no arguing over its effect on the roleplaying hobby and industry, however. Vampire represented a paradigm shift in thinking on what an RPG really was about. Instead of action and adventure, Vampire emphasized mood, setting, and to a large extent, psychological drama. Depending on your viewpoint, the game was either a revolutionary conceptual breakthrough or a hollow triumph of style over substance.

Vampire popularized a dark, brooding, introspective style of roleplaying. It was hip and it played directly to the angst-ridden zeitgeist of teenagers in general and the growing, black-clad goth subculture in particular.

As a result, RAVENLOFT experienced considerable pressure from outside the company to follow the trend and shift toward a darker, more psychologically sinister outlook. Inside the company, the idea never stood a chance. We played Vampire and enjoyed it, but we also liked RAVENLOFT just the way it was, and that's the way it stayed—traditional, classical, gothic but not goth.

WHO WERE IN NO DANGER THEMSELVES.

DARK SUN

BY STEVE WINTER

In 1991, TSR published the DARK SUN campaign set. DS was a departure from the established standard of campaign settings like GREYHAWK, FORGOTTEN REALMS, DRAGONLANCE, or even RAVENLOFT. It was different in so many ways that it's difficult to assemble a simple list of them. It will be better to start at the beginning and follow the world's development.

The first stirrings occurred in 1990 when it was decided at high levels that the company needed a new campaign setting. DRAGONLANCE Chronicles and Legends were four and five years old respectively, and DRAGONLANCE sales were slowing down overall. We needed a fresh, new campaign that could occupy that same position in both games and books.

We also had the second edition of the BATTLESYSTEM miniatures rules coming out, and it was considered essential to their success that they be tied into the game more actively than the first edition had. Or, more correctly, something about the AD&D game had to tie itself actively into the BATTLESYSTEM rules. Correspondingly, the project immediately received the working title of "War

World." That was all we knew about it when we sat down to start brainstorming.

In the nineties, when my two sons first started getting interested in playing AD&D, I got a lot of mileage out of telling them that DARK SUN was my idea. For some reason, that seemed to impress them a lot more than everything else I'd done at TSR over the years. In truth, my contribution was the suggestion during the first brainstorming session that the world should be a ravaged, dying desert world built on the crumbling ruins of a long-lost civilization. At the time, I'd been reading a lot of fiction by Clark Ashton Smith and DEN comics by Richard Corben. My contribution to the creation of Athas began and ended with that one notion. As everyone knows, ideas are cheap. The people who created DARK SUN are the ones who actually did the work, not the guy who tossed off a nebulous remark like "make it a desert." Still, even a scrap of glory has appeal, and I'm not letting go of that one.

That initial brainstorming session probably included about a dozen people. The AD&D creative group was there, plus a few other people

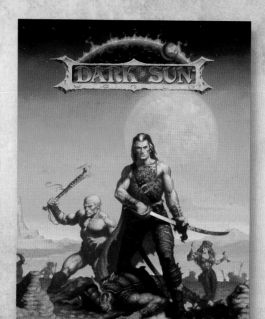

TITLE OF 'WAR WORLD.'
DOWN TO START BRAINSTORMING."

WORLDS OF IMAGINATION

DARK·SUN

who were particularly interested in the topic. It's impossible to recreate the full roster anymore. Two people I'm certain were there (besides myself) were Troy Denning and Tim Brown. Tim had been at TSR for less than a year at that time, and he remembers the scene clearly, for reasons that will become obvious.

I remember sitting in the old conference room when Steve Winter (the product group leader) asked the entire group who would like to work on the new campaign universe, at the time nothing more than a working title: War World. Now, I was sitting in a room with some pretty heavy hitters, as I recall. I remember looking across the large table at Zeb Cook and thinking what a lucky guy he was that he was going to get to create an original new world. But Zeb didn't raise his hand. No one did! I was shocked! In hindsight I think most of the veterans were either exhausted from previous projects or savvy enough to avoid "the eye of Sauron" [the

common euphemism for management scrutiny]. But I was no veteran, so I leaped to the fore. I don't remember my exact words, but they were something like "Ooh! Ooh! Pick me! Pick me!" In the end, Troy and I were the only ones to express an interest, so the job was ours.

I think that Tim is being overly modest here. He was a newcomer to Lake Geneva but he came to us from a long and lustrous stint at GDW. Troy had been with TSR since 1981 and was certainly one of the "heavy hitters" in the room. They were joined shortly by Gerald Brom (soon to become just "Brom"), another newcomer, who would contribute tremendously to Dark Sun's appeal with his edgy, atmospheric illustrations. Mary Kirchoff, managing editor of the books department, also joined the conceptual team because Athas was going to be the focus of a major fiction publishing effort. The project was in the hands of a terrific team.

As the team originally envisioned it, Athas would feature none of the standard AD&D races or monsters. There would be no elves, dwarves, dragons, or orcs. It was a world of humans, muls, half-giants, and even more exotic species. That notion eventually made the marketing department (one part of "the eye of Sauron") very uneasy, however, because it left the setting with nothing familiar to draw in players and readers. The designers relented and added dwarves, elves, halflings, dragons, and a few other familiar shapes back into the mix. Each was subtly or radically twisted in some way to give it a characteristically Athasian quality. Tim Brown recalled that ultimately "marketing's objection took us in a whole new direction that we might not otherwise have gone, and Dark Sun was stronger for it."

Troy agrees with that assessment. "We may have grumbled a bit about 'unimaginative' marketing people at the time, but it made all the difference.

WORLDS OF IMAGINATION

DARK·SUN

I don't think DARK SUN would have achieved the popularity it did without this touch."

The miniatures tie-in was a new endeavor for TSR. Athas was intentionally crafted to be a world at war. The city-states dotting the blasted landscape were ruled by amoral, egotistical dragon-kings that were perpetually in conflict with one another. The first few DS adventures included BATTLESYSTEM statistics for armies so that epic field battles could be integrated into the adventure plot. Even with that push, however, the BATTLESYSTEM miniatures rules never really caught on with roleplayers. Before long, the miniatures stats were dropped from the adventures and little was said about them again.

Psionics was included in a big way. Psychic powers were incorporated into every aspect of Athas. That was partly done to lend commercial support to the then-new *Complete Book of Psionics* and partly because psionic characters in general were

WORLDS OF IMAGINATION

DARK SUN

B·R·O·M

something new and exciting in the game. The inclusion of psionics—in fact, their integration into every fiber of Athas—made the setting a very different sort of place for AD&D adventures and fiction. "In retrospect," recalled Troy, "I think we went a little too far with this—every character and every creature had psionics, which meant that another whole system had to be dealt with in each and every encounter. If I had it to do over, I would save psionics for special characters PCs, important NPCs, really bad-ass creatures."

Brom's visual input was a key factor in the way Athas developed. The team members were committed to having an illustrator as a full participant in the process. When they strolled through the art department looking for compatible ideas and styles, they spotted Brom's painting of Neeva, a character who would become iconic of DARK SUN (her image appeared on the cover of the original box). This was a painting that Brom

had done with no prior knowledge of Athas or what the team had in mind for the setting. The picture captured what they were aiming for so perfectly that they knew immediately they had found their illustrator. Troy explains that Brom's "visual contributions served as a real touchstone for the project. Whenever we came up with something new, one of the first questions we asked was 'Can Brom make this look cool?'"

The answer to that, of course, is that there's very little Brom can't make look cool. When the initial concept, images, and map were presented to Lorraine and the company execs for review, there were no arguments at all. The images did such an outstanding job of capturing the mood of this proposed world that the descriptions were almost secondary.

That was also due, in part at least, to the company's commitment to making DARK SUN both a commercial success and a critical showcase.

"I've never had such resources at my disposal," Tim explained. "I was a kid in a candy store. If we wanted a sketch of something, a sketch was made. If we needed a map, we went to the mapping department. I could devote my entire attention to the creative process."

DARK SUN was a revelation when it was published in 1991. It took AD&D to a type of setting where it had never been before and made it darker, more threatening, even more relevant with its undercurrent story of a world in ecological collapse. It was the richest and most original setting to come from TSR to that date. It was, in Tim's words, "as ground-breaking as a new AD&D campaign world could be. We turned the game on its ear and had a hell of a good time doing it."

Athas was a wildly different kind of setting, and it attracted a different kind of player. "It seemed the more we distanced DARK SUN from other, more mundane fantasy worlds, the more [the fans] liked

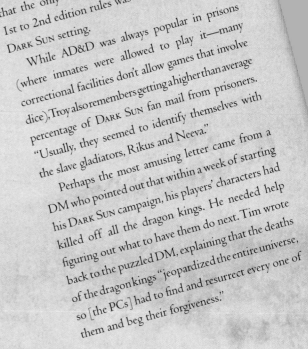

it," recalled Tim. People wrote letters pointing out that the only reason they made the switch from 1st to 2nd edition rules was so they could use the DARK SUN setting.

While AD&D was always popular in prisons (where inmates were allowed to play it—many correctional facilities don't allow games that involve dice), Troy also remembers getting a higher than average percentage of DARK SUN fan mail from prisoners. "Usually, they seemed to identify themselves with the slave gladiators, Rikus and Neeva."

Perhaps the most amusing letter came from a DM who pointed out that within a week of starting his DARK SUN campaign, his players' characters had killed off all the dragon kings. He needed help figuring out what to have them do next. Tim wrote back to the puzzled DM, explaining that the deaths of the dragon kings "jeopardized the entire universe, so [the PCs] had to find and resurrect every one of them and beg their forgiveness."

A HELL OF A GOOD TIME DOING IT."

Sharyn McCrumb

Statistics and Attributes: McCrumb is best known for her Appalachian "Ballad" novels, including *New York Times* best sellers *She Walks These Hills* and *The Rosewood Casket*, which deal with the issue of the vanishing wilderness, and *New York Times* Notable Books *The Ballad of Frankie Silver*, the story of the first woman hanged for murder in the state of North Carolina, and *The Songcatcher*, a genealogy in music. *Ghost Riders* (Dutton 2003), is an account of the Civil War in the Appalachians and its echoes in the region today.

McCrumb's honors include: The 2003 *Wilma Dykeman Award* for Literature given by the East Tennessee Historical Society; *AWA Outstanding Contribution to Appalachian Literature Award*; *Chaffin Award* for Achievement in Southern Literature; *Plattner Award* for Short Story; Virginia Book of the Year nomination; AWA Best Appalachian Novel; *SEBA Best Novel* nomination; St. Andrews College's *Flora MacDonald Award*; and the *Sherwood Anderson Short Story Award*. Her books have been translated into a dozen languages, and she has served as writer-in-residence at King College, Bristol, Tennessee, and at Shepherd College in West Virginia. In 2001 she taught fiction at the WICE Conference in Paris.

Sharyn McCrumb, a graduate of UNC Chapel Hill with an MA from Virginia Tech, has lectured on her work at Oxford University, the Smithsonian Institution, the University of Bonn, Germany, and at universities and libraries throughout the country.

McCrumb lives and writes in the Virginia Blue Ridge. Her latest novel *St. Dale* (Kensington, Feb. 2005) examines grassroots canonization, setting the *Canterbury Tales* within the culture of NASCAR.

Description: In the early 1980s when I was in graduate school in theatre at Wake Forest University, some actors of my acquaintance became interested in DUNGEONS & DRAGONS for its role-playing opportunities, since creating characters was what we were trying to learn how to do. I have always been interested in mythology and folklore, and D&D was as close as I could come to using that information in "real life." It also served as creativity practice for an aspiring writer.

I always based my adventures on Celtic mythology, so that anyone who was well up on British folklore would have had a great advantage. Now I think I'd broaden that base to include Cherokee and traditional Appalachian heritage, which would make it rather more interesting.

Since I was an aspiring novelist, I always preferred to be the Dungeon Master, writing the scenarios and crafting the NPCs. At some point I invented a character named Jingo. This fellow was a con man and a bit of a rogue but basically the good-hearted huckster. Years later when I saw the character of Salmoneus on *Hercules*, it was like meeting an old friend. Jingo turned up in almost every scenario I devised. He might be using an alias or passing himself off as some local authority figure, but sooner or later the players would recognize him. I remember how delighted they always were to meet a familiar face in a new adventure. The lesson in this was that if you create a memorable character, either in a roleplaying game or in a novel, people will react as if that character were a real person. Some of our best friends are imaginary.

My strongest connection with D&D was that I wrote a comic novel called *Bimbos of the Death Sun* in which a game of DUNGEONS & DRAGONS is instrumental in solving a murder. Here's how it came about.

In 1985, when I was a struggling graduate student in the Virginia Tech English department, the university science fiction club sponsored a short story contest, to be judged by my colleague and fellow writer, English instructor John Nizalowski. As a practical joke, I slipped an outrageous manuscript into the pile of story entries and waited to hear John's scream when he read it. The spoof was entitled, "Bimbos of the Death Sun." When John had recovered from reading a manuscript in which his dog and his office mate were depicted as evil aliens in a parody of *Moby Dick*, he returned it to me, saying, "You know, that title is really too good to waste on a practical joke."

"I know," I said, "but I could never write the book that went with that title."

I tucked the idea away in a few spare brain cells in the cortex and went back to writing satirical math section of my comic novels. A few months later, I did get an idea that fit the title: What if one of the university's engineering professors wrote a hard science fiction novel about the effect of alien sunspots on computer circuits, and what if he sold that novel to a cheap paperback house and they changed the title to *Bimbos of the Death Sun*. I pictured the professor going to a small regional science fiction convention to promote his book and trying to keep his students from finding out that he was the author of the paperback with the lurid bikini-clad girl on the cover. That book I could write, I thought.

I wrote the first two chapters for fun, drawing on a local science fiction convention for inspiration. The chapters were funny, and they were based on my observations of the local convention and on my husband's gaming friends. My husband the chem major loved all sorts of strategy games. Diplomacy was his first love, but he also played DUNGEONS & DRAGONS and variations thereof. There would be marathon gaming sessions at our house in those days, which gave me a good opportunity to observe the culture. Writing the novel was cheaper than therapy.

Still, since this wasn't the sort of book that I was writing for my New York publisher, I didn't submit it for publication. I put the pages in a drawer and went back to writing term papers on the Brontes in grad school, and chronicling the adventures of Elizabeth MacPherson. Then the university science fiction club had its own convention. It was being held one weekend at the Blacksburg Econo-Lodge, and the club had raised enough money to bring one – just one – author in to star in about eight hours of programming. Even as out of touch with reality as they were, they realized that this poor author would need to be given a recess every now and then, so they cast about for other ways to fill up the program schedule. One of them hunted me up on campus.

"You! You're a published writer!" he said accusingly.

"Well . . . not anything you guys read," I murmured.

"Doesn't matter. The real author will have to eat and so on. Why don't you come and do a one-hour session? A reading, maybe."

Since I didn't get many offers to give readings in those days, I agreed to do it, but I knew the science fiction club wouldn't be interested in a reading of my usual work. That's when I remembered those ten pages of *Bimbos of the Death Sun*. I dug them out of the file cabinet and took them to the Econo-Lodge.

The guest author, who was Margaret Weis, the DRAGONLANCE lady herself, stayed for the reading, laughed harder than anybody, and asked for a copy of the manuscript. I photocopied the ten pages for her, thinking that she wanted to pass them around the office when she got home.

She did — but the office was that of her publisher.

Six months later, I received a phone call at work from a strange man who said that he represented a company called TSR. He said, "We want to buy your book."

I said, "What book?"

The rest is history. I agreed to write the rest of the novel for TSR in fewer than eight weeks, so my memory of that autumn is a blur of computer screen and exhaustion, but I did finish on time. I drew on the sort of D&D scenarios we had played to craft the gaming chapter of the novel in which Jay O. Mega as Dungeon Master uses the game to trap the killer. *Bimbos of the Death Sun* was published in the spring of 1987, and it went on to win the Edgar Award that year for Best Paperback Original.

The book proceeded to have a life of its own.

At book signings in Hollywood, cast members of science fiction television programs turn up with battered copies of *Bimbos of the Death Sun*.

"We use it as a survival manual," one of them told me. "It's the best way to explain to guest stars what they'll experience when they go to a fan convention."

Science fiction fans discovered the book, and readers either loved it or were outraged by the description of fandom. Panel discussions debated the issues raised in the novel. I felt like the Salman Rushdie of science fiction. People from all over the U.S. and Canada would tell me that they recognized their friends in the book — people I had never heard of. I was able to keep track of which authors were being difficult in the genre by who Appin Dungannon was reputed to be — his identity kept changing in the popular mindset.

Bimbos of the Death Sun was intended to be an observation of the culture of fandom and a gentle warning. Science fiction writers build castles in the air; the fans move into them; and the publishers collect the rent. It's a nice place to visit, but I don't think we're meant to live there.

After fourteen years and two publishers, *Bimbos of the Death Sun* is still in print and is currently under option by a filmmaker. As a result of winning the Edgar, I got a hardcover contract and finally reached the *New York Times* best-seller list. So, because of D&D, I got to live happily ever after. ■

PLANESCAPE
BY STEVE WINTER

"WE WANTED SOMETHING

By 1993, SPELLJAMMER had run its course and we were looking for a new product line to replace it. We wanted something very different from SPELLJAMMER but still able to fill its niche—a setting that allowed characters to travel across wide distances to visit strange and wonderful lands that went beyond simple variations on a theme.

For some time, at department brainstorming sessions TSR designer Slade Henson had been promoting an idea for a product that he called Planescape. It was built around *The Manual of the Planes*, the hardcover manual written by Jeff Grubb in 1987. MotP (or Manuel of the Planes, as it was usually referred to internally) had been a popular book, and it was a tremendous concentration of creativity. We'd never updated it after 2nd edition was published, however. Jeff, Slade, and Dori Hein, their product group leader, worked over the proposal and kept it on the table. Their proposal was essentially to update the original book to the 2nd edition standard and expand it by filling in some of the gaps that resulted from trying to cover such

a huge topic in a single volume. Despite that idea's appeal, nothing came of it.

When the search for a new setting got seriously underway, the Planescape idea was still kicking around, and it got tossed onto the table. It had never really been considered as a setting up to that point. This cast it in a whole new light, and we all took a serious look at it. By the time the project got the final go-ahead to be placed on the schedule, almost everything about it was changed except for its name. That shouldn't be considered an indictment of the original proposal because it wasn't at all uncommon in a process like this. The name, though, which originated with Slade, was inspired. No other name would have suited PLANESCAPE half as well.

When the new schedule was laid out, the design job went to Zeb. He knew from the planning meetings that several concepts were key. One of the lessons from SPELLJAMMER was that the setting would benefit from having a real campaign base. A movable base, like a vessel of some sort (or an artifact, which was the original idea for the means of traversing the planes) wouldn't do it. It had to be a place that characters could come home to when they needed to, and it had to be central to the nature

of the setting. Also, Vampire: The Masquerade was a particularly hot game at that time, and one of the ideas in it that we really liked was the clans. Jim Ward wanted to be sure that players had something to identify with and to give them a sense of belonging in this alien venue. Those two concepts clearly led to Sigil and the factions.

As it turned out, PLANESCAPE is the most relentlessly unique setting TSR ever published. Like everything that came from TSR, it was the product of many inputs. At the same time, there's no denying that it was Zeb's AD&D masterpiece. Just where it all came from is a question that's come up many times since PS was published. "Standard fantasy" takes many forms, but until PLANESCAPE appeared, none of them took that form. According to Zeb:

By the time I started on PLANESCAPE I had pretty much given up reading fantasy (too many years spent working in it). For a long time I had been reading obscure history, but right around that time I picked up a batch of experimental fiction. Books like *Invisible Cities*, *Einstein's Dreams*, *Dreamtigers*, and the *Dictionary of the Khazars* had an effect. There were movies ranging from art house films (*Orphee*) to Hong Kong action and fantasy

Dave Meyers

Statistics and Attributes: Dave Meyers is a director of music videos and commercials. He lives in Los Angeles.

Description: DUNGEONS & DRAGONS was as important—if not more important—to my career than my college education. The game inspired and challenged my creativity and imagination at an early age and liberated my mind as I matured into adulthood. It is because of this freedom that I've been so successfully prolific in all forms of filmmaking and continue to rely on my own imagination for freshness and originality.

At the time, I far preferred to be a player instead of a dungeon master, but as life has moved on I have taken on the role of a dungeon master, not with the game, but with my career. I now influence and govern the rules for the imagination of MTV audiences (metaphorically speaking).

My most memorable and most frustrating moment was this pesky spectre that kept killing my most treasured character, Brightblade. In fact I threw such a fit, my dungeon master had to adjust the rules to allow for a higher-level spell to be used on me, even though I hadn't gotten that far, so I could be resurrected several times and kill that damn ghost. In fact, I think it was my sword that cast the spell (talk about a magical sword). I suppose he had to be creative, because I wouldn't let him go until I had completed that mission.

I also remember my dungeon master and I tried putting hot peppers under our fingernails because when engaged in the game, I bit my nails and did major damage to them.

Then there was Becky, the first girl I fell in love with, during senior year in high school. I went to her house once and saw her mother and mother's boyfriend playing D&D with some friends. I confessed my love for the game, and suddenly I was allowed to hang out as late as I wanted with her daughter. It was the D&D code of honor. They knew I was a gentleman just by that connection.

In ninth grade, I was studying one of the D&D manuals before my gym class. The hottest girl in the gym, Melissa, sat

down next to me and was actually intrigued by the game. I began to tell her all the wonderful aspects of the D&D world. My moment of glory was crushed by an obnoxious classmate of mine who showed up a few moments later and mocked me in front of her for being into D&D. Needless to say, I was humiliated and didn't get the girl. Fifteen years later, this classmate is now a good friend, and I remind him every time I steal the hottest babe in the room from him that he should have studied up. I got all my mojo from the game — and that's why he has none.

To sum it all up, I'd not be the man I am today if I hadn't been exposed to the wonderful world of DUNGEONS & DRAGONS. I hope to some day contribute to the legacy in some form or another, and until then, my personal experience and take on the game will remain in my head, and will stay my guiding light when times are tough. ■

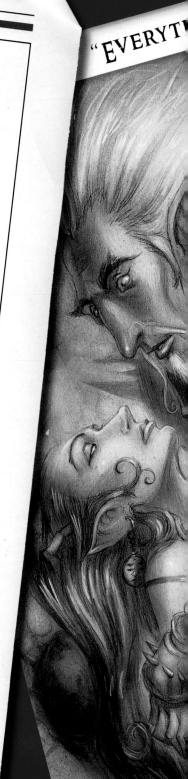

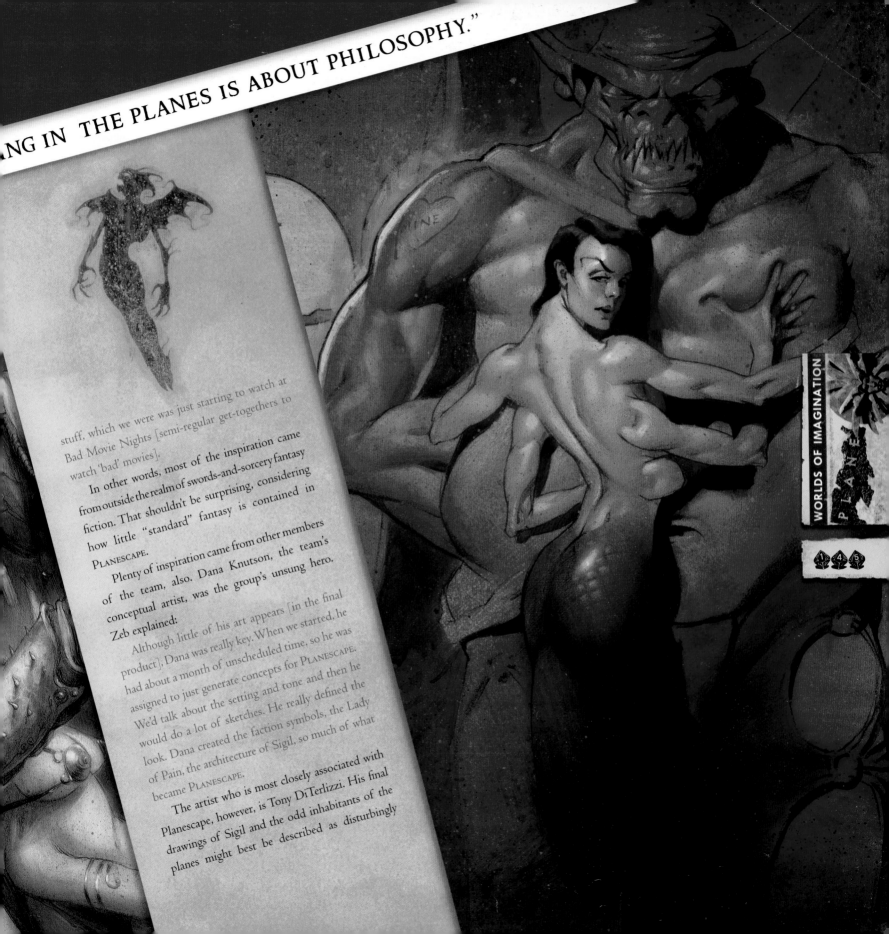

stuff, which we were was just starting to watch at Bad Movie Nights [semi-regular get-togethers to watch 'bad' movies].

In other words, most of the inspiration came from outside the realm of swords-and-sorcery fantasy fiction. That shouldn't be surprising, considering how little "standard" fantasy is contained in PLANESCAPE.

Plenty of inspiration came from other members of the team, also. Dana Knutson, the team's conceptual artist, was the group's unsung hero. Zeb explained:

Although little of his art appears [in the final product], Dana was really key. When we started, he had about a month of unscheduled time, so he was assigned to just generate concepts for PLANESCAPE. We'd talk about the setting and tone and then he would do a lot of sketches. He really defined the look. Dana created the faction symbols, the Lady of Pain, the architecture of Sigil, so much of what became PLANESCAPE.

The artist who is most closely associated with Planescape, however, is Tony DiTerlizzi. His final drawings of Sigil and the odd inhabitants of the planes might best be described as disturbingly

WORLDS OF IMAGINATION

whimsical, like something out of a Keebler elf's nightmare. "Tony … really took what was there and ran with it," said Zeb.

His people, the faces, their dress made these spiky landscapes personal and something that people could relate to—people players wanted to be…. It was a huge stroke of luck (and a good decision by our art director) to get Tony and have him fit in so well.

Dave Wise was the editor on the original set. He was particularly involved in helping to establish "the Voice," the unusual tone and language used in writing the rules. He and Zeb adhered to some specific rules in writing and editing "just to make the whole thing harder, I think," according to Zeb.

The books were liberally sprinkled with unusual jargon and slang terms. Some were created for the game but many were drawn from historical sources. Zeb had copies of *Cony-Catchers* and *Bawdy Baskets* and *The Elizabethan Underworld* on his office shelf for years before PLANESCAPE crossed his desk (he loaned them to me when I was working on *A Mighty Fortress*). Finally, in PLANESCAPE, he got to use them to full effect. Bashers, barmies, bloods, cutters, cagers, keyless Primes, sods, factols and factotums all populated the sooty alleys and dingy alehouses of the City of Doors. Atmosphere dripped from every page of these books. It could be overwhelming to clueless berks and leatherheads who didn't know the cant from the chant.

The heart of PLANESCAPE was Sigil, the City of Doors. This donut-shaped city floated mysteriously above the Spire, which rose to unimaginable heights above the circular plane of the Outlands. Many campaigns were built around Sigil alone and never, or rarely, left the confines of the city.

The most enduring icon of PLANESCAPE is the silent, enigmatic matriarch of Sigil, The Lady of Pain (whose original name was Our Lady of Pain). The sight of her knife-ringed face as she drifted silently through the quickly abandoned streets was enough to make even the stoutest bloods and high-up men scramble to get out of her—or more properly, its—way. Cross her and there's no telling what might become of you. If you're lucky, you'll get written into the book of the dead and the dustmen will cart you away. If you're not so lucky, you could find yourself wandering forever in an eternal maze, beyond all help from friends or gods.

Sometimes, however, you had no choice about leaving the city. Step through a doorway at the wrong time or with the wrong souvenir in your hand and you could unexpectedly find yourself on another plane entirely, and it might be even less hospitable than Sigil. The whole point of the setting was to get player characters onto the inner and outer planes, after all.

The planes were tough on intruders, though, and their inhabitants even more so. Figuring out a way to let PCs survive in such a dangerous environment was a big part of the design effort. That, in part, led to the concept of "philosophers with clubs." Everything in the planes is about philosophy. That doesn't mean it's calm and rational. It means ideology has real, physical effects, and the PCs can influence the shape of the world by helping to spread their views and those of their faction. The factions were designed along the lines of philosopher street gangs—or something like that.

All this textual and graphic oddness created a setting that was, to say the least, unique. When the PLANESCAPE boxed set was released in 1994, it caught the gaming industry by surprise. TSR, after all, was supposed to publish "standard" fantasy, whatever that might be. Cutting-edge RPGs emphasizing attitude as much as hit points were generally thought to be the province of smaller, fringe companies with less of a stake in the status quo. PLANESCAPE was proof that TSR still had the talent and the will to innovate and to stretch the creative envelope.

Ed Robertson

Statistics and Attributes: Ed Robertson is a founding member of the Canadian rock group Barenaked Ladies. Over the years the Barenaked Ladies have developed a reputation as one of North America's best-loved live acts and have sold over twelve million records worldwide. Ed has also appeared in several films; his most recent role was in the romantic comedy *Love, Sex and Eating the Bones.* Currently Ed resides in Toronto with his wife and their three children.

Description: I was introduced to DUNGEONS & DRAGONS at my school when I was in the fifth grade. I was ten. The teacher came into the class and told us we were all going to learn this new game, DUNGEONS & DRAGONS. He set the day aside and taught us all how to make characters and the basic tenets of the game. We were immediately hooked, of course. We were in a gifted school for accelerated learners, and I guess our teacher knew how much we would love it.

I vividly remember that day and wanting so badly to be a powerful, magical elf.

I had read Lord of the Rings in the fourth grade, so I was already pretty big into fantasy. I was already into video games, even though they were in their infancy. I loved board games, I loved crosswords, so when D&D came along it was like manna from heaven.

My characters never lasted long because I was too reckless. We played freestyle games at the time. We would make up a scenario and go in headlong, and when your character died, you'd just make another character. I was amazed when I first met some really hardcore D&D guys from TSR that they had these characters who'd been around for, like, seventeen years. I never had a character that lasted more than a month.

We played a lot of the modules. We'd run to the hobby store to get the latest module whenever it came out. More than that we played freestyle games where the DM would come up with an entirely new scenario and we would just improvise through the whole thing.

When I was eighteen or nineteen, Steve and I used to open up for this comedy troupe, Corky and the Juice Pigs. They toured across the country doing campuses and colleges. They won awards at the Edinburgh comedy festival, and were favorites at the Just for Laughs festival in Montreal. One of the members was a Canadian comedian named Sean Cullen, who's now the lead in Mel Brooks's *The Producers* in Toronto. Sean was a big D&D fan, and he used to DM while we would travel. One of my favorite DUNGEONS & DRAGONS experiences was with Sean, this master comedian, as a dungeon master.

I remember we had come into this harbor, four of us. We had snuck aboard a ship, and through a series of impossible exploits, we had managed to sneak aboard a fully equipped rogue pirate ship. We snuck up to the crow's nest undetected, again through a series of elaborate rolls. Phil, a guy who was with us, in a daring

move slid down the sail with his knife – just to be cavalier. Then we besieged this little tavern. We armed ourselves in the tavern, and fought off all these people and planned to escape on the boat... but we had forgotten Phil's daring knife slide entry that rendered the sails useless. We were slaughtered on the deck. It was just one of those memorable things where everything was going insanely well and we were managing insurmountable odds, and then this cavalier move that none of us had even thought about destroyed us in the end.

Barenaked Ladies played in Milwaukee about eight years ago, and a bunch of guys from TSR came out to a show. A security guard said to us, "A bunch of guys from "T S R" are here. Do you know TSR?"

I was like, "Yeah, I know what TSR is."

So I met these guys after the show and chatted D&D with them, and over the years they just kept coming to the shows, and I kept in touch with them. Then I got to like other Wizards of the Coast games. There's a great game called Guillotine. We just kept in touch over the years.

I haven't gamed in ages, but I just called up a bunch of friends that I used to play with, and we're getting together a game. In preparation for the interview I was going through my Monster Manual and my Monstrous Manual. I actually have a Silver Anniversary edition. I still have tons of modules in my basement and lots of little lead figurines. I'm a hoarder—my wife hates me for that—but even though I haven't played D&D in seven or eight years, I have a huge collection of D&D stuff. It's the first great RPG, the first fantasy RPG, and it's important in that respect. I can't wait until my kids are old enough to be interested in it, and then I'll be the DM. ■

SECOND EDITION
BY STEVE WINTER

The biggest decision of 1987, of course, was one of the biggest moves ever in the history of TSR, D&D, and the whole gaming industry. That was the decision to publish a revised edition of ADVANCED DUNGEONS & DRAGONS.

With three and a half editions of the game under our belts now it's more difficult to appreciate just how groundshaking that decision and its announcement were at the time. The ADVANCED DUNGEONS & DRAGONS game was the undisputed king of the roleplaying market – top of the heap, cream of the crop, leader of the pack. It spawned the entire industry. AD&D was more than ten years old, DUNGEONS & DRAGONS older than that. Players who'd picked up the game in college during the early years were teaching their children to play. The game had evolved considerably during its lifetime but never been revised. In the eyes of many role-players, the game rules were sacred text that should be left untouched. A revision would be tantamount to adding a fifth president to Mt. Rushmore

— however great and beloved the choice might be, is he really necessary on the mountain?

In reality, of course, the rules of AD&D were no more sacrosanct than any other living document. They had been undergoing constant revision for years. It was guerilla revision, however, disguised in the form of accessories, expansions, and optional rulebooks. Unearthed Arcana was the biggest and most visible entry in the revisionist sweepstakes but there were many others. Every hardcover book after the Dungeon Masters Guide, Players Handbook, and Monster Manual contained rules alterations. These usually came in the form of optional rules intended to expand the players' alternatives, redress imbalances, fill gaps, or otherwise repair a perceived imperfection.

While well-intentioned and individually creative and successful, these changes were still of the worst kind: slow, unheralded, and unguided by any overarching principle or ultimate goal.

The growth of gaming worlds like FORGOTTEN REALMS and ORIENTAL ADVENTURES exacerbated

the situation. Their unique, world-specific character classes, races, spells, and weapons inevitably found their way into other campaigns where they didn't always mesh smoothly or fit logically.

When ORIENTAL ADVENTURES was designed, new methods were developed to handle many problematic aspects of AD&D. In some ways, OA was a trial run for a larger AD&D revision when it was published in 1985. That idea was never put forward generally in the company because it would have tripped alarms all over management and the marketing department, and we always tried to fly as low under the radar as possible. A few examples of how OA broke the AD&D mold are its treatment of piecemeal armor, martial arts styles, character kits, and proficiencies. Not all or even most of OA's innovations made it into 2nd edition, but they laid the foundation for the intellectual work that would go into revising the game.

People immediately recognized these changes for what they were, which is to say, improvements over the original. Even if no one wanted to acknowledge it publicly, behind the walls of TSR's R&D division, we were acutely aware that the game was slowly transforming, and we were keen on somehow incorporating all those new, fringe ideas into the established core of the game.

By 1987, the science and/or art of roleplaying game design (whether it's art or science is an ongoing argument) had progressed significantly since AD&D's first appearance. Games such as Runequest, The Fantasy Trip, Chivalry & Sorcery, Paranoia, Pendragon, Warhammer Fantasy, Star Wars, Call of Cthulhu, and many others (including games from TSR such as Marvel Super Heroes and The Adventures of Indiana Jones) showed that there were innumerable ways to build a quality, innovative RPG.

It was important for TSR to stay on top of that curve. We were the industry leaders, the ones who'd created roleplaying games in the first place. We were always happy to see other companies produce innovative products because we really believed that whatever was good for the hobby was good for everyone involved in the hobby. (That philosophy carried right through to Wizards of the Coast, too, as demonstrated by the Open Gaming License.) But whatever AD&D's popularity might have been, we also knew that it wouldn't stay on top forever if we didn't keep it up to date or straighten out the confusion and controversy that we ourselves had created in the game by publishing expansion rules.

Which is not to say that everyone in the company was on board with this idea from the beginning. The notion of revising the game that formed the company's backbone clearly involved some risk. It was not only a question of customer reaction. There was the question of where the resources would come from – such a huge undertaking would tie up key personnel for a long, long time. (When all was said and done, Zeb Cook and I spent almost two and a half years apiece on this one undertaking. No accurate records were kept during the creation of the original AD&D manuals but it's almost certain that more man-hours were spent creating 2nd edition than were spent on the first set of books, and they were published over several years.) Fortunately, despite some devil's advocacy, Lorraine Williams, the head of the company, seemed to be on the side of revising all along. The form and intent of the revision was subject to debate, but we always felt that we had her support for the undertaking.

The project evolved significantly as we got further into it. Initially, it was to be primarily an

SECOND EDITION
2nd Edition

"I LITERALLY SLICED THOSE BOOKS INTO PIECES..."

editing task. The goal at that stage was to clear up the inconsistencies between all the various manuals and reorganize the information to make the game easier to learn and simpler to reference during play. That alone was a laudable goal and a sizable task.

It was also a bit of guerilla marketing. The idea of even a minor revision to the company's bread and butter product was enough to make a lot of people queasy. Several key company officers were opposed to the undertaking entirely. They felt that the potential for backlash among dedicated players, confusion in the market, and inevitable inventory problems made a revision too risky. On the other hand, a simple reorganization to make the game more accessible to new players was an easier sell to upper management and the people who handled the business aspects of the company.

To one extent or another, we were all concerned about the effect a new edition of the game would have on the market. TSR had a huge product backlist and it was a source of dependable, necessary income. People were right to be concerned about the potential effect on the business of making ten years' worth of products obsolete.

To us in R&D, however, the business concerns seemed distant and secondary. We believed in our hearts that the game had to be revised sooner or later if it was to survive in the changing industry, and the sooner the better. Whatever the short-term pain might be — angry gamers, unsold 1st edition books returning to the warehouse, moms confused about what to buy — we knew that in the long run, a revision would prove to be the right business decision. All of us wanted to keep working for TSR for many more years, so we took the long view.

Beyond that — we wanted to do it! Who could resist the lure of getting to remake the greatest game of all time? As Zeb said:

Writing 2nd edition was one of those career moments. We all knew it was a big responsibility. ... I didn't realize just how much my name would be attached to 2nd edition when it was said and done. People still from time to time know my name because of 2nd edition. When I started, I had no idea that would be one result.

With editing as the primary idea, at least initially, my work on the project began by getting a ream of three-hole-drilled paper, many rolls of tape, scissors, and several copies of the Players Handbook, Dungeon Master's Guide, Unearthed Arcana, and ORIENTAL ADVENTURES. I literally sliced those books into pieces, paragraph by paragraph, and reassembled them by taping the pieces, in more logical order, to blank pages in three-ring binders. (This was 1987, remember. Computerization would have made the job much easier, and TSR had been using computerized word processing for quite a few years. Both the Players Handbook and Dungeon Masters Guide, unfortunately, predated desktop publishing. Neither of those books existed in electronic form. Having them scanned and optically converted to electronic text would have taken months, and with the technology of the time, they still would have been loaded with typos and scrambled tables. It was more efficient, given our computer system, to handle it the old-fashioned way—more efficient, but still a lot of work.)

Before that work could be completed, or even significantly started (given its size), the scope of the project changed. Instead of just a reorganization and cleanup, the game would be

able to speak the following lan... goblin, kobold, and orcish; in addition, for their alignment tongue," of all human... more than two additional languages (see **ALIGNMENT**)... ability. regardless

Similarly, dwarves have exceptional constitutional... toxic substances, ingested or injected. Therefore, ... make saving throws against magical attacks from w... spells.

Dwarves are miners of great skill. They are able t... facts when within 10' or less of the particular p...

Dwarves are able to see radiation in the infra-red spectrum... see up to 60' in the dark noting varying degrees of heat ra... ability is known as "infravision."

classes; in the dark noting varying degrees of heat ra... a thief when performing any functions of that class. Experi... be divided between the two classes also, even though the... longer advance upwards in fighting ability level. (Comple... regarding this subject is given hereunder in the section **CHARACTER CLASSES**.)

also the medieval Catholic Church which used Latin as a... **D**, alignment and communication base to cut across national boun... words which intelligent creatures use to inform other in... tures of the same alignment languages are NEVER flaunted in public. ...ment languages are NEVER flaunted in public.

...bulary and deal with the ethos of the alignment... ...ssion of varying subjects cannot be conducted in general... Furthermore, alignment languages are of lim... ...munications language is used to establish cred... desperate of situations have been established by other means. Only... ment tongue otherwise. It must also be noted that alignment... necessarily empower a creature utter something in t... ment language which is general in the ethos. Thus, blink dogs... gent; lawful good creatures who have a language of their own... good human, ...municate with blink dogs, however, will be absolutely at a... on-aggression, non-fear, etc.) without knowledge of... guage of lawful good but are of the... tually embrace the ethos of lawful good but are of the... ctually; therefore, they do not speak the tongue used... s is not true of gold dragons, let us say, or red dragon... ir alignment, who speak their respective alignment

START

SECOND EDITION
2nd Edition

of demi-gods, demons, and devils are whether... level characters prince, an arch-devil, or a demi-god. While there is a point where the... into most characters, singly, in small or part humans with the co-operation the group so doing, it is certain that the leaders will be some near... beings of other planes human. In co-operation the group so doing, it is certain that the leaders will be some near no upper limits as to level or acquired power from monsterdom, for they have... adventurers. Yet, there is a point where the... can challenge a demon

FIGHTERS TABLE ← FIGHTERS - DWARVES?

Experience Points	Experience Level	10-Sided Dice for Accumulated Hit Points	Level Title
0—2,000	1	1	Veteran
2,001—4,000	2	2	Warrior
4,001—8,000	3	3	Swordsman
8,001—18,000	4	4	Hero
18,001—35,000	5	5	Swashbuckler
35,001—70,000	6	6	Myrmidon
70,001—125,000	7	7	Champion
125,001—250,000	8	8	Superhero
250,001—500,000	9	9	Lord
500,001—750,000	10	9+3	Lord (10th Level)
750,001—1,000,000	11	9+6	Lord (11th Level)
1,000,001—?	12		

250,000 experience points per level for each additional level beyond th... 11th.

The Fighter

The principal attribute of a fighter is strength. To become a fighter, a character must have a minimum strength of 9 and a constitution of 7 or greater. ... strength above 15, he or she adds 10% to experience ... If a fighter has ... the Dungeon Master. Also, high strength gives the fighter a better chance ... hit an opponent and causes an increased amount of damage.

...ghters have a ten-sided die (d10) for determination of their hit points per ...vel. No other class of character (save the paladin and ranger (qq.v.) sub-...sses of fighters) is so strong in this regard. Fighters are the strongest of ...acters in regards to sheer physical strength, and they are the best at ...-to-hand combat. Any sort of armor or weapon is usable by fighters. ... first level of the dungeon ...the upper ruins

not merely a meaningless dungeon and an urban base around ... plopped the dreaded wilderness. Each of you must design a wo... by piece, as if a jigsaw puzzle were being hand crafted, and e... section must fit perfectly the pattern of the other pieces.

rewritten from the ground up. I don't think anyone was actually saying "redesigned" at that time; the idea was that the rules could be clarified most easily if they were rewritten in a single voice and following a coherent outline. While we were at it, we might as well incorporate those improvements and developments that had gotten popular. That meant cleaning up the contradictions between the old and new material — which meant that substantial design decisions had to made. Once you open that door, it's only a short step to "it would be so much better if we did it this way."

One of the first big questions was how to divide the material between the Players Handbook and Dungeon Masters Guide. Traditionally, the Dungeon Masters Guide was the larger of the two books. We decided to flip that relationship and place most of the rules that everyone needed to play the game in the Players Handbook, whose title implied it was the natural place to look for standard rules. The Dungeon Masters Guide would contain rules that applied specifically to the DM, rules that players didn't need to know, and advice and tools to help the DM do his job better or more easily. Whether you think that was the best solution or not, rest assured that we argued about it a lot.

One of the eternal questions when assembling any rulebook is whether it should be primarily an instruction book or a reference book; should it be structured so that it does a good job of teaching the rules to beginners or so that experienced players can find specific rules easily. Of course, the ideal would be to do both but the two approaches are mutually exclusive.

Our solution on that score was to make the manuals as useful as possible as reference books. The best way to learn AD&D was, is, and always

will be to find someone who already knows the game and learn from him. The concept of roleplaying is difficult to explain but very easy to demonstrate. With that as our guide, the reference book model seemed the natural choice. That decision was easier than how to split the books.

Probably the biggest debate of all centered around AD&D's character classes. Everyone seemed to have a compelling argument why classes were a bad idea from the beginning and should be stripped from the game. They were simplistic, artificial, childish, constraining, or obsolete. Skill-based rules were more flexible, more progressive, or more mature, whatever that means.

For every argument against classes, we could put forward another in their favor. Two weighed in most heavily (beyond "that's the way it's always been," which carried a lot of weight, too). The first was that the classes are archetypes of fable and mythology. We wanted characters to fit the archetypes, so defining them made perfect sense. It also gave us leeway to change the definitions slightly to accommodate different campaign worlds. A cleric in DARK SUN (which didn't exist at the time, of course), might be very different from one in the FORGOTTEN REALMS. We could enforce the differences easily with character classes, thereby focusing attention on the differing natures of the campaign worlds. What better way to emphasize subtle differences than by altering the archetypes? The second argument was that a character class gave a player an immediate handle on his or her character and smoothed the entry into what was otherwise a completely different sort of game from what most people had known previously. A character class isn't a straitjacket; there are many different kinds of archetypal fighters, for example, beyond the brooding barbarian with rippling

"PROBABLY THE BIGGEST DEBATE OF ALL CENTERED AROUND AD&D'S CHARACTER CLASSES."

muscles. Still, everyone immediately has a pretty good idea what you mean when you say "fighter" or "magic-user."

Ultimately, the fact was that few things in the rules said "AD&D" as loudly as the character classes. Without the classes, the game simply would not be AD&D any longer. That would violate the first principle of the revision. This whole argument really was as simple as that. No matter how many good alternatives people urged on us, none of them could be considered seriously. In our mandate, AD&D equaled character classes, period. In other words, "That's the way it's always been" carried the day.

That's not to say we didn't look at significant changes to the way classes worked. We considered things that were nothing short of radical. One proposal (made by me, and one that I still like, by the way) was to revamp thieves so that they functioned more like magic-users. That is, they would have a selection of skills divided by difficulty levels and a table that indicated how many skills of each difficulty level the character could earn at each character level. A third-level thief, for example, could know three 1st-level skills and one 2nd-level skill. This idea was rejected in favor of a less structured skill system. It's a good example, however, of the far-ranging alternatives that received serious consideration.

We looked at other changes that everyone agreed would be improvements, yet they still didn't happen. Zeb recalls two:

The most basic mechanic we wanted to change was the order of Armor Class, making I the worst and going up. It was an absolutely sensible change,

but ultimately it was decided that took things too far from what players were accustomed to. There was also the idea of getting rid of saving throws and using the ability scores instead. That just never seemed to work.

Some of the changes that were bandied about in DRAGON magazine were geared purely to get reactions. Zeb's "Game Wizards" column in DRAGON number 118, for example, the infamous "Who Dies?" essay, was purposefully inflammatory. No one had any intention of doing away with the core classes. His remarks had their intended effect, however, in that everyone started talking about the proposed revisions and writing letters to the editor, to Zeb, to the other game designers, to the company directors — I wouldn't be surprised if the Pope received one or two.

One of the most interesting and revealing responses came from a long-time player of the game who was upset about all of the changes as a whole. Zeb recalls that he was not calmed by our claims that all we were doing was making the game more accessible. This fan "wrote to say that we had ruined the game because we had made the rules understandable. Now anyone would be able to play the game!" AD&D's complexity gave it an air of elitism that kept out the riff-riff, apparently.

Generally, in talking to players before the release, there was a lot of concern. Nobody really knew for sure what we were doing, so there was a sense of relief from most when the changes were explained. The best comment [came from] a gamer in Montana who said that it seemed like we were just incorporating the changes they had already made in their house rules.

Offi
Dun
ORI

This fascinating sourcebook contains all-new information for players and Dungeon Masters, ages 10 and up.

ADVANCED DUNGEONS & DRAGONS, the TSR logo, and PRODUC

"WERE NOTHING SHORT OF RADICAL."

Dungeons & Dragons
2nd Edition

2102

Monstrous Compendium

VOLUME ONE

The perfect range
of creatures to play
the game.

TSR, Inc.
PRODUCTS OF YOUR IMAGINATION

Advanced
Dungeons & Dragons

AL ADVENTURES

Gary Gygax

All the necessary inform... ...on to
add Oriental Adventures to your
AD&D® campaign, for beginning
to advanced players.

...AGINATION are trademarks own...

Official **Advanced
Dungeons & Dragons**

UNEARTHED ARCANA

by Gary Gygax

2017

SECOND EDITION
2nd Edition

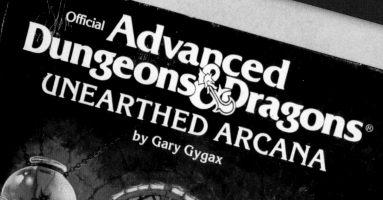

This a...

Advanced Dungeons & Dragons®
2nd Edition

2100

DUNGEON MASTER™ Guide

This newly revised and updated version of the AD&D® game provides everything Dungeon Masters need to create thrilling role-playing challenges. For intermediate through advanced players, ages 10 and up.

TSR

Advanced Dungeons & Dragons 2nd Edition

Tome of M

by Cook, Findley, Herring, Kubasik, Sarg

TSR

This supple AD&D® 2nd E details hund wizard and p and sco mag

Tome of Magi light spectacular effects

Besides clarifying and integrating the rules and cleaning up their presentation, a few conceptual or philosophical issues were dealt with, too. Chief among these was the question of dogma.

At various times in the past, Gary Gygax had written essays in which he claimed that the rules were only guidelines for DMs to bend and alter to suit their whims. Unfortunately, he also wrote other essays in which he explained that while the rules could be altered, DMs did so at the cost of imperiling game balance and at the cost of playing pure AD&D.

In the revision, the rules were divided into three levels: standard rules, optional rules, and tournament rules. The standard rules were the "basic" version of AD&D. Tournament rules added additional detail and would be standard in official, competitive AD&D play such as Gen Con tournaments. The optional rules were variants and details that could be used or ignored freely. Using them would sometimes slow things down; ignoring them would allow fewer options to the players. ("Fewer options" and "faster play" almost always go hand in hand.)

In line with those categories, the idea that the rules were only guidelines was (ironically) enshrined in stone. In tournament play, rules would be followed to the letter. In your own game, however, you were not only allowed but encouraged to customize to your heart's content. As hard-core rules tinkerers, we were all pleased with that decision. Zeb noted that he was "amazed when I [heard] about people who actually used every rule. We never did."

The work on this project was challenging and exciting but it was also difficult and demanding.

The sheer volume of words involved, not to mention the overwhelming number of tiny details that had to be tracked, was a grind. Zeb felt that the hardest part was . . .

. . . trying to sort out all the ugly little systems that didn't integrate with each other and work through the rule contradictions and interpretations. Some of them were really minor in the scheme of things—non-lethal combat never worked right, for example. Others like weapon speed and spellcasting times were things I never supported anyway but I still had to try to make them work within the game.

A side benefit of being assigned to this project was that Zeb and I got moved out of our cubicles in the R&D department and into actual offices in a section of the building that was mainly empty (typesetting had been located there previously but was in its new location by then, and marketing and graphics had yet to move in). We got real offices with real doors in an area that was real quiet. When we finally finished our work on AD&D two years later, our great relief and elation were tempered by the fact that we had to leave our private offices and come back to the bullpen.

Eventually, after two and a half years of outlining, dissecting, writing, editing, rewriting, re-editing, playtesting, critiquing, getting critiqued, arguing, and writing and editing some more, the books finally came out. It was a massive effort that involved at some point, in some way, almost every one of the several hundred people working at TSR and a host of outside volunteers and freelancers. When the books appeared, it was obvious that all our work was worth it because they blew off the shelves as fast as TSR could ship them.

Ed Castillo

Statistics and Attributes: Ed Castillo is the president of Liquid Entertainment and is working on the forthcoming Dungeons & Dragons real-time strategy game.

Description: I remember it like it was yesterday, even though it was more like twenty-one years ago. . . . A friend of mine had been talking to me about this cool game called Dungeons & Dragons, explaining that if I saved up my paper route money and bought the Players Handbook, he would save up and buy the Dungeon Masters Guide.

Now, at the time, I was deep into video games, especially Galaxians, Galaga, and Pacman, but I had seen the Bass & Rankin Jr. animated *The Hobbit* (you know, the one with the fire-drooling Smaug), was beginning to read for pleasure, and, for the first time, my imagination was beginning to bubble and pop.

I bought the book. My pal bought the other book, and we started to read. It was slow going at first. We would read, then we'd talk about what we'd just read, argue, then agree about how it was going to work in our upcoming game. I poured over those books until the pages fell out.

I played D&D all through high school. In the summers we would play in the garage (since anywhere else kept my parents awake) until we fell asleep at the table. All the neighbor kids would go home. We slept, woke up, and it was back to the garage and the sawed off ping-pong table until we fell asleep again.

During school, if my parents were unhappy with my grades, the D&D books were the first things to get taken away and always with devastating effect.

My brother and I bonded more during this time than ever before, and I came to know the true measure of my friends (believe me, sitting around a table all day will test friendships as sure as anything).

So now it was the first week of college and the local pub was having a free video game night. It was there, around a Gauntlet machine that I met some life-long friends. It would be these same people who would later get me into the video game business.

To this day I still play D&D, and I have my very first

character, as well as all subsequent characters that I played or campaigns that I ran. Each one is a marker. Each one is a juicy reminder of the times I shared with an ever-changing group of people. Like a scrapbook that comes to life, every time I pull them out, all those memories come flooding back.

D&D hasn't just influenced my life; it's been a constant part of it. It's served as companion and hobby, education and gateway to unforgettable social experiences. In the game, I've been hero and villain, monster and myth. It's kept me out of trouble and brought me closer to my ideals. D&D has let me be other people and by doing so, taught me a lot about myself.

As with all things, you get out of something what you put into it, but in this day and age, imagination is a dwindling resource, and social interaction on the decline. Playing Dungeons & Dragons can be a whetstone that sharpens both imagination and creativity, a workshop on team interaction and heroism.

David X. Cohen

Statistics and Attributes: David X. Cohen has served as executive producer and head writer of the Emmy Award-winning series *Futurama* since its inception. Previously, he was a writer and an executive producer of *The Simpsons*. While earning a bachelor's degree in physics from the Harvard University, he also served as president of Harvard Lampoon.

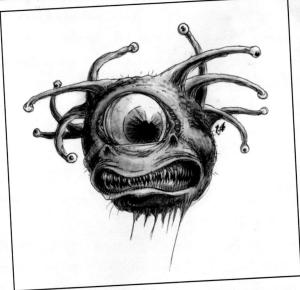

Description: I was in middle school when I first heard vague whisperings of a game called DUNGEONS & DRAGONS. I had no idea what it was, but I was pretty sure it was weird and complicated — and therefore, I wanted to play. I received the Basic Set as a present from my cousins in 1979, when I was in eighth grade.

Initially, my friends and I could not process the concept of a boardless board game, so we constructed a board with a dungeon on it, the contents of which we would vary from game to game, while the physical layout of the dungeon remained the same. Eventually, we figured things out and dispensed with the board. I played with my good friends Roy Carvalho, David Borden, and several others. Roy and I would alternate adventures as Dungeon Master, so both of us would get to play some of the time.

We were fairly conservative with the experience points, requiring significant effort to move up in level. Another friend of ours, David Schiminovich, was in a rival group that played fast and loose with the experience points. They were constantly beating up gods and finding priceless artifacts under every rock. We looked down our noses at their hyper-inflated game. In retrospect, though, our game might have been a little too stingy, as we all graduated from high school and went our separate ways without ever getting to do any of those crazy things the other group was always doing. Sigh.

My main character was an elf fighter-magic user named "Sho-Rembo," a name I got from the Basic Set handbook before I realized I was allowed to make up my own name.

Technically, Sho-Rembo is still alive somewhere. Hello, Sho-Rembo!

Once, when my friends and I were in high school, I was DM'ing *The Ghost Tower of Inverness*. After several days of extremely tense adventuring and seconds from death, the group suddenly made it out alive. They were so happy that they began jumping up and down excitedly, forming a human bouncing ball that went out of control and smashed into my friend Roy's basement wall, knocking a huge hole in it. I just checked with Roy, and he has confirmed that the hole is still there. So this is not just the thirtieth anniversary of D&D but also the twenty-second anniversary of the hole in Roy's basement wall.

I'm probably one of the only people on planet Earth, outside of the gaming industry, to have actually used my knowledge of D&D on the job — and not gotten fired. In the writers' room at *Futurama*, our shelf of reference books included a full D&D library (God forbid we should misspell ixitxachitl). And the job itself bore striking resemblance to a D&D game — a bunch of nerds sitting around a table, stuffing candy in their mouths and talking about monsters. (I'm allowed to describe it that way because I was one of them.) At one point, there was even an occasional game after work, but I missed out on it because I was editing at that hour. The following statement from *Futurama* writer Eric Kaplan was tacked up on our "quote board," where we posted memorable remarks. It perhaps best sums up the years of heavy wear put on our D&D library:

"My Monster Manual is starting to smell."
— Eric Kaplan

Many of the writers on *Futurama* and *The Simpsons* were D&D fans, and Futurama paid on-air homage to the game on numerous occasions. One *Futurama* episode entitled "Anthology of Interest I" features a guest appearance by Gary Gygax and culminates in a quadrillion-year-long game of D&D. Gygax guest-stars alongside then-Vice President Al Gore, physicist Stephen Hawking, and actress Nichelle Nichols, a.k.a. "Uhura" on the original *Star Trek*. This intellectual squad of "Vice Presidential Action Rangers" is charged with preventing the destruction of the universe — a task at which they fail miserably. When the D&D game starts, Al Gore refers to himself as "a tenth-level Vice President."

There are at least three other episodes of *Futurama* that make reference to D&D, and I could probably think of more if I weren't so lazy and forgetful.

I'm still friends with members of my old gaming group, David Borden, David Schiminovich, and Roy Carvalho. When we get together now, we usually play cards. However, none of us will ever forget the many hours we spent exploring dank caves together, risking our lives on each other's behalf or for no particular reason. ■

PHBR

PLAYER'S HANDBOOK REFERENCE BOOKS

2113

The
Complete Book of
ELVES

TSR

Advanced
Dungeons & Dragons
2nd Edition · Rules Supplement

The
Complete
Priest's
Handbook

TSR, Inc.

The PHBRs, or Player's Handbook Reference Books, were an integral part of the AD&D 2nd edition plan. We knew pretty much from the beginning of the project that we would do those books. They served two purposes:

First, the PHBRs held the gate open for continual revision and expansion of the rules. Even though 2nd edition had a two-year development track, we knew that no feasible amount of development and playtesting was going to produce a perfect game. Once it hit the shelves, a hundred thousand fans would inflict more playtesting on it in a week than we and our "legions" of playtesters could in years. No good avenue for publishing errata existed outside of DRAGON magazine, and even it had limited penetration. Avalon Hill had hit on a good scheme for disseminating errata for its magnum opus, Advanced Squad Leader. The game came with two coupons that could be mailed in to the publisher after certain dates (about eighteen and thirty-six months after first publication, if I recall correctly—mine were mailed in years ago, of course). Avalon Hill would then mail replacement pages to the purchaser with all the updates and corrections incorporated. The old pages could be pulled out of the binder and tossed and the new pages slotted in. This was a terrific, high-end solution to the age-old errata question.

Unfortunately, AD&D was going to be published in two hardcover rulebooks, not a three-ring binder. A binder was considered but the idea was rejected because of cost and durability considerations. AD&D books are subjected to a lot of hard use that would leave most binders in ruins. The Monstrous Compendiums were considered good candidates for a binder because the monster books don't get used as hard as the rulebooks. We also believed that having the monsters on individual pages would let a DM pull the pages he intended to use out of the binder for easier reference during the game. The binder was essentially a filing system. Whether anyone actually used the MCs that way I can't say. It seemed like a good idea at the time.

Second, the PHBRs represented a significant source of revenue for the company. We knew from years of business experience that campaign worlds and rules expansions were the biggest sellers. Anything that was targeted at players would sell many more copies than something intended solely for DMs. That was the primary problem with adventures—players had no reason to buy them except to fill a collection. Even if everyone played a particular adventure, you could expect to sell only one per gaming group. PHBRs were aimed specifically at players. Ideally, a PHBR could sell as many copies as the *Players Handbook*, the eternally

best-selling RPG product. Between the races and the classes, we had fifteen potential sales chart busters on deck in the PHBRs.

On both of those counts, the PHBRs were sterling performers. Gamers gobbled them up like candy.

Sadly, there was a downside, too-much-power spiral.

Anyone who plays music in a band knows about volume spiral. When the guitar player performs his solo, he turns up his amp just a bit for a little more punch. When he's done, he doesn't turn it down again. When the bass solo comes around, the bass player turns up a bit to be heard over the now slightly louder guitar. Now the drummer can't hear his beats over the guitar and bass monitors, so he plays a bit louder to compensate. After one complete cycle, the entire band is playing a few decibels louder than before. At the next guitar solo, the guitarist turns up again—just a little bit—and the whole cycle starts anew. By the end of a set, the band is playing noticeably louder than when it started. That's one reason why so many bands take volume control out of the hands of the musicians and give it to a sound man who sits in the audience. You can't trust musicians with something as important as volume.

It turns out that you can't trust game designers with something as important as designing games,

either. When you sit down to write a book like *The Complete Fighter's Handbook*, you need to figure out how you're going to fill 128 pages with interesting, useful material. What can you state about fighters that will hold someone's interest for 128 pages? More importantly, what can you state that will leave the reader feeling like his or her fifteen dollars was well spent? (That might not sound like much money in the twenty-first century but in 1992, fifteen dollars was a significant gaming purchase.)

One thing you can do that's guaranteed to hold the reader's interest is give more power to the character. It doesn't have to be a lot—just enough to give the character a little more punch. This is the character's solo, after all, and it's important to be heard when you're at center stage.

So *The Complete Fighter's Handbook* gave the fighter a bit more punch: some new combat options, a few new proficiencies to choose from, and some character kits that allow PCs to be fine-tuned in ways that the standard rules don't allow.

Kits deserve their own discussion. The idea for character kits originated with Zeb, and it was a core concept behind the PHBRs. It's not stretching the point to claim that kits were the notion that made the PHBRs work as a product line. We struggled for some time to figure out how we would fill these books before kits were suggested. Once they were on the table, everything else fell into place.

We were well aware of the danger of runaway power inflation. We knew that unless the PHBRs were closely managed, there would be a tendency for each new book to ramp up the power ever so slightly from the previous book's level. The result would be that by the tenth book, characters would be getting significantly better bonuses than were given out in the first book. We knew all that, and we planned against it.

Our plan didn't work.

The plan was to keep a very close watch over the first four books (fighters, thieves, wizards, and priests) and then use them as the benchmark for all subsequent books. It was a good plan but it fell apart quickly.

The first problem popped up when the plan ran into the reality of scheduling. The initial PHBRs were slated to appear in 1990 and 1991,

two books per year. That meant there would be significant overlap in their production schedules. (From the time the author typed the first word until the printed book arrived from the printer, a 128-page sourcebook took over a year in development.) In other words, all four books couldn't be done by the same team or even by the same editor. The designer/editor team working on the fighter book (Aaron Allston and myself) would be separate from the team working on *The Complete Thief* (John Nephew, Carl Sargent, Doug Niles, and Scott Haring), *Wizard* (Rick Swan, Anne Brown), and *Priest* (Aaron Allston and Karen Boomgarden). The only person with any overlap was Aaron Allston, a freelancer from Texas. All of the authors were freelancers, in

fact. They represented the best freelance talent available, which is why they got this job. Only the editors were full-time TSR employees. It was our job to make sure these books were in accord with each other and with what we projected for the line.

In that regard, and despite the difficulties, I think we did a pretty good job with those first four books. That took us through the first two years of PHBRs, and we felt that the mold was set. Everything from that point on should be smooth sailing.

PHBR5, *The Complete Book of Psionics*, was different from the first four. First, it was written by an in-house author (me). We decided it had to be kept inside instead of being farmed out to a freelancer because of the second thing that made it different from the first four PHBRs; it wasn't an expansion to an existing class but a reintroduction of a character type that had been excluded from 2nd edition. (Also, I really, really wanted to write this book, and I pestered my boss, Jim Ward, incessantly until he agreed to rearrange the schedule and let me do it. I had to make a lot of promises to get that commitment. Deadlines were king at TSR, and if you had a record of hitting yours, people believed anything you said. That may sound facetious but it's actually a pretty good system for

rewarding results. As it turned out, I promised too much in a "Name that Tune" way: "I can write that book in ten weeks!" I had to bring in Blake Mobely to help out toward the end. He designed the metapsionic powers, and Andria Hayday pulled it all together in editing. Andria was also responsible for the clever captions on the illustrations. I liked that idea so much that I thought it should have been continued in all subsequent PHBRs. We seemed to be the only two who thought that way, though, so the *Complete Book of Psionics* was the only book in the series to have amusing captions.)

Psionic characters were rebuilt from the ground up. Aside from some terminology and a few key concepts (like psionic points), very little was carried over from the original psionics rules. More importantly, though, the book was completely different in its structure and content from the four that preceded it. It distracted attention from the core principle that we had worked hard to establish, that the PHBRs had to introduce new material while maintaining balance. I don't think the psionics handbook was unbalanced at all. Letters of complaint ran fifty-fifty between "psionics are too powerful" and "psionics are too weak," a pretty good indicator that we got it about right. Nevertheless, the book broke the format chain.

Or maybe the distraction resulted from simple ennui. By the time *The Complete Book of Psionics* appeared in 1991, we'd been publishing PHBRs and their blue-covered companion DMGRs for over two years. They were becoming old hat. We were moving on to exciting new projects like the *Tome of Magic*, the historical reference books, Ravenloft, and Dark Sun. With the PHBR format so well established, surely that line could look after itself, couldn't it?

"EVERY RULE IN THE PHBRs WAS OPTIONAL..."

Of course not. None of us would have agreed with that statement at the time, had anyone spoken it aloud or even thought it consciously. Anyone would have agreed that shepherding the development of the game rules and carefully overseeing their evolution was an important job, possibly one of the most important responsibilities we had.

Unfortunately, we also had product catalogs to fill out, games to design, and deadlines to meet a thousand short-term priorities to swamp far-off chores like "make sure the PHBRs don't drift off the balance beam." The upshot was that the PHBRs were allowed to continue on autopilot.

Remember volume spiral? Here's where that parable becomes important. Slowly, almost imperceptibly, the new powers and abilities being granted to the classes and races in the ten remaining books began climbing. Each new book offered just a little bit more than the last. That's not to state that the books were poorly written or didn't have terrific new ideas. All of them had plenty of value to offer AD&D players. The problem was that each one offered just a little more than its predecessor.

Every rule in the PHBRs was optional, so the DM could nix anything he didn't like. That wasn't really sufficient, though, because players and DMs tend to assume that anything in print is official, and official means mandatory. Who wants to have rules you can't use?

Taken as a whole, the PHBRs had a major unbalancing effect on the game. By the end of their run in 1995, we had a situation much like that which led to the need for 2nd edition in the first place. Besides the core *Players Handbook*, fifteen books of expansion rules offered significantly better powers than the *Players Handbook* in ways that sometimes conflicted with each other. Playing a character straight out of the *Players Handbook* would get you sneered at by the power munchkins.

Revising the books was not economically viable and was never seriously considered. Like any genie, once these were out of the bottle, there was no acceptable way to put them back in. The solution to this problem would have to wait until the appearance of D&D 3.0.

HISTORIC
SOURCE

9425

Advanced
Dungeons&Dragons
2nd Edition   Reference

HR5

Historical

The Glory
of Rome
Campaign Sourcebook

9376

Advanced
Dungeons&Dragons
2nd Edition   Reference

HR3
Celts

Historical

Celts
Campaign Sourcebook

Beginning in 1991, TSR published seven historical sourcebooks for AD&D. These were 96-page softcover books that included a fold-out poster map. The seven books were: *Vikings* by Dave Cook (1991); *Charlemagne's Paladins* by Ken Rolston (1992); *Celts* by Graeme Davis (1992); *A Mighty Fortress* by Steve Winter (1992); *The Glory of Rome* by David Pulver (1993); *Age of Heroes* by Nicky Rea (1994); and *The Crusades* by Steve Kurtz (1995).

These books were well liked by the creative staff even though they never went over very well with the buying public. They were particular favorites of mine for several reasons.

First, because of my interest in history. That link is fairly obvious and shouldn't need much explanation.

Second, because they brought a different type of creativity to AD&D. That is, they required the authors to bend the AD&D rules to make them describe the real world. The AD&D game was designed primarily to deal with mythological "reality," which is quite a different thing from real-world reality. Previous campaign supplements for AD&D had ranged from almost cartoonishly stereotypic western European, late medieval settings to flights of pure fantasy. The historical sourcebooks called for a different approach. Instead of adapting AD&D's archetypes to a fictitious setting, the archetypes of the time had to be adapted to the rules. Rationales had to be found for magic. Mythological monsters, which are often very different from standard game monsters, had to be adapted in ways that were challenging and that made sense.

Those requirements combined in ways that produced unusual, intriguing campaign settings. The best of the bunch, in my opinion, were *Vikings*, *Age of Heroes*, and my own *A Mighty Fortress*.

Being the first of the series, *Vikings* suffered from the usual birthing pangs that afflicted new endeavors—the format was not established, and no one was sure what to expect from the line, what to include, or how to approach the material. Zeb did a terrific job of pulling it all together, partly because he was good at that sort of thing and partly because the subject was a particular interest of his (Zeb was the only person I knew who routinely walked around with dog-eared Penguin editions of Nordic sagas stuck in his hip pocket). It was clear from the text, however, that he had a good time writing the book.

9408

Advanced
ns & Dragons
nd Edition

Reference

# of Heroes
paign Sourcebook

HR3
Celts

9376

Advanced
Dungeons & Dragons
2nd Edition

Historical

Reference

Celts
Campaign Sourcebook

HISTORICAL SOURCEBOOKS

I can't say whether Nicky Rea had fun writing *Age of Heroes* because she was a freelancer who lived several states away. The golden age of Greek mythology was such a natural choice for an AD&D setting, though it's surprising how seldom it has been tapped. The Homeric tradition of heroic storytelling is the basis for much of what makes AD&D so compelling. Great heroes like Odysseus, Perseus, and Jason stride gigantically through their tales much like D&D characters. The combination was nearly perfect.

A Mighty Fortress was a later setting than standard D&D. In the years 1550-1650, firearms were prominent, armored knights were waning, and scientific reasoning was just beginning to challenge mysticism. It was also a period of incessant warfare, rampant superstition, and far-ranging exploration of the rapidly expanding world—a perfect setting for bold adventurers.

Initially these books were planned to appear in related pairs: *Charlemagne's Paladins* and *Vikings*, for example, allowed players to take sides in the long, bitter struggle between the Christian Carolingians and the pagan Norsemen. Likewise, *Celts* and *Glory of Rome* were meant to build a complete campaign along the Gallic frontier of

9475

Advanced
Dungeons & Dragons
2nd Edition Reference

The Glory
of Rome
Campaign Sourcebook

HR1
VIKINGS

9322

Advanced
Dungeons & Dragons
2nd Edition Reference
Historical

Vikings
Campaign Sourcebook

A Mighty Fortress
Campaign Sourcebook

HISTORICAL SOURCEBOOKS

the expanding Roman republic. Had the series continued, a companion volume to *The Crusades* would have been very likely, drawing heavily on *Arabian Adventures*. A Mighty Fortress was meant to stand alone, however, as was *Age of Heroes* (no one saw much potential in the market for a setting based on ancient Persia, and the Greeks had their hands full just dealing with their fellow Peloponnesians through most of their history).

Other subjects that got consideration were the Rus (plenty of two-fisted adventure and another tie-in to *Vikings*), the Balkans (Rumania, Transylvania, rampaging Wallachians and

Mongols, and a possible tie-in to *Crusades*), and Arthurian England (constant fighting against the Welsh, Scots, and rebellious Saxons after the Roman withdrawal).

All of that became moot, however, because by 1995, sales on the historical settings had fallen below the point at which we could justify continuing the line. It was a particularly sad demise for me because the HRs had been my pet project. They had a good run, though, and I'm still quite proud of the quality, depth, and creativity of some of those books.

Genndy Tartakovsky

Statistics and Attributes: Genndy Tartakovsky brought the STAR WARS epic to television with *Star Wars: Clone Wars* and is currently working on new episodes of the mini-series for March 2005 to air on Cartoon Network. In addition, Tartakovsky created the critically acclaimed animated series, *Samurai Jack*, as his follow-up project to the massive success of *Dexter's Laboratory*. He has been named one of Variety's "50 To Watch" as a future leader in the entertainment industry.

Description: I moved to America from Russia in 1977 and was introduced to DUNGEONS & DRAGONS in the early 1980s by my friends. I always wanted to be the knight, the guy wielding the sword. I always had that inner warrior spirit.

I played with a couple of kids from school and a couple of kids from the neighborhood. Mostly we just came up with our own worlds. I didn't grow up with a lot of money, so we ended up making up a lot of our own stuff. When I was a kid I'd always argue with my brother, who was two years older, because I would want to be the DM but I would never get it right.

I think D&D helped build my imagination. At an early age you start thinking about situations and how your characters get out of situations. It started building my story talent.

When I was doing *Dexter's Laboratory*, we came up with the idea that we've got to do a D&D episode. Dexter's the kind of character that would be into D&D. Paul Rudish who did the storyboards for the show was a big D&D player, so we talked about a little storyline and how we wanted to have D&D messing up the story as it went along. So we included the stuff about who was going to be the Dungeon Master—all those things we remembered having frustrations over when we were kids. Then we figured out how it would affect Dexter.

I played until I was about fourteen, kind of in and out.

At one point it turned into less playing and more about doing comic book panels of the adventure. We'd start talking about it and run out of time, so I'd go home and do a drawing of what would happen and give it to my friend, and he would do a drawing of it.

A couple of the guys here at Cartoon Network Studios started playing D&D. It's really cool. I come in in the morning and see all the drawings. Everybody can draw well now, so you can see the adventures all detailed out in drawings. It's really cool!

I think what came out of D&D for me was memories, memories of really fun times and friendships that lasted through my childhood. Just a lot of fun times and friends.

Marc Haimes

Statistics and Attributes: Marc Haimes is a production executive with DreamWorks S.K.G. Some of his projects include *Men in Black, Win a Date with Todd Hamilton,* and *Collateral.*

Description: We were halfway through "U-1," attempting to uncover the sinister secret of Saltmarsh, when he introduced himself and asked if he could join in the adventure. Regretfully, we said yes. He claimed he was a Ranger with no less than 2,034 hitpoints . . . a number that we eventually discovered was as arbitrary as his arsenal of more than 150 weapons and, in fact, his commitment to hygiene. Indeed, he was the first in a long line of "hit point inflators" (or "H.P.I.'s" for short) who blustered their way into our all-weekend DUNGEONS & DRAGONS marathons only to make things a little less fun for everybody else.

What was truly annoying about H.P.I.s, beyond their absurd degree of indestructibility, was that they seemed to be missing the entire point of the game. For them, it was about bragging rights. It was about tales of adventures that were never actually had, boasts of victories that were never actually won, and ludicrous accumulations of spurious wealth.

Of course, somebody who has never rolled a twelve-sided die might ask the obvious question: "Isn't that all DUNGEONS & DRAGONS really is anyway?"

The short answer is, of course, no.

The longer answer is that DUNGEONS & DRAGONS came at a time in my adolescence when I believed that all creative indulgences were more or less passive ones. Reading books, comics, watching movies, sitting in front of the television . . . yes, these things provided inspiration and fueled discussion, but they did not supply a more proactive outlet. One could read and watch and absorb the fantasy without ever being certain how to more actively participate in it.

DUNGEONS & DRAGONS was a clarion call for those of us who wanted a more hands-on experience but who weren't yet confident or disciplined enough to sit in isolation, confronting a blank piece of paper with fiction of our own. It brought like-minded comic book readers and fantasy fans together, provided us with a common template, and taught us a brand new vocabulary of creative collaboration.

And then, as we continued on our adventures together, something miraculous happened. Our creativity grew! We became more confident. More disciplined. Now, thirty years later, it seems clear to me that D&D invented or, at the very least, legitimized a type of creative play that helped build mental muscles in an entire generation of future fantasy scribes, screenwriters, and filmmakers.

Today I have had the good fortune of landing what I think is a very cool job. As an executive for the feature division of DreamWorks, I spend a good deal of time in creative meetings with writers, producers, and directors. Together, sometimes in all-weekend marathon sessions, we work to shape simple ideas into fully rendered, emotionally satisfying journeys. Often in these meetings, the cadence of our discussion, the back and fourth springboarding of imaginations takes on a familiar rhythm. This should probably come as no great surprise. An extraordinary number of our collaborative partners cut their creative teeth in the Demonweb Pits . . . and can still say quite readily what the sinister secret of Saltmarsh actually was (the "haunted" house was actually a front for weapon smugglers).

The most challenging part of the job is when I'm stuck dealing with certain (not all) negotiators who lie and manipulate and are generally more concerned with closing big deals than producing good movies. These people bluster their way into Hollywood only to make things a little less fun for everybody else. "Exaggeration-prone agents," I call them. "E.P.A.'s" for short.

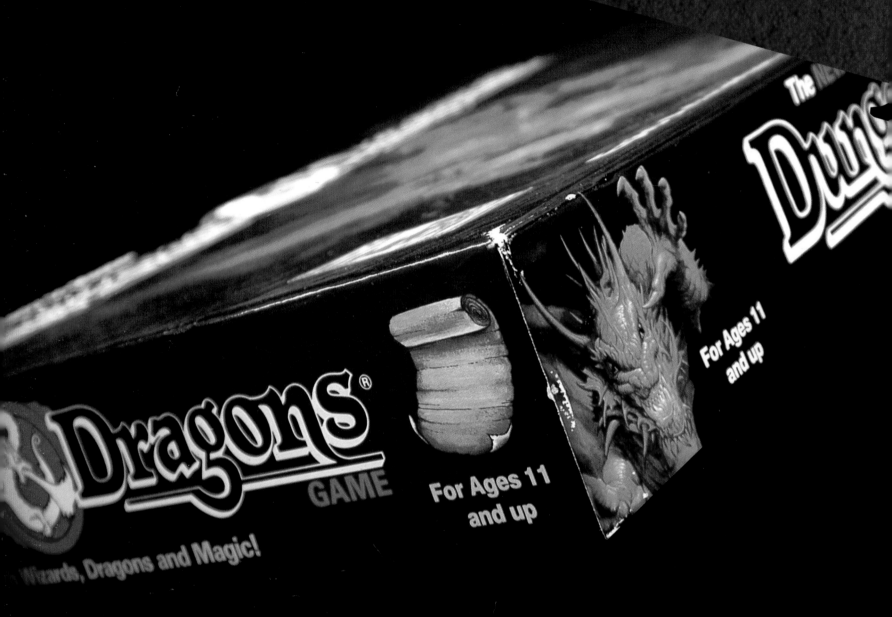

A perennial question at TSR was how to attract new players to the game. This was an important issue for the future of the company and we took it seriously, but coming up with an answer was a tough problem.

A big part of the reason why it was a tough problem was that while we had tons of theories and anecdotal evidence about who our customers were, we had very little in the way of hard, empirical, statistical evidence about who they were. The commonly held view was that the typical role-player was a boy, twelve to fifteen years old. "Bright" ten and eleven-year-olds

weren't uncommon if they had older siblings who could explain the game to them.

This idea of "brightness" is actually fairly important in the story of D&D. The idea that you had to have above-average intelligence to play D&D was a commonly held conceit, not just by TSR insiders but throughout the hobby and even by many people who never played the game but who had seen the mass of rulebooks. What's probably more true is that D&D players liked to believe that if you play D&D, you must be smarter than most people. This viewpoint is common to every special-interest group, whether

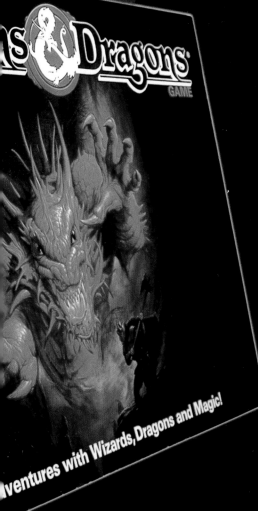

it's model railroaders, Barbie doll collectors, bird watchers, or sports car enthusiasts. To belong to a group, you must be privy to the special knowledge that gives the group its unique character. That, pretty much by default, makes you at least a little bit smarter than everyone else—in the eyes of your fellow group members, if no one else. What limited surveys were done tend to confirm that D&D players read more and at a higher level than the average person, and they have a good grasp of math. Does that make us "smarter" than everyone else? If you value the ability to read quickly and divide three-digit numbers in your head, then yes,

it does. If you value the ability to dance gracefully and sing karaoke, then D&D players as a group might look like a pack of stumbling, howling idiots to you and your friends. "Brightness" comes in a multitude of forms.

The common wisdom held that once our young, male barbarians and wizards hit the magic age of sixteen, they discovered cars, girls, and jobs. Caught between social pressures and hormones, they would drift away from D&D. We might get a few of them back again when they moved on to college. We might get a few more back when they graduated from college and got jobs. We'd

probably lose them again when they got married and had children. Maybe they'd drift back when the children went to school or, better yet, when the children got old enough to "discover" D&D for themselves and rekindle their parents' interest. (I've always loved this scenario: (Dad) "What'cha got there, junior?" (Son) "It's this great new game where you play elves and wizards and fight monsters!" (Dad, smiling) "Let me tell you about my 12th-level druid . . .")

There were two schools of thought within TSR on how to deal with this issue. The first was that it would be easiest to bring lapsed players back to the fold, because they already knew the rules and understood the concepts. The trick was creating a product that would lure them back and then getting that product in front of them.

The second was that it was easier to attract new players because the game had such strong appeal for middle school and early high school students. The trick was teaching them the game.

It's no secret that the easiest and best way to learn D&D or any roleplaying game is to play it with experienced players. To people accustomed to games like checkers, Monopoly, and Parcheesi.

RPGs are so foreign that they hardly look like games. In fact, I'd argue that they really aren't games in the traditional sense. They're systems for organized play, more akin to cooperating at building a huge, tumbling domino pattern than actually playing dominoes.

Every new roleplaying game always started with a short section describing what a roleplaying game is and how to go about learning to play. In every case, "find someone who already knows and is willing to teach you" was the first and best choice. The reason is simple. Roleplaying as a concept is hard to explain but easy to demonstrate. Over the years, I wrote those "What is roleplaying" chapters for at least a half-dozen different RPGs. Each one got a little better (I think) but there never was a really satisfactory way to explain it short of giving a lengthy example of play. Using an example is little more than cheating, frankly, because it works as a substitute for sitting in with experienced players—sort of a virtual roleplaying experience. It still isn't as good as actually playing but it's better than an essay.

As a company, we couldn't passively rely on word-of-mouth to spread our product's popularity and fill our coffers with cash. The problem became especially acute when console and computer games started catching on in the late eighties. Some of the most successful electronic games called themselves roleplaying games. We could argue about whether they were or weren't, or whether any electronic game can really be a roleplaying game. We can't argue about whether they presented a challenge to traditional, pencil-and-paper RPGs. They did.

Even without the challenge from electronic games, however, the problem of AD&D's steep learning curve remained. The game just looked daunting to the novice. Stack up all those rulebooks. No one wants to read such a mound of twaddle just to play a game that he or she might not even like! Cut it down to just the *Players Handbook* and it's still too much. Finding a way to make the learning curve less steep was an ongoing company concern.

For years, DUNGEONS & DRAGONS Basic was the best answer we had to offer. The game was much simpler than AD&D. Options were fewer, character creation was faster, and overall play was more straightforward. In those ways, the game

THE BLACK BOX

Dungeons & Dra

1 8 9

was better suited to beginners than was AD&D with its stacks of rulebooks and endless options. Each succeeding new edition of D&D was geared toward making the game more accessible to beginners.

To a large extent, these efforts were successful. D&D, over the years, became better organized and easier for neophytes to get into. There was a seeming paradox working against us, however. The players who wanted simplified rules with less structure (like those in D&D Basic) were not the beginners who hadn't yet mastered the intricacies of RPGs but rather the veteran players who had the experience and inclination to "wing it." The fact that D&D was filled with holes and abstractions made it attractive to experienced players who enjoyed coming up with their own field expedients. Conversely, AD&D's wealth of rules covering every situation gave rookies a sense of security: when the game moved into unfamiliar territory, somewhere in those books would be a rule to cover the situation. If, that is, the new players could wade through the mass of rules and stick with the game long enough to learn it before frustration drove them away.

We could see no way to overcome the complexity of AD&D in a way that would make it suitable for beginners. (The problem started with the name of the game itself—"Advanced" Dungeons & Dragons. That alone told prospective buyers, "this game is difficult to play,"

Who knows how many people it drove away: people who might have enjoyed the game if only they had tried it.)

Sometime in 1990, a different solution was proposed by TSR's CEO, Lorraine Williams. That was to follow the format established by the SRA reading programs. SRA (Science Research Associates) changed the way children learned to read in 1957 when it published the first of its individual instruction packets. In this format, lessons are broken down into small, self-contained steps. Each lesson fills a single, double-sided card. The student reads the lesson on one side, then immediately applies what he or she just learned by working through the exercises on the reverse side of the card. Each student can proceed at a comfortable, individualized pace.

Lorraine wanted to apply that same method to D&D.

Each card (they were called "Dragon Cards") would introduce the new player to one or two game rules on the front side. On the back was a small portion of a solo adventure focusing on the rule the player had just learned. The adventure was a simple scenario in which the character, who had been captured and imprisoned by orcs, had to escape from his cell, find a weapon, overpower some guards, and make his way out of the orcs' stronghold.

The job of adapting D&D to this instructional format went to Troy Denning. Troy had started

working at TSR in 1981, just a few months after me. He left the company in the mid-eighties to help start up Pacesetter, Inc. (publishers of Chill, TimeMasters, Space Ace, and Wabbit Wampage, among many other fine roleplaying and board games). By the late eighties, Troy was working independently as a freelance author and editor for TSR and other companies. He was lured back to TSR full-time by Jim Ward in 1989. There was never any doubt in Lorraine's mind that she wanted Troy to create this version of D&D.

For some reason, although this game was officially the fifth edition of D&D, it was always known throughout TSR by its stock number: 1070, pronounced "ten-seventy." It's the only

product that ever earned that distinction. (The people who dealt with "inventory" rather than "games," such as the fine and dedicated folk in shipping and purchasing, always used stock numbers rather than names when referring to products but this practice never carried over to most other departments.) D&D sets in general were usually referred to by their colors or other distinguishing package graphics. The original set was "small-box D&D" or "brown-box D&D." The 2nd edition was "blue-box D&D." The 3rd edition was "red-box D&D." When the 4th edition appeared, also in a red box, it assumed the name of red-box D&D and 3rd edition became "the Erol Otus set." Erol Otus (those who worked with Erol knew

him as Ool Erts) was the artist who painted the unique images on the 3rd edition Basic and Expert box lids. Most people either loved or hated Erol's highly characteristic style. I'm proud to proclaim that I was and remain a big fan.

The 5th edition, then, should have been called "black-box D&D," and sometimes it was. Most often, though, it was just Ten-Seventy.

The Ten-Seventy box contained: a DM's screen with a pocket to hold the dragon card learning pack; the dragon card learning pack itself, consisting of fifty-two SRA-style cards with the step-by-step instruction program; two sheets of cardstock fold-ups of characters or

monsters; a 21-inch by 31.5-inch map printed on both sides and made of heavy, linen-based, wear-resistant paper; six polyhedral dice; and a sixty-four-page rulebook. The rulebook served as a handy reference after you had learned the rules (trying to look up a specific rule on the dragon cards once you were familiar with the game would have been a terrible hassle). The rulebook was put together by Tim Brown, who along with Mary Kirchoff and Brom was one of Troy's partners on the budding DARK SUN design team. Because of the importance of Ten-Seventy, Lorraine insisted that it be completely finished before Troy could really dive into working on DARK SUN. Even though Ten-Seventy wasn't Tim's project, he pitched in to help wrap it up so that the DARK SUN project could begin in earnest.

TSR put as much marketing push behind Ten-Seventy as it could muster when the game was published in 1991, and the payoff was tremendous. Distributors ordered what they thought would be a three-month supply and sold out in weeks. Ten-Seventy was one of the hottest products TSR ever produced, with something over half a million copies sold worldwide. Hundreds of thousands of people who might never have tried D&D in another form, or who knew about it but were intimidated by the rules bulk, bought Ten-Seventy for themselves, as presents for friends and relatives, or even as a means of introducing reluctant friends to a game that they themselves were already playing. It was one of the great TSR success stories.

Reflecting on that success, Troy explained that "the dragon cards were Lorraine's idea; what to put on them was my call. She gave us the resources to do the job right. [Ten-Seventy] was the first time upper management and design really worked together on a project" with a clear, common goal, and the effort paid off with one of the biggest-selling RPG packages ever.

THE BLACK BOX

Dungeons & Dra

Matthew Rhodes

Statistics and Attributes: Matthew Rhodes is a producer, whose credits include *An Unfinished Life, Auggie Rose,* and *September Tapes*.

Description: Fifteen years old is a great age to fantasize because the mind runs wild with endless possibilities. I whisked through fantasy books instead of reading schoolbooks. I often stayed up all night reading under the bedcovers with a flashlight, and on more than one occasion I hid in the basement and skipped school to finish a story that I had started. I wanted to fly, breath underwater, scale walls, and fight with swords and magic. I always wanted to be a hero and have always been frightened by the villain. It was at that point in my life when I was introduced to DUNGEONS & DRAGONS. I learned about another world that exceeded my imagination and creativity. I became many different heroes who challenged and defeated many different villains. My imagination exploded, and my life changed forever.

My first summer job was as a caddy at a nearby country club, where I met a new group of friends. The only thing we had in common was DUNGEONS & DRAGONS. I quickly realized that's all you need.

There were about twenty caddies in the shack, and we all played "the game." We were all different ages, different backgrounds with different experiences. The Dungeon Master was a fifty-year-old man and the most experienced caddy. We all fell into ranks from there. I was a new guy and the lowest rank. My first game and my first time caddying. It lasted for the next seven summers.

Creating my characters has been and will forever be my favorite part of the game. Everything that I ever wanted to be I was. Anything I wanted to do I did. I raced across different lands, fought wars that lasted days, and met characters so real that they are forever burned in my mind. I died. I lived. I loved. I felt pain and passion. I wished and longed for things that I never imagined. I was a child and an adult surrounded by centuries of young and old. The game took me to places that one can only go in the mind.

D&D is the most interactive game that I have ever played. It has been an endless experience that sharpened many of the skills I still use in my daily life. It enhanced my ability to communicate, my responsibility to others, and the general understanding and compassion for mankind, the daily battle of good versus evil. Most importantly, I have learned when to fight for what I believe in and when to lay down my sword.

DUNGEONS & DRAGONS expanded my mind and imagination, enabling me to visualize something long before I saw it in the Monster Manual or Players Handbook. In the maze of life, I chose to be in the entertainment business and produce motion pictures and television shows. This has allowed me to continue to be creative and imaginative. I am never far away from my +3 sword, and my d12 still sits at my desk.

Some would say that D&D is a richer world of color and life than the one we live in. I am and forever will be that child. ∎

Tom DeSanto

Statistics and Attributes: A self-described pop culture junkie and longtime D&D fan, Tom DeSanto is a writer/producer who has worked on various films such as *X-Men*, *X2: X-Men United*, *Apt Pupil*, and the upcoming live-action Transformers film. He currently lives in Los Angeles.

Description: There are two types of people on the planet: those who have never played DUNGEONS & DRAGONS and those of us who were not like the other children. We were the kids always daydreaming in algebra class, sketching spaceships and monsters when we got bored. Don't get me wrong—we were smart, just in a way that is underappreciated by standardized tests. We had something teachers couldn't measure on a pie chart . . . we had imagination.

I remember when I was in eighth grade, rushing home from football practice so I could play D&D. That was sign number fourteen that I was never going to grow up and play middle linebacker for the Steelers. Reality just wasn't exciting enough for my twelve-year-old imagination. And who wanted to be stuck in suburban New Jersey when with a few books, some funny-looking dice, and a pencil (pens didn't erase hit points), you could be transported to Gary Gygax's world of DUNGEONS & DRAGONS. I couldn't wait to leave behind the humdrum land of manicured lawns, homework, and paper routes and enter into a realm of wizards, green slime, and gold pieces. Don't ever forget the gold pieces. Yes, it was good to be twelve.

Danny Carroll was my best friend in seventh and eighth grade, and I have him to thank for starting my obsession with throwing dice. Danny was the Dungeon Master, and I was the player. Seeing as there were only two of us, I got to play all of the characters, fighters, thieves, and magic users – all mine to command. It made me realize, why just live one life? With D&D you could be whoever you wanted, limited only by whatever your imagination could create.

As I entered high school my time spent with roleplaying games grew. Danny went to a different school, but a new fellowship arose with Rob Hoitela, Tim McKiernan, Brian Barclay, and Mark Sojak. Frodo and Gandalf had nothing on us. We not only had history class together, we also battled invading orc armies, outsmarted assassin guilds,

and explored the astral plane. We expanded out into other realms such as the wild west, Capone's Chicago, and comic book Metropolis but we always returned to our roots in D&D. We were highly caffeinated teenagers.

I appreciate those hours spent with those guys more than anyone can ever understand. Those lessons learned and skills developed help me more in Hollywood than any film class I have ever taken. From character development through complex plotting, those adventures helped me become a better storyteller.

To anyone who's never picked up a twenty-sided die, those of us who played D&D seemed a little crazy. Well, American novelist Charles Bukowski wrote, "Some people never go crazy. What truly horrible lives they must live." I want to thank Gary Gygax and all those who continue to expand the D&D legacy for creating an outlet for my insanity and the insanity of many a kindred spirit around the world.

By the way if anyone knows of a good game, I still have my dice. ∎

THE BLACK BOX

30 Years
of
Adventure

FROM TSR TO

BY PETER ADKISON
WITH ED STARK

DUNGEONS & DRAGONS

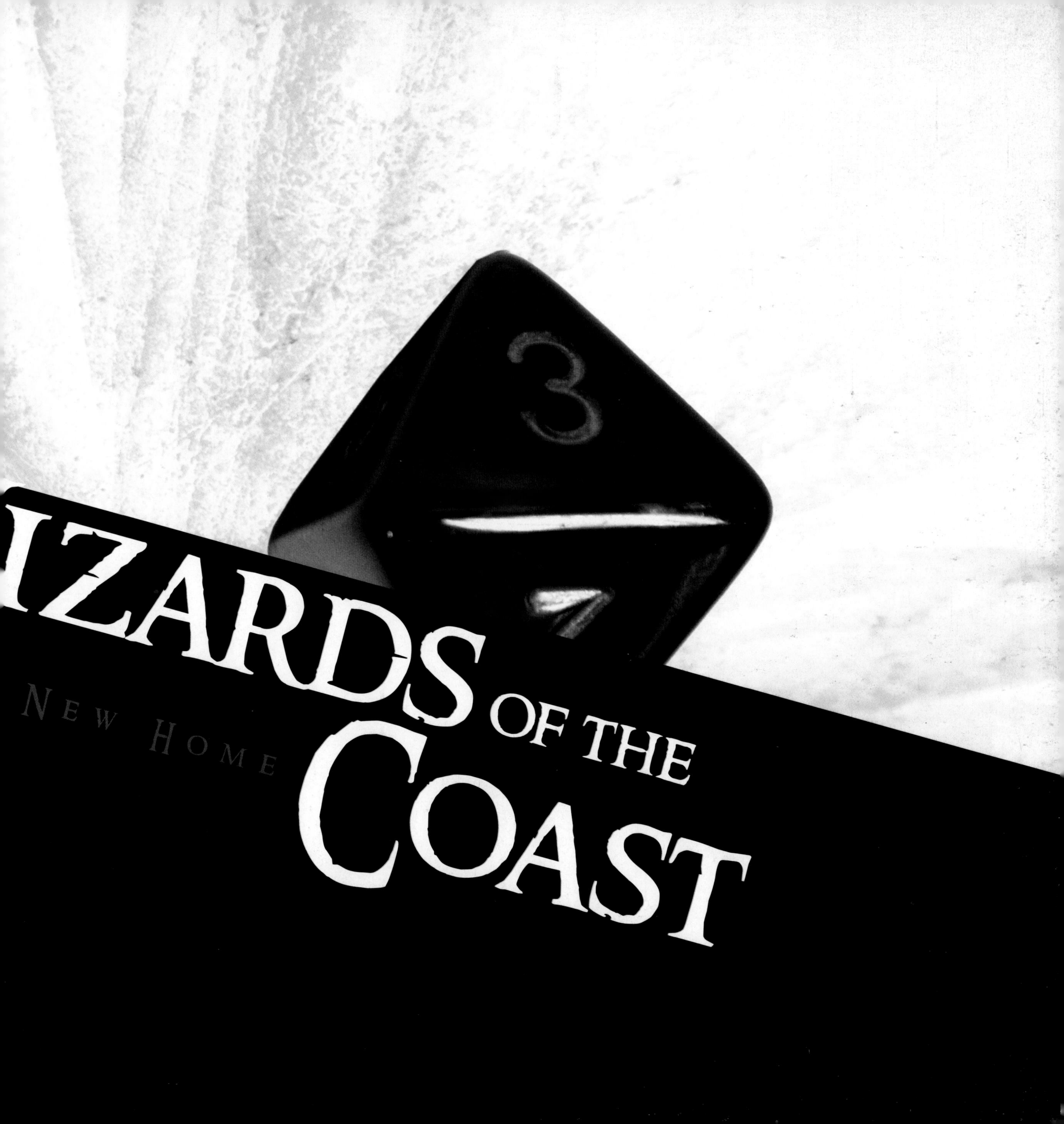
IZARDS OF THE
COAST
NEW HOME
3

HOW I BECAME A D&D FAN

I have loved games for as long as I can remember. My earliest memory of games isn't Chutes & Ladders or some other game of random luck. My earliest gaming memory is that of playing Rook with my mother. I was probably about four or five years old, and instead of sitting at a table we were sitting on my parents' bed. Rook is a card game with a deck that's very similar to a Poker deck, except that instead of face cards (jack, queen, and king) it simply carries the numbering sequence up from 10 (11 through 14), with an extra card thrown in for some reason that's probably lost to antiquity. My parents were, at the time, strict fundamentalists, and we weren't allowed to own Poker cards because people at the church might think we were gambling. So, we played a game that was essentially a trick-taking game like Hearts, but we played with Rook cards. My earliest memory is playing Rook with Mom, sitting on my parents' bed, laying out my cards behind a pillow because a starting hand of fourteen cards was way too many for a little boy to hold on to. I even remember being nervous that if I wasn't careful, Mom would see a card over the pillow, or from around the edge. Perhaps that's why, years later, I feel so comfortable behind a Dungeon Master's screen.

Eventually I graduated to playing Rook at the table with the adults, especially when visiting my grandparents because then we'd have enough players to play partners. My favorite partner was Grandma; somehow she always seemed to know my next play. In those early years my mom was always a faithful gaming companion. We played many games of Rook, and many other games as well—Aggravation, Battleship, Scrabble, and Monopoly were our favorites. Our family had a television of course, but my parents believed strongly that watching TV together wasn't really "family time," so we played games.

I like to trace my history of my love for games by those moments when I was introduced to a new game that totally awed me, times when someone showed me a new game and the game had such a profound effect on me that it totally revolutionized my way of thinking about games and games that took my understanding of games and what they could be to a whole new level.

The first time this happened to me was in 1972 while I was in fourth grade. My father was a teacher at a local high school, and he brought a few of his students over on a Saturday night and showed us a game called Risk. I immediately fell in love with this game. The game with all the strategic depth of Rook but played on a map! With armies! What is it about being male that makes us fantasize about wars and guns and ships? I really don't know. As I've gotten older I've felt less and less comfortable playing games that are tied too closely to real-world conflict, preferring fantasy, or at least fictional conflict. But at the age of eleven you'd think I'd discovered ice cream!

It wasn't long before I discovered that as amazing as Risk was, there were far better military board games. The very next Christmas I was in the mall with Grandma when she asked me what I wanted for Christmas. I really had no idea there were games like Risk out there. Since

I Blame My Sister
BY ED STARK

I have three sisters, the youngest of whom is ten years older than I. Fortunately, they aren't vain about their ages, so I don't expect repercussions from making this statement. Still, it'd probably be best if I moved on to how this all ties into DUNGEONS & DRAGONS.

My youngest sister, I'm told, really liked me when I was a baby and a toddler. She liked to take care of me and dress me up and do all the sorts of big sister things you'd typically expect from a teenage girl. I say "I'm told" because I don't really remember all that much about those years. Perhaps I just have a bad memory, but knowing Lynn I've probably just blocked out traumatic images that will come back to haunt me later in life, perhaps in deep therapy.

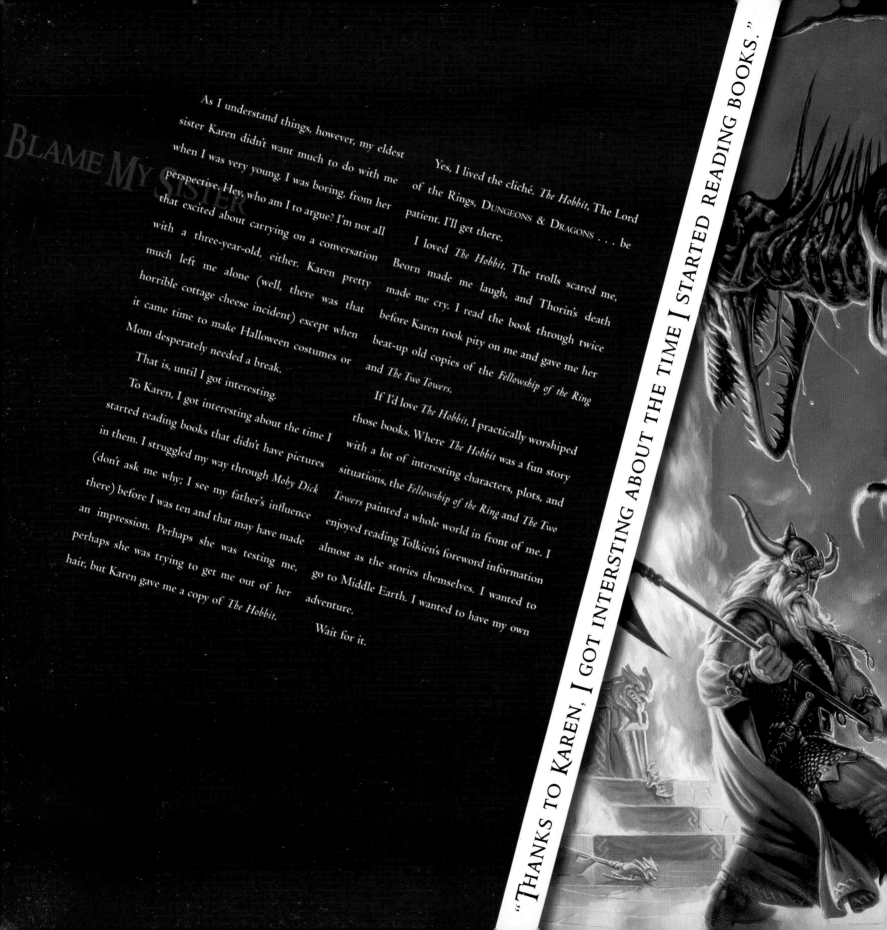

BLAME MY SISTER

As I understand things, however, my eldest sister Karen didn't want much to do with me when I was very young. I was boring, from her perspective. Hey, who am I to argue? I'm not all that excited about carrying on a conversation with a three-year-old, either. Karen pretty much left me alone (well, there was that horrible cottage cheese incident) except when it came time to make Halloween costumes or Mom desperately needed a break.

That is, until I got interesting.

To Karen, I got interesting about the time I started reading books that didn't have pictures in them. I struggled my way through Moby Dick (don't ask me why; I see my father's influence there) before I was ten and that may have made an impression. Perhaps she was testing me, perhaps she was trying to get me out of her hair, but Karen gave me a copy of *The Hobbit*.

Wait for it.

Yes, I lived the cliché. *The Hobbit*, The Lord of the Rings, DUNGEONS & DRAGONS . . . be patient. I'll get there.

I loved *The Hobbit*. The trolls scared me, Beorn made me laugh, and Thorin's death made me cry. I read the book through twice before Karen took pity on me and gave me her beat-up old copies of the *Fellowship of the Ring* and *The Two Towers*.

If I'd love *The Hobbit*, I practically worshiped those books. Where *The Hobbit* was a fun story with a lot of interesting characters, plots, and situations, the *Fellowship of the Ring* and *The Two Towers* painted a whole world in front of me. I enjoyed reading Tolkien's foreword information almost as the stories themselves. I wanted to go to Middle Earth. I wanted to have my own adventure.

Dad and I were also into model railroading at the time we went to the local hobby store and I pointed out some train things. But while perusing I found the Avalon Hill section of the store. Based purely on the cover art I requested U-Boat, Gettysburg (the old square-grid version), and Bismark. Come Christmas I knew I would be getting one of them, and the curiosity about which one was killing me.

Gotta love Grandma—she got me all three.

Fortunately my father loved these games as well, and we both launched into a serious wargaming phase that would carry on quite intensely for about four years, until 1976 when he moved to Korea on a one-year "hardship tour" (meaning, no family allowed) and Mom and I moved to Idaho to live with my grandparents. For the next two years I kept playing wargames just as intensely, but with no opponent to play against, I played them solitaire. I'd set up several games and rotate between them, with the notion that by the time I got back to a given game I'd "forget" what my opponent (me, an hour or day earlier) had been strategizing.

By 1978 DUNGEONS & DRAGONS could hardly be called new still, as the astute reader of this book can attest. Sure, I'd heard of it, but nothing I'd heard about D&D sounded interesting. Before I got hooked on D&D I had to get hooked on fantasy. That happened in the fall of 1978 when I went to stay a weekend with my older brother, Lonnie. Lonnie was never a gamer (I love him anyway), but he liked to read. When I arrived—soon looking

bored I'm sure—Lonnie suggested I might like this book called *The Hobbit*. I loved it immediately. Three days later, pausing only for naps and nourishment, I'd finished it and all three books in The Lord of the Rings.

For Christmas that year I went with Mother (my parents were divorced by now—the Korea "hardship tour" lived up to its name) to visit relatives in Portland, Oregon. I had just gotten my driver's license, and Mom—knowing how bored I'd be in a house with only adults—let me use the car and gave me a little spending money. I learned to drive on the freeways and streets of Portland, searching for game stores. Eventually I found one. I was just about to purchase another SPI "monster game" (wargames with oversized maps)—I was actually in the checkout line—when I saw the DUNGEONS & DRAGONS blue box set.

On total impulse, I purchased the DUNGEONS & DRAGONS game instead.

(Buying wargames based on cover art? Purchasing D&D in the checkout line on impulse? I'm a real life case study for marketing!)

For the second time in my life I encountered a game that shook my whole awareness of what a game could be.

I mentioned earlier that there have been three times in my life when this has happened, when I was introduced to a game so different from anything I'd experienced that I emerged from the encounter with a sense of awe, a sense of wonderment and

"…MY CHARACTER IS NOT CONSTRAINED BY ANYTHING

I BLAME MY SISTER

You may have noticed I make no mention of The *Return of the King*. That's because Karen had lost her copy of the last book in the series. I didn't know that until I was almost through with *The Two Towers*. I mean, I suppose I knew there was a third book, but, hey, I was ten. I trusted my sister. She wouldn't do that to me. Would she?

Yep.

Nowadays, we've got Barnes & Noble, Borders, amazon.com, and a whole mess of other ways to get books in a hurry. Well, I grew up in a small northeastern Pennsylvania town called Montrose. We did have a local library but their fantasy section at the time was, shall we say, non-existent. We also had a bookstore, though . . . it was about as big as my bedroom. Did they have a copy of *The Return of the King*? Not a chance.

"We'll be happy to order it for you."

"When will it come in?"

"About a month."

Erg.

I was frantic. I reread *The Hobbit* again, then the other two books. That took up about four days. I tried to find other things to do. My mind kept going back to those books. I haunted the bookstore, hoping something would come in.

No luck. A month was a month.

I started looking around. I found The Chronicles of Narnia by C.S. Lewis. I found *Dragonriders of Pern*, by Anne McCaffrey. I found a host of other fantasy fiction to read while I waited for *Return of the King* to come in. I kept looking for other things to read, and other things to do.

excitement about entire new dimensions of game possibilities. The third time was in 1991 when Richard Garfield explained to me the concept of a trading card game, a concept that would later be realized through a game called MAGIC: THE GATHERING.

There were (and still are) so many things about D&D that appealed to me. What I like most is the idea that my character is not constrained by anything other than the laws of the universe. If there isn't a rule to cover what I want to do, there is the Dungeon Master to make an arbitrary ruling. I don't have to move pegs around a board along a pre-ordained path, or pick the next step of my adventure based on a menu of options. If my character is in a bar and he wants to jump up on the table and start singing, or pinch the butt of a serving girl strolling by, he's free to do so, and the DM will tell me what happens.

Very quickly I also came to love DUNGEONS & DRAGONS as an outlet for my creativity. At first I took the three levels of the dungeon that came with the basic game and added my own levels, expanding the number of levels to nine. At the bottom of the dungeon was a gate to hell. I thought that was so cool! Though thousands of Dungeons Masters had done the same thing before me, it didn't matter; the game was developing as I wanted it to. Eventually I figured out that D&D could be more than a dungeon, and I started my very own D&D campaign, called Chaldea, which I run to this day. I liked the name

OTHER THAN THE LAWS OF THE UNIVERSE."

HOW I BECAME A D&D FAN

I FOUND REFERENCES TO A GAME CALLED DUNGEONS

And here we go. . . .

I found references to a game called DUNGEONS & DRAGONS. It was in some magazine I picked up. The magazine talked about "roleplaying games" and I had no clue. It talked about "adventure supplements," and I didn't know what that meant. It talked about "creating your own world," and . . .

Hey.

Hey, hey, hey.

That sounded pretty good.

I BLAME MY SISTER

The Return of the King arrived, and I read it. For good measure, I read The Hobbit and the entire Lord of the Rings trilogy over again. In the meantime, however, I began making a Christmas list. On the top of that list was the DUNGEONS & DRAGONS game. My parents, not knowing any better, got it for me. Heck, it was something like twelve dollars. A bargain.

What did my sister get me for Christmas? Karen, I'm sure, bought me a book. I don't remember what it was, but that hardly matters.

Thanks, sis.

& DRAGONS."

Chaldea because of the theories in our own world about it possibly being the home of the Garden of Eden, the origin of human life. Building on this tradition, Babylonian and Sumerian deities have always played a prominent role in my campaign's mythology.

I spent a tremendous amount of time developing Chaldea and running it throughout the 1980s. By the time I graduated from college in 1985 my DMing skills had developed sufficiently that I had a great following of players, was running several different gaming groups, and was approached regularly by players looking to get into my game. When I moved to Seattle after school many of my gaming friends moved to Seattle as well, and the gaming continued on. Many of my friends, including my first wife, also ran D&D campaigns, and these campaigns were all linked together through a portal system so that characters could hop from universe to universe, wreaking havoc along the way. While I'm sure there must be other gaming groups with inter-connected D&D campaigns as intricate as the ones we played, I have yet to run across one.

HOW I BECAME A D&D FAN

MEETING PETER
BY ED STARK

"I DECIDED TO START A

Thinking back on my own entry into the gaming industry I recall my first meeting with Peter Adkison. It was in 1991, I believe, and the place was Las Vegas. Every year the hobby game industry held the Game Manufacturer's Association (GAMA) Trade Show.

I attended GTS as an employee of West End Games and,

more importantly, a "game design flunky" for WEG's sales and marketing manager. I was there to interact with retailer hobbyists and answer game-related questions while our sales manager did "the real work."

A lot of the "real work" involved going off to the bars and lounges in the Tropicana, apparently, so I often found myself stuck alone at the single booth space we had, talking

By the end of the 1980s our campaigns were intricate enough to have stock markets, fluctuating prices for commodities across portal trade between campaigns, numerous campaign-unique elements (races, artifacts, character classes, maps, etc), a regularly published newsletter, and so many house rules that the typeset version we had printed and bound at Kinko's was almost the size of the Players Handbook. By this time all of the "first generation" player characters were demigods (or some powerful equivalent) and many of the second generation characters were well on their way, and I was spending more time playing D&D or working on D&D than I was at my "real job" as a systems engineer at the Boeing Company.

Coming into 1990 I had a career breakdown. I was spending so much time on D&D that I decided, along with many of my friends, to start a gaming company—Wizards of the Coast (WotC).

Many people think of WotC as originally a trading card game company since MAGIC: THE GATHERING was our first big hit. But WotC's first products were roleplaying games: *The Primal Order*, written by yours truly and the Talislanta

GAMING COMPANY—WIZARDS OF THE COAST "

211

roleplaying game and campaign setting, formerly published by Bard Games. Unfortunately neither of these lines did that well commercially, and the company was on the verge of bankruptcy when MAGIC was released.

As everyone in gaming knows, MAGIC became a huge hit and soon it took over all our attention. With MAGIC making around a hundred million dollars in sales and the roleplaying games making less than one million dollars, we decided in 1994 to abandon our efforts in RPGs and focus on MAGIC. While this was certainly a smart decision from a business perspective, it was a very painful one for the company to make as it resulted in numerous layoffs, and we alienated a lot of roleplaying fans who were supporters of our RPG products.

Fortunately, three years later we would re-enter the RPG market—and in a big way!

MEETING PETER

to whomever deigned to come by. West End Games being a small game company, we didn't have a lot of traffic—not like TSR, a company that commanded several booth spaces and drew lots of attention. As a newbie in the game industry and GTS in specific, I felt a little intimidated by the "big boys" of the hobby game industry . . . so I started looking around for others of WEG's stature.

And there was Wizards of the Coast.

Wizards had a cool logo and a friendly looking guy sitting in a booth that had just as much traffic as WEG's . . . that is to say, very little. He had a few products there, and we struck up the typical "industry conversation." Nothing deep, but that was my first meeting with Peter.

Imagine my surprise when six years later I was working for the industry "big boy" and Peter was buying the company.

Boy, was I glad I hadn't made a poor first impression!

HOW I BECAME A D&D FAN

TSB

NEEDED HELP

Nineteen-ninety six was a very strange year for TSR. From a financial point of view 1996 was the best sales year in the history of the company with over $40 million in sales. Unfortunately, in spite of these huge sales, TSR ended up losing money, and losing big.

To understand how this happened it's necessary to understand TSR's relationship with the book trade. TSR sold (and now, as part of WotC, continues to sell) a large percentage of their products through stores like B. Dalton and Waldenbooks. All of these sales were managed by a distributor and publisher, Random House. The contract between TSR and Random House required very careful management or it could backfire.

As provided for in the contract, at the end of each year, Random House could return to TSR any products they didn't sell, and TSR would have to return the money that Random House paid for those products, plus a handling fee.

During 1996 TSR bet big on two product lines: the collectable dice game Dragon Dice and hardcover novels. Dragon Dice started off strong and was critically acclaimed as a great product. It sold well at first in the hobby market so TSR started pumping out the expansions and used special provisions of

"IT WAS A VERY ROUGH, VERY CONFUSING TIME"

AN INSIDE VIEW
BY ED STARK

It was a very rough, very confusing time to be employed by TSR. Only two years before we'd celebrated TSR's anniversary with a huge party out on the side lawn. We'd just been given a new benefit—our first 401(k) plan—and we'd launched another new campaign setting, BIRTHRIGHT: THE LEGACY OF KINGS.

In 1996 I was the lead designer on the BIRTHRIGHT team (the campaign setting's original designers, Colin McComb and Rich Baker having moved on to other things) under Harold Johnson. Through the summer and fall we'd heard the occasional rumor that things weren't going as well as we'd hoped for the year, but nothing much happened until Jim Ward, the Vice President of Creative Services left the company.

Then winter came, along with the layoffs. At the end of 1996, TSR cut back a significant number of its staff, including deep cuts to its Creative Services department. I, in fact, was let go . . . for about an hour and a half. Fortunately for me, Harold Johnson objected so strenuously to my departure (leaving him without a designer in his entire group) the company called me back.

TSR NEEDED HELP

217

their Random House contract to place tons of dice into the book trade. In parallel with this TSR decided to aggressively expand the number of hardcover novels they released that year. Whereas in previous years two or three hardcover novels per year was the norm, in 1996 TSR released twelve, placing these books aggressively into the book trade.

Neither line of products did as well as TSR expected. Dragon Dice peaked quickly and died off in the hobby market and never caught on in the book trade. Twelve harcover novels turned out to be about ten too many. In spite of having its best year ever in sales, TSR ended the year with a small cash reserve.

And then the roof caved in. Random House informed TSR that almost a third of their TSR products for the year had not sold at the store to a customer and that these products were being returned for a fee of several million dollars.

To say TSR was in shock would be no understatement. When I came back after my thankfully brief layoff, I saw folks stumbling around in a daze, wondering what was going to happen next. Our immediate superiors, people like Harold, did their best to try to get us to focus, but when the end of the holiday break rolled around, things were still pretty rough. The much-reduced Creative Services staff did its best—some members of the team worked extraordinarily hard on new projects like ALTERNITY, while others focused on creating solid product for existing lines.

But then January came and went with no product releases. No DRAGON, no DUNGEON, no new game books. A book I'd written and turned in late in 1996 finished editing, went to typesetting, and then sat. As Peter commented, the printers weren't going to print without getting paid.

This lasted for six months. Most of us wondered when we'd show up to locked doors, or maybe when our paychecks would bounce. Neither of those things happened, however, but we weren't getting any information on why.

"TSR ENDED THE YEAR WITH A SMALL CASH RESERVE."

Meanwhile TSR had fallen behind payments to the logistics company that handled all of TSR's pre-press, printing, warehousing, and shipping. When TSR got too far behind in these payments the logistics company refused to do any more work for TSR. Unfortunately, this meant that TSR could not ship products because their inventory was housed in the logistics company's warehouse, nor would the company print products that had run out of stock. Since the logistics company had all the production plates for key products like the core D&D books, TSR couldn't secure short term financing and print somewhere else.

TSR was broke, in debt, and had no way to generate revenue, with their exclusive printer and warehouse refusing to print or ship products and their largest distributor refusing to sell them.

Lorraine Williams immediately started looking for someone to purchase her company and assume these debts, a process that typically takes many months to complete. Meanwhile what little income TSR was able to generate from existing inventory through sales in the hobby games trade went to keeping the lights on and paying employees. These sales were not sufficient to even keep up with the interest on their debts to their distributor and printer. It was clear that if TSR didn't find a buyer by springtime it'd be out of business.

Problems at TSR were further exacerbated by a funk that the entire RPG industry was going through during the early nineties. Roleplaying games simply were not selling like they used to. Throughout the eighties TSR had been top dog, but in the early nineties both Games Workshop and Wizards of the Coast passed them in terms of sales volume, leaving them in third place. As a result, TSR was sliding into a lower level of relevance in the gaming industry—but was not declining gracefully. Not only did TSR come on some hard times due various problems within the company, the industry itself was changing, and TSR's plans to keep up with these changes, through admirable efforts like the collectable card game SPELLFIRE and DRAGON DICE, just didn't quite do it.

Then the rumors began again. This time, we were hearing people talk about a possible sale. No one in senior management would say anything, but that only fed the rumors. One of my co-workers asked me if I thought TSR would be sold. I replied cynically, "No. Why buy TSR? Wait until we go bankrupt, then buy DUNGEONS & DRAGONS." That tells you how low we were all feeling.

Fortunately, Peter wasn't nearly as cynical as I was, and he went on to purchase not only D&D but TSR. Many of my fellow employees followed him out to Seattle and Wizards of the Coast and even some of the folks who'd lost their jobs the year before came back. We arrived on the West Coast still stunned . . . but that feeling soon gave way to hope.

DUNGEONS & DRAGONS would live on, and we'd still be a part of it.

AN INSIDE VIEW

TSR NEEDED HELP

ACQUISITION OF
TSR

Anyone who's followed the history of D&D even slightly knows how this chapter of the story ends—Wizards of the Coast buys TSR. But very few people know the details of how this happened. In fact, if it weren't for this book, the various parts of the story might never have been brought together.

The story of the actual acquisition itself, however, doesn't start off as a story about Wizards of the Coast and TSR. Rather, it begins with Five Rings Publishing, the company that originally published the Legend of the Five Rings trading card game, and TSR. One of the central characters in that story is Ryan Dancey, who will at this point tell the story in his own words, a story he calls "The Million Dollar Fax."

THE MILLION DOLLAR FAX
BY RYAN DANCEY

It all started in the winter of 1996.

My trading card game company, Five Rings Publishing, was finishing its first year of business. We had some ups and some downs like any startup company but on the whole the year had been fairly good from the standpoint of growing the business. Unfortunately, a combination of investment in new products requiring a lot of up front capital and a lot of continued softness in the core hobby market had made it necessary to either raise additional capital or make some pretty drastic operational cuts to staff and salaries in 1997. A cash crunch was looming, and hard choices would need to be made in a fairly short period of time.

My formal role as Vice President of Product Development for Five Rings Publishing was to keep the pipeline filled with new releases. My informal role was to represent the interests of the majority shareholders on a day-to-day basis.

As the year of 1996 came to an end, we started to hear that TSR had run

into financial problems. I had been working with TSR since 1993 when I co-founded a mail-order hobby gaming company called RPG International and begun placing ads with TSR's DRAGON and DUNGEON magazines. Prior to that, my relationship with the company was as a consumer. I had been a player of TSR's roleplaying game DUNGEONS & DRAGONS since the sixth grade. While TSR made public denials that there was a problem, my industry sources were telling me that something was very wrong with the company. Ship dates were being missed, something TSR had never done in my experience with them, and resumés were circulating from some very big names who in other circumstances would never have considered leaving the company.

The CEO of Five Rings Publishing, Bob Abramowitz, was at a convention of booksellers late in the year meeting with distributors and trying to explore the opportunities to grow the business when he had a chance encounter with the CEO of TSR, Lorraine Williams. Bob had worked for TSR in the 1980s in sales, but had been working in the toy industry for nearly ten years. He parlayed his familiarity with TSR into a meeting with Lorraine to talk about the business, and behind closed doors she indicated that TSR was in dire straits and would be receptive to an offer to buy the company.

I got a call around midnight the next day telling me to come to the office with my bags packed for an extended trip. In the morning, I was sworn to secrecy regarding the nature of Bob's conversation with Lorraine, and handed a one-way ticket to Lake Geneva, Wisconsin, the home base of TSR. Bob was worried that if word leaked that TSR was considering a sale that other bidders would come out of the woodwork and raise the cost of an acquisition beyond a reasonable price. He was also certain that if word leaked and it came from Five Rings Publishing that the skittish Lorraine would walk from the negotiating table. Bob insisted on such tight secrecy that I could not even tell my wife exactly where I was going, and we jokingly named the location "Destination X".

Later that day I was in a cramped seat in coach, winging my way east to Chicago, and thence to Lake Geneva by rental car. I arrived at "Destination X" around midnight, found my hotel, checked in, and crashed for the night. In the morning, I began one of the most interesting, if stressful jobs I have ever had: The job of buying TSR.

These events took place in late November. Lake Geneva itself was frozen over, and the lake was dotted with the huts of ice fishermen, and covered with a thick fog as I awoke early in the morning to go to TSR. I carefully worked my way through the icy streets and found myself at a low, gray, nondescript building on the edge of town. I was later to learn that the building had originally been a Q-Tip factory, but at the time the only things that really surprised me were the lack of external windows and the fact that the only signage indicating the nature of the business was a small, simply lettered plaque near the mailboxes. Coming to TSR as a longtime fan of their products I expected a little more grandiosity and maybe a dragon or two.

THE MILLION DOLLAR X

I walked in the front door and introduced myself to the receptionist. I had been told to give neither my company name or state my purpose for being at TSR but to simply ask for Lorraine, which I did. This got me a raised eyebrow and a puzzled look not the last such reaction I was to receive in Lake Geneva. She called via the interoffice intercom for Lorraine, who appeared shortly to escort me into the executive suites. Walking through a doorway from the drab off-white reception area, I was ushered into a world of rich wood paneling, skylights, glassed offices, and comfortable furniture. Lorraine escorted me into a large conference room where a sample of all of TSR's products had been arranged as if a presentation was to be given of the company's history.

Lorraine seated me and presented her agenda for the meeting. I would be given a nondisclosure agreement to sign and afterward, she would lead me through the company's financials and explain its current difficulties. My role would be to tour the facility, ask questions about the company and its documentation, then report back to Bob with my recommendation regarding moving forward with a purchase.

Within the day, I had determined that this was a once in a lifetime opportunity. A combination of management style, need for speed, and a lack of liquidity made it possible to do an acquisition in a few months at most, and the company's core brand of DUNGEONS & DRAGONS was strong and could be rehabilitated with a new vision and better marketing. On my way home I drafted an extensive memo to Bob outlining the crisis TSR faced and what I would do to fix it.

Bob, when motivated by the prospect of an exciting deal, is a whirlwind of action. In less than a week after my return, we had assembled a due diligence team consisting of himself, myself, a forensic accountant and a lawyer, and the four of us had returned to Lake Geneva, which was, if possible, even colder than when I had left it last.

After completing our due diligence, Bob worked his magic. He locked himself in a small conference room with Lorraine for about an hour, and when he emerged, he had a letter signed by both CEOs that gave Five Rings Publishing an option to buy TSR for a fixed price. Smiling triumphantly, he announced that it was time to go home to arrange the necessary financing.

At the time, Five Rings Publishing was about one-tenth the size of TSR. Under ordinary circumstances it would have been impossible to pull such a deal together. However, Seattle and the Northwest region was in the early stages of the dot-com bubble in 1996, and capital was available to fund all sorts of deals that would ordinarily be off the table. Returning home after winning the right to buy TSR, Bob made a fateful phone call that changed the deal, and the gaming industry, forever.

We had cordial relations with our largest competitor, Wizards of the Coast. In fact, earlier in the year, discussions between the two companies regarding an acquisition of Five Rings Publishing had nearly succeeded and had been called off at the last moment by Wizards of the Coast's board. Bob and Peter Adkison, CEO of Wizards, had a working relationship and had maintained contact

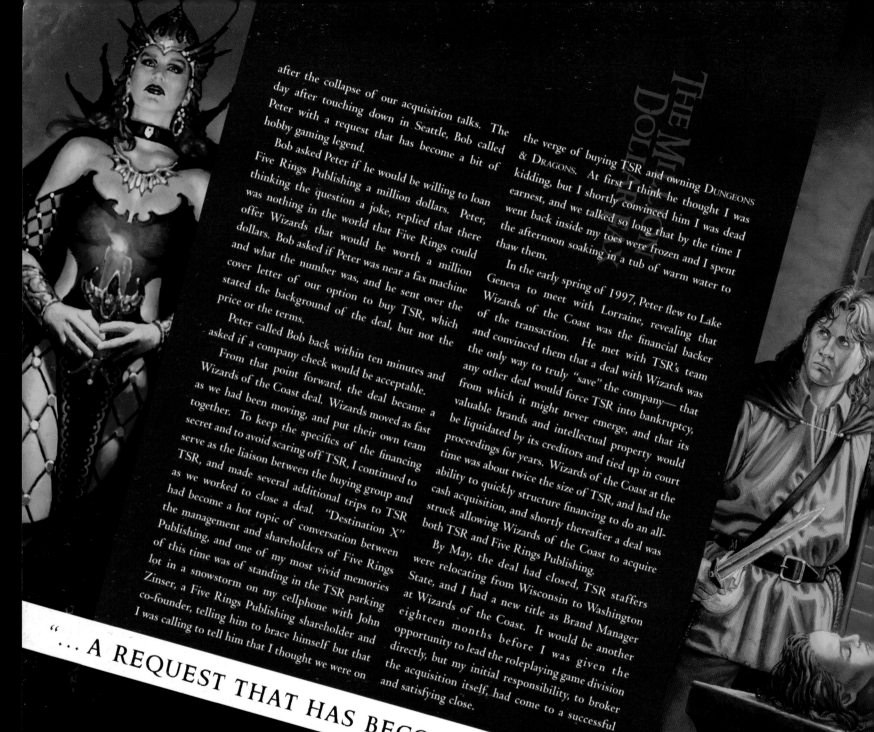

after the collapse of our acquisition talks. The day after touching down in Seattle, Bob called Peter with a request that has become a bit of hobby gaming legend.

Bob asked Peter if he would be willing to loan Five Rings Publishing a million dollars. Peter, thinking the question a joke, replied that there was nothing in the world that Five Rings could offer Wizards that would be worth a million dollars. Bob asked if Peter was near a fax machine and what the number was, and he sent over the cover letter of our option to buy TSR, which stated the background of the deal, but not the price or the terms.

Peter called Bob back within ten minutes and asked if a company check would be acceptable. From that point forward, the deal became a Wizards of the Coast deal. Wizards moved as fast as we had been moving, and put their own team together. To keep the specifics of the financing secret and to avoid scaring off TSR, I continued to serve as the liaison between the buying group and TSR, and made several additional trips to TSR as we worked to close a deal. "Destination X" had become a hot topic of conversation between the management and shareholders of Five Rings Publishing, and one of my most vivid memories of this time was of standing in the TSR parking lot in a snowstorm on my cellphone with John Zinser, a Five Rings Publishing shareholder and co-founder, telling him to brace himself but that I was calling to tell him that I thought we were on

the verge of buying TSR and owning DUNGEONS & DRAGONS. At first I think he thought I was kidding, but I shortly convinced him I was dead earnest, and we talked so long that by the time I went back inside my toes were frozen and I spent the afternoon soaking in a tub of warm water to thaw them.

In the early spring of 1997, Peter flew to Lake Geneva to meet with Lorraine, revealing that Wizards of the Coast was the financial backer of the transaction. He met with TSR's team and convinced them that a deal with Wizards was the only way to truly "save" the company— that any other deal would force TSR into bankruptcy, from which it might never emerge, and that its valuable brands and intellectual property would be liquidated by its creditors and tied up in court proceedings for years. Wizards of the Coast at the time was about twice the size of TSR, and had the ability to quickly structure financing to do an all-cash acquisition, and shortly thereafter a deal was struck allowing Wizards of the Coast to acquire both TSR and Five Rings Publishing.

By May, the deal had closed, TSR staffers were relocating from Wisconsin to Washington State, and I had a new title as Brand Manager at Wizards of the Coast. It would be another eighteen months before I was given the opportunity to lead the roleplaying game division directly, but my initial responsibility, to broker the acquisition itself, had come to a successful and satisfying close.

"... A REQUEST THAT HAS BECOME A BIT OF HOBBY GAMING LEGEND

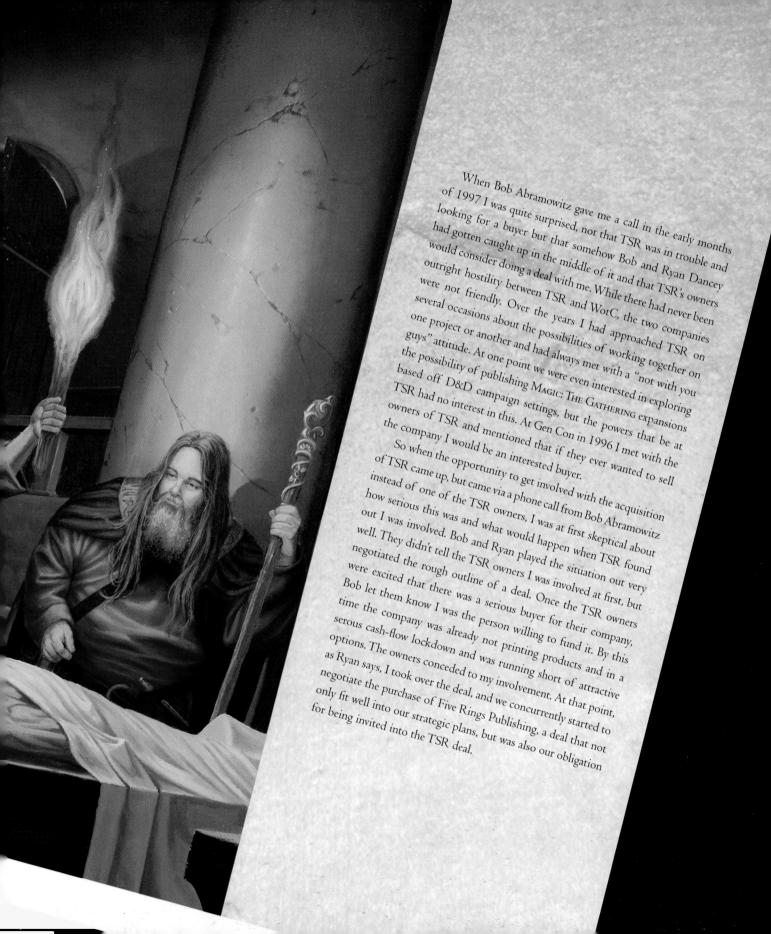

When Bob Abramowitz gave me a call in the early months of 1997 I was quite surprised, not that TSR was in trouble and looking for a buyer but that somehow Bob and Ryan Dancey had gotten caught up in the middle of it and that TSR's owners would consider doing a deal with me. While there had never been outright hostility between TSR and WotC, the two companies were not friendly. Over the years I had approached TSR on several occasions about the possibilities of working together on one project or another and had always met with a "not with you guys" attitude. At one point we were even interested in exploring the possibility of publishing MAGIC: THE GATHERING expansions based off D&D campaign settings, but the powers that be at TSR had no interest in this. At Gen Con in 1996 I met with the owners of TSR and mentioned that if they ever wanted to sell the company I would be an interested buyer.

So when the opportunity to get involved with the acquisition of TSR came up, but came via a phone call from Bob Abramowitz instead of one of the TSR owners, I was at first skeptical about how serious this was and what would happen when TSR found out I was involved. Bob and Ryan played the situation out very well. They didn't tell the TSR owners I was involved at first, but negotiated the rough outline of a deal. Once the TSR owners were excited that there was a serious buyer for their company, Bob let them know I was the person willing to fund it. By this time the company was already not printing products and in a serous cash-flow lockdown and was running short of attractive options. The owners conceded to my involvement. At that point, as Ryan says, I took over the deal, and we concurrently started to negotiate the purchase of Five Rings Publishing, a deal that not only fit well into our strategic plans, but was also our obligation for being invited into the TSR deal.

Not only did TSR need to be bought, Wizards also needed to buy. By 1997 Wizards had been enjoying the success of MAGIC: THE GATHERING for four years. MAGIC is an incredibly profitable game, in spite of the corporate waste that's inevitable in a young company that experiences such rapid growth, Wizards was starting to generate a lot of cash. We had several million dollars in the bank above and beyond what our operational budgets required, and the future was looking bright. But when a corporation has a lot of money sitting around that introduces some new challenges that we didn't have when we didn't have excess funds—challenges that are a lot more fun to work on, but challenges nonetheless.

With MAGIC: THE GATHERING as our "only" hit product, we felt we could dramatically increase the company's value for our shareholders if we had a second hit product in our portfolio. It seems silly now, with the continued success of MAGIC after all these years, and the subsequent success of POKEMON, but at the time one of the pressures that wore heavily on my shoulders was the idea that Wizards of the Coast was a one-hit wonder. We had tried breaking

out of that mold through a long series of new product introductions beyond the extensions to the Magic line: ROBO RALLY, NETRUNNER, JYHAD/VAMPIRE: THE ETERNAL STRUGGLE, EVERWAY, and so on. Some of these products would go on to become classics in the gaming industry, but none of them provided a stable, significant revenue opportunity for the company. We told ourselves that eventually one of these products would take off and become a big hit, that we just needed more times at bat to hit a home run, but doubts were starting to creep in as to whether this would ever happen. A growing contingent of the board and management team started to say things like, "What would happen if we cancelled everything we're working on except for MAGIC? What would that do to our profitability?"

I felt that Wizards was at a crossroads, very close to a junction where perhaps we should rename ourselves "The MAGIC Company" or some such thing. Don't get me wrong—I love MAGIC—but I had always dreamed of having a portfolio of games, not just one. No one loves MAGIC more than Richard Garfield, and he was committed

AT THE RIGHT TIME."

to the same vision. As a game designer, he wanted a vehicle that would publish his new games. Without that opportunity the best designers would leave Wizards and we'd lose our creative edge. So we remained committed to the strategy of continuously introducing new products, chasing the next hit, but I wanted to cover my bets. I wanted to buy a hit.

But I wasn't having much luck. I'd made the overture to TSR's owners in mid-1996 and their reception left me thinking that was a dead end. By the time I got the call from Bob Abramowitz, I was just starting to think about distribution companies, retail chains, and electronic games publishers. Thankfully, the call from Bob came when it did.

Financially and strategically the TSR deal came just at the right time. But Wizards of the Coast was not in a great position to purchase a big company. Our operational systems were not fully developed, and our management team had some significant gaps in it. I was working very hard running Wizards of the Coast as a full time job and I knew that the job of acquiring TSR, relocating it to Seattle, integrating it into Wizards of the Coast, and returning it to profitability would collectively be a full time job all on its own. I needed help at a level that no one on my management team at the time was in a position to provide.

Enter Vince Caluori. Before starting Wizards of the Coast I had been an employee of The Boeing Company. I worked in the aerospace division on a series of programs that were tasked with studying the future launch vehicle needs of the U.S. and various scenarios for fulfilling those needs. The group I was in changed names and priorities a few times while I was there but it each time it was around the same theme and the group was consistently led by a senior Boeing executive, Vince Caluori. I didn't know Vince really well as he was about four levels of management above me, but I knew what it was like to work in an organization run by him. All his subordinates loved him, we all knew what our priorities were, we always knew that we could get a straight answer from him, and one of his priorities that he'd tell us about was "protecting us from corporate bullshit." I considered Vince the "model manager" and when I left Boeing to start my company we stayed in touch and I regularly asked him for advice.

I found Vince's advice so incredibly helpful that I eventually asked Vince to sit on Wizards' board of directors, an offer he accepted.

By 1997 Vince had retired from Boeing and on a couple of occasions I had suggested to Vince that he come work for me at Wizards. He declined these early offers in favor of skiing around the world. He liked to say, "I'm really good at retirement." But when the opportunity came up to acquire TSR I sent to him again and laid it on the line. "I can't do this without you." I told him. "I'm working eighty, ninety hours a week managing Wizards of the Coast, and it's going to take another eighty or ninety hours a week to run TSR, at least for six to twelve months during the transition." Anytime before then when I'd go to Vince and say "I can't do this," he'd say, "Sure you can," give me a pep talk and some good advice, and I'd go out and get the job done. But this time I was right: it really was too big a job for me to do on my own.

Vince was hooked. He ended up staying at Wizards even longer than I did. Convincing Vince to work fulltime at WotC was probably the most important thing I did in terms of getting support for the TSR acquisition from the Wizards Board of Directors.

Eventually all the major deal points were agreed upon by both parties. This was a big deal, with a price tag in excess of $30 million when combining the money that went to the owners with the amount of debt we assumed by making the purchase.

Once our press release went out and we didn't have to keep the deal a secret any longer things really started to pick up. I started going out to Lake Geneva, Wisconsin, the home of TSR on almost a weekly basis. I conducted extensive reviews of the entire business and brought out several people from Wizards to

help me with this analysis. We still had to be careful because we couldn't "interfere" with how the company was being managed. But of course the word was out among the employees that I would probably be their new boss so they were naturally curious how I would weigh in on various issues. I tried to be as neutral as possible "officially" while still giving an occasional "wink, wink" on things that I felt were very important. One thing I'm very thankful for now is that I insisted we not miss a Gen Con. Limited preparation had been done to get ready for this enormous event (there wasn't even a contract signed with the convention center, only three months before the show!) and before the deal was final I told Gary Smith (who was managing our conventions at Wizards) to start working on his plan so that as soon as the deal was done we could "flip the switch" and go into high gear and make Gen Con happen.

Well, I wouldn't be writing this story if the deal hadn't gone through. The timing of the deal had some symbolism to it that was unrelated to TSR. About two years earlier, feeling overwhelmed and unqualified for the job of CEO, I had enlisted in the Executive MBA program at the University of Washington. I finished my MBA the same week as the TSR deal was finally executed. I actually had to miss my last day of MBA residency so that I could be at TSR on the day of the change in ownership.

I'll never forget going in to TSR that first morning. I drove up to the building, saw the TSR sign out front just like I had many times by now, and pulled over to the side of the road to collect my thoughts. When it comes to dealing with management teams and boards of directors and shareholders

the typical dynamic is for people to ask tough questions. That's fine, and it's normal, but psychologically it puts the CEO in the position of fighting hard to get something done. For several months I'd been fighting the good fight, pushing this deal through, winning over the hearts and minds of everyone I could about how wonderful this would be for TSR, for Wizards, for the gaming industry, for various industry celebrities, and so on.

But now that the deal was done, all the fears crept up. "Okay, Peter, we let you have your way, now you gotta deliver!" I suddenly felt the weight of an immense burden of responsibility shift to my shoulders. I'd just paid over $30 million for a company that was bankrupt and I'd inherited more than seventy employees whose livelihoods I was about to seriously disrupt by either terminating them or asking them to relocate to Seattle.

And I had asked Lorraine's assistant to start the first day off with an "all hands" meeting, a meeting with all the employees of the company.

Knowing that everyone was waiting for me I "pulled it together" and somehow got myself psyched to go in and hold the meeting. It wasn't that I was unprepared. Hell, I'd been waiting for this day for months! But when I walked into the room and saw more than seventy anxious faces looking at me expectantly, I almost got physically sick with anxiety. Knowing that throwing up wouldn't make the best first impression or instill the confidence I needed them to have in my leadership, somehow I swallowed the urge and launched into it. The next couple hours are a blur. I don't remember

THE MARRIAGE CEREMONY

anything about the meeting other than teaching the TSR employees how to sing the Wizards of the Coast company song. You have to understand that the Wizards company song (at least while I was there) was a dark humorous song, really designed to make fun of more typical company songs. See the sidebar.

I think from day one the TSR employees knew that things were going to be a lot different.

What happened over the next three to six months is a blur in my head. This time was an emotional roller coaster for everyone involved. I would alternate between the joy of a kid with a new toy and the fear of screwing it up. Employees would alternate between the joy of being back in production with the fears associated with having to relocate to Seattle and integrate into a larger corporation.

Some of the tasks were pleasant, others less so.

Of course a big part of "fixing" TSR was simply to pay off their debts and put money into the system so that they could get products printed and sold to distributors, especially Random House. This got the engine running, but not necessarily efficiently. We had to combine TSR and Wizards into one game-publishing entity with a shared overhead. I had to lay off almost everyone at the company who was in any sort of administrative position. I was also worried that TSR had too many product lines so I also laid off a few people in product development positions as well. The remaining employees were given job offers in the new combined company, but, except in a couple of cases, with the requirement that they move to Seattle. Not everyone was willing to make the move, but most did, and we started the very complicated but exciting project of having over fifty families pick up their bags and cross the Rocky Mountains.

Verse

It was a head

It was a human head

Pappy held it up

This is what he said

Chorus

Take it to your room

Water it every day

Chain it to the wall

So it don't get away

Repeat verse but change "head" in the first line to some other body part and then change the fourth line to whatever you like in order for it to rhyme with the new body part. Then repeat the chorus. Repeat both for as long as you can think of clever rhymes involving body parts, or until those around you demand silence!

THE WIZARDS OF THE COAST COMPANY SONG
BY JESPER MYRFORS

BUILDING TSR TO LAST

With TSR having been off the market for so long the distribution channel was hungry for new products. And with nothing else to do at TSR, the employees had designed lots of new products with the hopes of getting back into the game soon. Once the floodgates were opened the gaming industry responded to TSR's product lines with renewed vigor and a sense of relief that TSR was back on the scene.

We got TSR running by fixing these operational issues, but we needed a well managed organization that could help us build a firm with a long term vision and strategy that would grow into the next century. My memory's a bit fuzzy on the exact sequence of events, but eventually three personalities emerged into leadership positions within the overall TSR franchise: Mary Kirchoff, Bill Slavicsek, and, one of the people who'd made the whole thing possible in the first place, Ryan Dancey.

One of the positions that I needed filled most urgently was the job of managing the book publishing division of TSR. It's easy to think of TSR as primarily a games company with a nice book business on the side. But it quickly became obvious that the novels business at TSR was extremely important. And this was something we at Wizards didn't know much about. I asked around about who had originally been responsible "back in the day" for the success of TSR in the book trade, and the name that kept coming up was Mary Kirchoff. She was easy to find—at the time she was married to a TSR employee, Steve Winter. A series of meetings and interviews were set up, and I quickly made up my mind that I had to have her on board. I even let her stay in Wisconsin for a while. My persistence and charm worked. Mary signed up and is running the DUNGEONS & DRAGONS brand at the time of this writing.

Another area where we felt we needed to find someone very special was in the area of RPG game design and development. This was a topic of a lot of debate. Lots of people had very strong opinions on this topic as Wizards had always been a product-driven

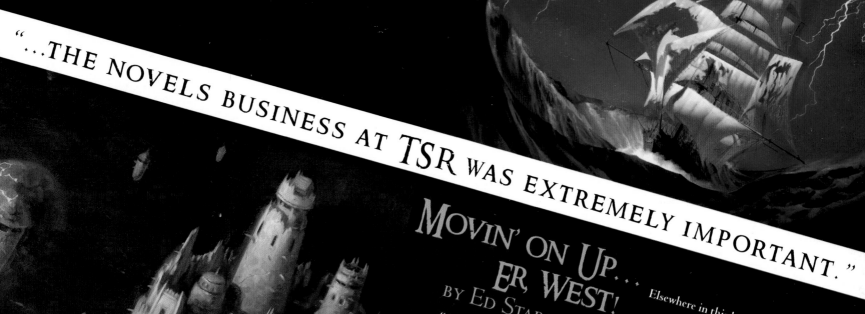

MOVIN' ON UP... ER, WEST!
BY ED STARK

Elsewhere in this book I talk about the effects TSR's layoffs and "down time" had the folks still working at the company prior to the acquisition. Peter's given a business account of what went on during the acquisition itself. Here's how some of these things affected the people involved and, of course, the DUNGEONS & DRAGONS game.

The first step in the relocation involved taking the Creative Directors and other management staff out to Wizards of the Coast to look around Seattle and to meet with some of the people many of us hoped to be working with soon. Harold Johnson, Thomas Reid, Bill Slavicsek, and many others flew to the West Coast while the rest of us waited in Wisconsin, wondering how things would continue to shake out.

Peter and company kept us entertained in the meantime. We had all hands' meetings, and we actually talked about getting product out the door. Oh, and Gen Con was only a few weeks away. Roughly 25,000 folks would be showing up to play D&D, and we had to run the show.

company where we essentially would look to R&D for good games and then rally behind the effort of getting those games to market, nicely produced, with good sales and marketing to back it up. R&D was expected to really provide a leadership role in this area. Instead of making this decision in isolation I decided to form a committee to interview various candidates and debate the merits of each. One of the people who was on the committee (not a candidate) was Bill Slavicsek. About halfway through the process I had a conversation with Skaff Elias, also on the committee and one of the power-thinkers of Wizards R&D. We said to each other, "Hey, we should hire Bill for this job." Like Mary, he's still doing that job as of the time of this writing.

With both Slavicsek and Kirchoff I hired people who'd had experience with TSR. I wanted to send the message that I valued the experience that TSR people had. But I decided that for the next key position of responsibility within TSR I would appoint someone who did not have a background with TSR, someone who would bring

in fresh, perhaps even radical, ideas. This person would have over all responsibility for building the budget, marketing strategy, and product strategy for the business. Basically, the job I'd been doing. To me the choice was obvious: Ryan Dancey. I think Ryan is one of the most innovative thinkers about the business aspects of our industry.

Ryan, with significant help from Mary and Bill and the rest of the TSR staff, went on to tackle some very important issues relating to the TSR business. Probably one of the most difficult was culling the product line. Before the acquisition TSR had been publishing so many game lines that it was cannibalizing itself. All the various campaign settings were dividing up the TSR market into different segments. With my complete blessing, Ryan made the difficult decision to cut back the number of campaign settings TSR would support, and, accordingly, dramatically reduce the number of new products that TSR published. As Ryan predicted, the business became more profitable due to these changes.

"…THE BUSINESS BECAME MORE PROFITABLE DUE TO THESE CHANGES."

So, naturally, we spent a lot of time playing CORPORATE SHUFFLE, a card game based on the GREAT DALMUTI and published by Wizards of the Coast with a DILBERT license. Somehow a game of corporate backstabbing and one-upsmanship seemed cathartic at the time.

The Creative Directors returned, and I still remember everyone going in shifts to watch a video Thomas Reid made of the trip. I can still remember the first frame, shot from inside a rental car through a—naturally—rain-streaked window as the car drove into Seattle.

We saw pictures of Wizards' bright-white building, its large windows, and its centrally located courtyard fountain. Did I mention TSR was located in a former Q-tip factory, a brick building with few windows? No, it wasn't a big six-sided die, no matter what Phil Foglio might say. Now you know.

There was still some amount of trepidation. We all knew everyone wouldn't be coming out to Wizards. Two of the best and most professional editors I'd ever worked with—Carrie Bebris and Anne Brown, both members of the BIRTHRIGHT/D&D Worlds group—would not be moving to Seattle. They had families in the Midwest and other commitments.

My wife and I, however, were starting to think how we'd find somewhere to live on the West Coast. I'd received a nice job offer and done some looking around on the internet, searching for apartments, but I'd moved into living spaces sight-unseen before, and that was no joy.

Then Wizards bowled all of us over.

Soon after acquiring TSR I sat down and made a list of "the most famous celebrities ever associated with D&D." The top five people on my list, in no particular order, were the following people: Gary Gygax, Dave Arneson, Margaret Weis, Tracy Hickman, and R.A. Salvatore, two game designers, and three authors. Now, we could have a fun debate about this list. Perhaps some of the famous artists like Jeff Easly, Larry Elmore, or Keith Parkinson should be on this list. Or what about Zeb Cook? Or James Ward? Or Jeff Grubb or Ed Greenwood? Okay, I get the point. There are lots of good suggestions for such a list.

No one on that list was working with TSR at the time Wizards acquired the company. The two game designers who had designed the company's most important game were prohibited from working for TSR due to outstanding legal constraints, and the three authors who'd written numerous *New York Times* bestsellers were writing for other publishers. One of my priorities after acquiring TSR was to reinvolve these people in D&D.

Arneson was easy. He was supposed to get a royalty off any product TSR published in the DUNGEONS & DRAGONS line. Previous owners "got around" this royalty by publishing everything as "ADVANCED DUNGEONS & DRAGONS." To me this always seemed silly. I talked with Dave, and we agreed that he would release all claims to DUNGEONS & DRAGONS if I simply gave him a big check. I did, and later, when we launched 3rd edition, we had the freedom to drop the "Advanced" from the game's title, and we chose to do exactly that.

The situation with Gary Gygax was a bit more complex. Again, we wrote a couple of big checks to settle some legal disputes. Wizards owned all rights to D&D free and clear, and Gary was free to work in the gaming industry however he liked.

Wizards of the Coast gave everyone interested in moving out to the West Coast a plane ticket—and one for their spouse or significant other as well—and paid for us to fly out, stay in a hotel, and spend a few days searching the area for someplace to live. They didn't ask for a commitment; if someone didn't like Seattle after going and looking, she or he didn't have to move.

I went with the second wave of TSR staffers to look around. My wife and I toured the Wizards facility, met lots of fine people (Jonathan Tweet was assigned to be my "host" while we were there—

that was a nice touch), and found an apartment nearby we could afford. I still remember finding out there was a movie theater within walking distance of the building. (That may not seem like a big deal, but for most of the time we lived in Wisconsin the nearest decent cinema was about forty-five minutes away.)

Wizards then picked up the tab for movers to bring all of our stuff out to Washington State. If the moving company thought they'd hit on a soft touch, though, they were mistaken. We had a certain amount of space we could occupy in a truck and most TSR staffers

filled their boxes with books—heavy books. I remember more than one muttered complaint from the movers, but they took it in good stead.

The roughest part, however, was saying good-bye. I'd grown up on the East Coast, so I didn't have family out in Wisconsin . . . at least, not blood relatives. I was leaving a lot of friends behind, though. On my office wall at Wizards I still keep a picture we took during that last week with nearly all the remaining TSR staffers standing by the old sign by the road. Some of them moved out with me, but more stayed behind or have since gone on to other things. TSR had its problems, but it was the home of D&D and, for many years, the home of the folks who made the game what it was. That made it special.

I suppose it helped, though, that our "final good-bye" to the Midwest would be at Gen Con 1997. The sale was announced, Wizards and TSR were one, and we still had a convention to put on. It was the first time Wizards and TSR staff worked together at the show and it was amazing. Peter threw a huge block party on Saturday night, and everyone spent most of the show saying "hello" to new friends. Everyone wondered what would come next for TSR and, especially, D&D (the good money was on a MAGIC/DUNGEONS & DRAGONS crossover product—boy, I wish I'd taken some of that action!).

We said good-bye the very first day after Gen Con and drove out to Seattle. And that was that.

MOVIN ON UP
ER VIII

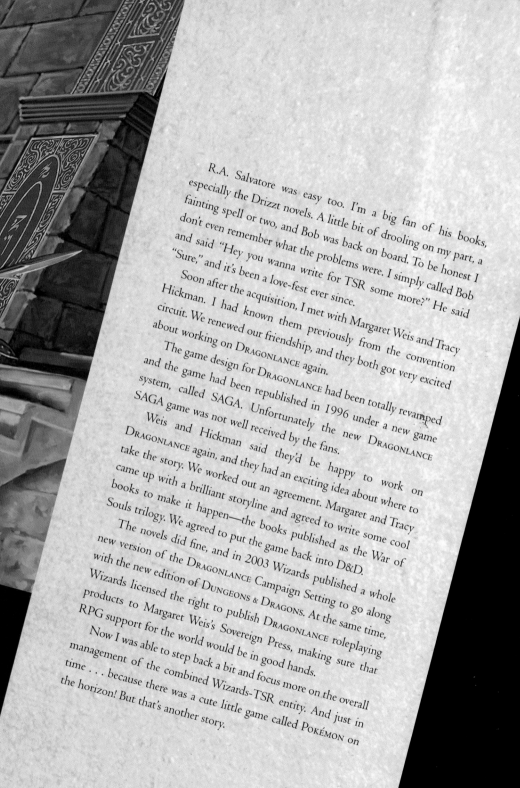

R.A. Salvatore was easy too. I'm a big fan of his books, especially the Drizzt novels. A little bit of drooling on my part, a fainting spell or two, and Bob was back on board. To be honest I don't even remember what the problems were. I simply called Bob and said "Hey you wanna write for TSR some more?" He said "Sure," and it's been a love-fest ever since.

Soon after the acquisition, I met with Margaret Weis and Tracy Hickman. I had known them previously from the convention circuit. We renewed our friendship, and they both got very excited about working on DRAGONLANCE again.

The game design for DRAGONLANCE had been totally revamped and the game had been republished in 1996 under a new game system, called SAGA. Unfortunately the new DRAGONLANCE SAGA game was not well received by the fans.

Weis and Hickman said they'd be happy to work on DRAGONLANCE again, and they had an exciting idea about where to take the story. We worked out an agreement. Margaret and Tracy came up with a brilliant storyline and agreed to write some cool books to make it happen—the books published as the War of Souls trilogy. We agreed to put the game back into D&D.

The novels did fine, and in 2003 Wizards published a whole new version of the DRAGONLANCE Campaign Setting to go along with the new edition of DUNGEONS & DRAGONS. At the same time, Wizards licensed the right to publish DRAGONLANCE roleplaying products to Margaret Weis's Sovereign Press, making sure that RPG support for the world would be in good hands.

Now I was able to step back a bit and focus more on the overall management of the combined Wizards-TSR entity. And just in time . . . because there was a cute little game called POKÉMON on the horizon! But that's another story.

THIRD EDITION

BY PETER ADKISON

After I got Ryan's "Million Dollar Fax" and the idea of acquiring TSR began to swim around in my mind it took me maybe thirty seconds to decide, "We've got to do a third edition of DUNGEONS & DRAGONS."

Okay, maybe a bit more thought went into it than that, but it didn't take long to conclude that it would be a great idea. Then I began to worry about what the designers at TSR would think. Fortunately, when I met them during the acquisition process I found out that that they already had plans in the works for doing exactly this.

Months later, sometime during the summer of 1997, after the acquisition was complete, the TSR folks had relocated to Seattle, and the production lines were back up and running, we revisited the topic and confirmed that this was a great idea. It had been over ten years since the release of 2nd edition so no one could accuse us of coming out

with new editions too quickly. Obviously we had a strong economic incentive for publishing a new edition; sales for any product line tend to spike when a new edition comes out, assuming the new edition is an improvement over the first. And given the change of ownership we thought this would be an excellent opportunity for WotC to "put its stamp on D&D."

Once the decision was made to publish a third edition of D&D the question quickly became, "What should 3rd edition D&D be like?" I've always been a fan of company-wide discussions, so we set up a discussion "room" within the our online email and discussion board system. The initial post invited everyone in the company to post their ideas of what they thought 3rd edition should be like. Employees were encouraged to discuss anything from game design issues to marketing strategies to artistic "look and feel."

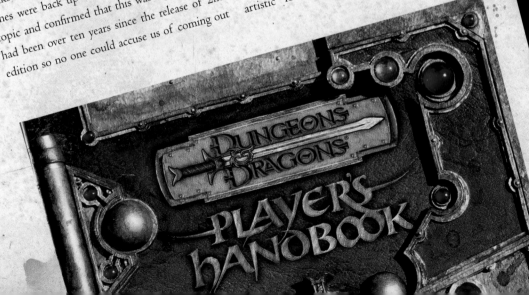

What to Name It?

Back in 1978 the decision had been made to undergo a serious revision to the rules of Dungeons & Dragons to produce the game Advanced Dungeons & Dragons (AD&D). Despite some complicated legal posturing that was involved in the name change, I felt it was best to think of AD&D as an upgrade to the original D&D and that it was silly to support two separately game lines. Shortly after acquiring TSR I settled an outstanding lawsuit with Dave Arneson so that the rights to the name Dungeons & Dragons were free and clear. Once that was taken care of it seemed very natural to drop the "Advanced" adjective from the title and simply call the new game, Dungeons & Dragons, along with an indication that this was a new edition. There was a brief discussion about what edition number the game should be labeled as. Some purists love to point out that if in the new order of things we considered AD&D as a new edition of D&D instead of a new game, then the new version of the game that WotC came out with should really have been called "4th edition." While arithmetically correct, it might have confused many people to progress from a game called 2nd edition to 3rd edition, so we fairly quickly reached consensus that we would simply call the new game Dungeons & Dragons. Ed Stark commented, "It was nice to get back to just calling the game D&D again, with no modifiers."

Sacred Cows
by Ed Stark

I remember the day we went from "we should do a third edition of D&D" to "we're doing 3rd edition." Bill Slavicsek, the head of RPG R&D, made the announcement to the department and told us he'd be choosing design and editorial teams over the next few weeks. Bill gave everyone in the RPG R&D department (somewhere between twenty or thirty people at the time) a few days to do nothing but consider what they did and didn't want to see in a

3rd edition of D&D. One part of this exercise was to identify "sacred cows"—game elements we absolutely positively couldn't change if D&D were to remain D&D.

Everyone took part. Bill received a barrage of emails and memos. Many of the design ideas, I recall, were pretty interesting. A lot of the sacred cows made sense. Here are a few I recall in particular:

- Armor class goes down. "AC 0" and "AC −10" are iconic touchstones. They resonate with our audience.

- Don't change the races! Dwarves, elves, half-elves, gnomes, halflings, and humans are iconic to D&D. Keep them the same and don't add or delete any.

- Ability scores go from 3-18. This is an easily managed, specific range. Our audience understands what an "18" means in character terms.

Any wonder why I remember these "sacred cows"? That's right. They got sent to the butcher pretty quickly. Oh, and one of these was one of mine. I'll let you guess which one.

DESIGN PHILOSOPHY

Deciding on an overall design philosophy for the new edition of D&D was a much more challenging question. For months the debate raged on within the WotC internal online discussion forum, with no clear consensus emerging. Broadly speaking, there were three schools of thought.

Some felt that changes in 3rd edition should be kept fairly modest. This camp had strong justification for its views, pointing out that changes from AD&D to 2nd edition had been fairly slight and that by keeping the changes minor there would be more continuity in the product line. Whenever a company releases a new edition of its game rules there are always some dissenting fans of the old game who don't want to see their game system changed. The more significant the changes, the higher the risk that current fans will reject the new edition of the game and either continue playing the previous version or jump ship to a different game altogether.

Another school of thought was to simplify and streamline D&D. The justification for this line of thinking was that D&D, as a game that had grown out of wargaming, was too rules heavy and played more like a miniatures game than what a roleplaying game "should" play like. Since the 1970s when AD&D was released there had been numerous advances in roleplaying game "technology" with much of those efforts directed toward more of

a free form format. Companies like White Wolf, for example, had been successful by advocating a more strongly based "storytelling" approach to roleplaying game design. A very compelling case was made for dramatically overhauling Dungeons & Dragons, making it a simpler game with a focus on fast, streamlined mechanics, emphasizing roleplaying and story development.

The third school of thought said that complexity was okay as long as it made sense. What we really needed to do was create a system that was more modular and supported more styles of play. Jonathan Tweet once said, "D&D is the game that dares to define everything." From stats on unicorns to listings of hundreds of monsters and spells to mass combat to charts on how to randomly generate dungeons, cities, or nations, one thing that had been consistent throughout the history of D&D was its daring attempt to reduce everything to numbers, charts, and rules. But many of the rules in AD&D and 2nd edition AD&D were inconsistent in application and needlessly limiting. Like the previous camp, this school of thought argued that after twenty-five years D&D was due for a major overhaul but that the changes to the game should make the games rules more consistent, more elegant, and support more possibilities for different styles of play.

While this debate over design philosophy raged on in the discussion forums the designers forged ahead toward the first draft of the new rules. But without a clear consensus on which of these strategies to undertake the results were far from acceptable. While each author's section was

fine on its own, in aggregate the approach was inconsistent. Some sections were very close to 2nd edition, but with some improvements. Other sections were greatly simplified, following more of a storytelling approach. Other sections retained the detail and complexity of previous editions but were more elegant and permissive of a wider range of character concepts.

At this point I became more personally involved in the project and read the 3rd edition draft carefully. I noticed what was also clear to the designers and everyone else in R&D: Someone needed to break the deadlock. Someone in authority had to make the call—which design philosophy would win out? That someone had to be me. Besides, what fan of D&D could resist? Was this not why I got into the gaming industry to begin with? Had I not led Wizards of the Coast successfully for years with a solid track record of good decisions? Nevertheless, I was filled with trepidation. This was serious business. I was assuming a responsibility for something very important to, literally, millions of fans around the world. If I made the wrong decision, a lot of gamers would be very disappointed. My biggest beef with the older rules were the consistent limitations on what characters could become. Why couldn't dwarves be clerics? Why could wizards of some classes only advance to some pre-determined level limit? Why couldn't intelligent monster races like orcs and ogres pick up character classes? In my mind these restrictions had no place in a rules set but should be restrictions established (if at all) at the campaign setting level.

THIRD EDITION

In other cases the rules had restrictions that did a good job of reinforcing play balance but still didn't make sense. A good example of this was the old rule establishing that wizards couldn't wear armor. That's a great rule for play balance: fighters and clerics need some sort of advantage like this over wizards and rogues. But my feathers were always ruffled at the notion of a rule in a roleplaying game that says, "You can't do this." A big part of what's cool about roleplaying games is that you can do anything you think of, as long as it's plausible and obeys the laws of physics in the campaign.

"So, what happens to my wizard PC when I put on a set of armor?" I argued in one meeting. "Do I explode, or what?"

The response was, "No, but you can't cast spells as well because armor limits your movement."

Well, if that's the case, instead of rule that says wizards can't wear armor, why not substitute a rule that explains what happens if a wizard does wear armor?

Yeah, I admit it, I was solidly in the third camp from the very beginning. D&D has always been complicated, and that never stopped it from becoming popular. Complexity wasn't the issue—the problem was that too many rules just didn't make good sense. I believed that what D&D players wanted was a great set of rules. Rules that made sense, while retaining the "feel" of the original works by Gygax and Arneson. With that as an over all philosophy I took the lead in developing a design philosophy for 3rd edition DUNGEONS & DRAGONS.

Goal. 3rd edition should be an elegant, solid game that is well thought out and thoroughly playtested. Our goal as designers is to improve the existing AD&D game better in any way possible while retaining the flavor and feel of the previous editions.

1. In order to retain this flavor, the following list includes the primary, inviolate elements of ADVANCED DUNGEONS & DRAGONS that must be preserved.

Stats. The standard six ability scores, generated (essentially) by rolling 3d6.

Level-based game mechanics. AD&D is arguably the only level-based game that really works.

Classes. The four archetypal character classes: warrior, wizard, rogue and priest must remain in the game as such. To a lesser degree, AD&D would not be AD&D without paladins and rangers, either.

To-hit rolls. Attack rolls made with a d20, desiring high numbers

Spells. Many spells, such as fireball, magic missile, and others, carry a significant amount of AD&D flavor.

Monsters. Orcs, beholders, mind flayers, liches, and other monsters have created a place for themselves in the genre of fantasy (even beyond gaming) as AD&D-ish. We do not want to lose that.

Magical Items. Along with spells and monsters, various items contribute to making AD&D the game it is (gauntlets of ogre power, staff of the magi, rod of lordly might, etc.).

Initiative-driven combat. The feel of AD&D combat should be kept, regardless of changes made.

Alignments and planes. These need to exist in the core game.

Polyhedral dice. Gotta have them funky dice.

Armor Class.

Hit Points.

2. Three overriding concerns drive each decision made by the team as they strive to achieve the above-stated goal.

- Make the game easier to learn initially and understand fully.
- Give the game "legs." Keep people playing the game longer.
- Create a game that will intrigue and interest those who currently play the game as well as those who have stopped.

3. In order to improve the game, the following large (and intentionally vague) issues, among many others, shall be considered.

WIZARDS OF THE COAST, INC.   CORPORATE OFFICE   P.O. Box 707, Renton, WA 98057-0707   PHONE (425) 226-6500   www.wizards.com

Streamlining. AD&D contains many redundancies. Further, perhaps certain things (like ability score bonuses) can be made more universal.

Portability. AD&D should be able to be utilized by a DM to create the fantasy setting of his choice. The Base Campaign. That said, we have to come up with a baseline on which we base our presentation of "setting" material races, equipment, skills, magic, etc.

Hard Choices. The game should contain hard choices rather than restrictions, where possible. Thus, rather than restricting a character class from an option, we give them all possible options, show them the up-side and down-side to each, and let them choose. Making various options (like the value of the various ability scores) more or less equal increases the likelihood of the choices being harder.

Making AD&D More AD&D. Certain aspects of the current edition do not capture the over-riding flavor of the game as well as they could. For example, certain aspects of this level- and classed-based game do not take this all-important factors into account.

Combat Enhancements. Combat needs to be made more interesting, with more options available to players, without becoming more cumbersome.

Character Options. Built within the class system, each would have various options to choose from as levels are gained to increase power and/or flexibility.

Spells. While we want to keep the Vancian system, a number of the spells need reconsideration and modification. Further, we can create new ways of using the existing spell system and spell lists to showcase its flexibility.

Skills. The current proficiency system needs a lot of work, and perhaps can carry more of the system's load than it currently does.

Formatting. The rules need to be straightforward and clear, without a lot of chit-chat (which can come after the rule is presented).

Templating. By using templating, we can make things much easier to follow. Rules, abilities, and functions which could be similar probably should be to decrease contradictions, confusion and make things like computer game translation easier. Templating through classifications for things like monsters can be created to keep our ever-increasing game from picking up contradictions and problems down the road.

Arming the DM. Tell it to them straight. Give them the "why" behind the rules, so that they can make their own calls.

Optional Rules. All rules given in the PHB will be a core set of rules. Options will be left to the DMG. Low Level and High Level. These are the weakest areas of the game and the mechanics may need to be altered to make these levels more playable (and enjoyable).

Playtesting. Gotta have it. Lots. And lots. Period. Not so much a design consideration and just a point that needs to be stressed at every opportunity.

WIZARDS OF THE COAST, INC.   CORPORATE OFFICE   P.O. Box 707, Renton, WA

Once this was set the designers had some guiding lights to turn to regarding the over all design philosophy, and I earned a place in the design credits for "Additional Design & Direction."

At this point I started coming to design meetings on a regular basis. In a few cases I was even able to share house rules I'd come up with in my Chaldea campaign for various topics that I thought previous D&D rules had not handled well. A couple of those ideas even made it into the published game.

One of the ideas that as far as I know came solely from my D&D house rules was an idea I had developed to address the "stacking problem" of magical items (the questions of what magic items work with what other magic items). In previous editions of D&D there weren't any systemic rules that covered what magic items worked with what other magic items. You would simply come across seemingly random rules like "Bracers don't stack with armor." I recommended having a "type" associated with each bonus that would hint at how that bonus worked. For example, a ring of protection would provide a "deflection" bonus to your armor class, where as armor would provide an "armor" bonus to armor class. Players would instantly know that these would stack because their bonuses come from different types of effects, whereas if you have multiple sources that give you the same type of bonus, only the best one works. The design team agreed that this was a much more elegant solution than a big "exceptions" list of what doesn't work with what and the idea was enthusiastically incorporated, much to my delight.

In other cases my idea on how to solve a problem wasn't necessarily a great solution, but I could point to it and say, "Well, at least design me something that's as good as this!"

This happened with the multi-class rules. I've never met a gamer who thought the multi-class rules from previous editions were good. Most gamers I've met along the way feel that a character should have some penalty or restriction on picking up new classes but in general should be able to do so without getting totally messed up. As drafts of 3rd edition D&D came in, this important topic kept getting "glossed over" with multi-class rules that in my opinion just didn't make much sense. So I wrote some multi-class rules myself based on my house rules and shared them with the team. These rules were better than what was in the current draft at the time in that they gave players more flexibility in terms of combining classes, adding classes during their career, dropping classes, or simply maintaining a class or two while advancing in others. This had the flexibility I was looking for, but it still needed refinement.

By this time Jonathan Tweet was on the team and he took this call to action seriously and made what I think was one of the biggest breakthroughs in 3rd edition D&D design: multi-classing rules.

The idea of designing hit points, to-hit bonuses, and saving throw bonuses in such a way that you simply add these bonuses from all your classes together is brilliant. It seems so obvious now, but it wasn't that obvious then or I think it would have shown up as a published variant years ago.

Maybe it did and no one noticed.

Johnathan Tweet Joins the Design Team

One of the fundamental reasons I felt there would be significant synergies in combining TSR and Wizards of the Coast was that each company had strengths to complement the other company's deficiencies. Wizards of the Coast had maintained dominance in the trading card game market through superior design and development skills—no one had been able to match the game design behind Magic: The Gathering. But Wizards' attempts at developing the world of Magic into a successful world or story had been met with only modest results. Conversely, while I had been critical of TSR's rules development for D&D, I greatly admired their success in developing a line of novels and a presence in the book trade.

Consequently, while I felt that the initial TSR rules designers had a great command of the AD&D game as it stood, I was worried that most of them had spent most of their careers designing source material instead of hard core rules development. I

The Fifth Beatle?
by Ed Stark

At the time Jonathan took over the lead designer position for 3.0 we had a major shift in RPG R&D's organizational structure. The brand team, led by Ryan Dancey, separated itself from the R&D process. Ryan, Cindi Rice, Jim Butler, David Wise, and others became the new RPG Business Team while Bill Slavicsek headed up the R&D side of the show. Rich Baker, who had been on the 3rd edition Design Team, became the Alternity Creative Director, Thomas Reid became the FORGOTTEN REALMS/Worlds Creative Director, and I became the D&D Creative Director. This was the first time in my knowledge that the heads of the RPG R&D design and editing

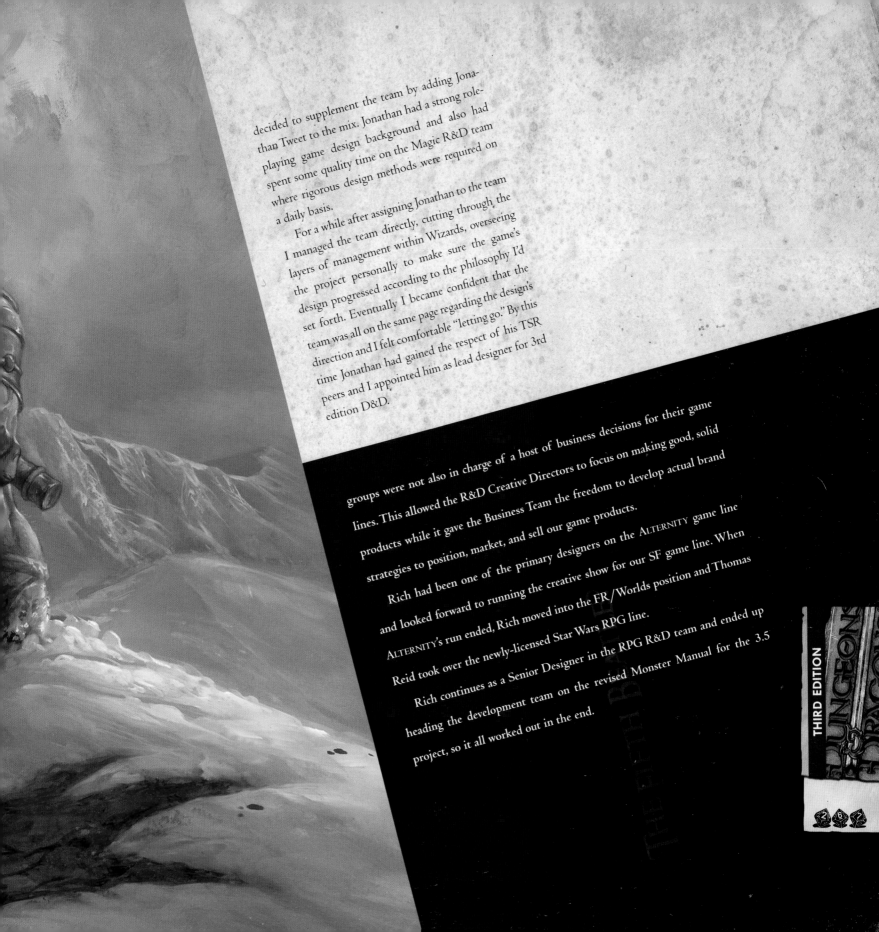

decided to supplement the team by adding Jonathan Tweet to the mix. Jonathan had a strong role-playing game design background and also had spent some quality time on the Magic R&D team where rigorous design methods were required on a daily basis.

For a while after assigning Jonathan to the team I managed the team directly, cutting through the layers of management within Wizards, overseeing the project personally to make sure the game's design progressed according to the philosophy I'd set forth. Eventually I became confident that the team was all on the same page regarding the design's direction and I felt comfortable "letting go." By this time Jonathan had gained the respect of his TSR peers and I appointed him as lead designer for 3rd edition D&D.

groups were not also in charge of a host of business decisions for their game lines. This allowed the R&D Creative Directors to focus on making good, solid products while it gave the Business Team the freedom to develop actual brand strategies to position, market, and sell our game products.

Rich had been one of the primary designers on the ALTERNITY game line and looked forward to running the creative show for our SF game line. When ALTERNITY's run ended, Rich moved into the FR/Worlds position and Thomas Reid took over the newly-licensed Star Wars RPG line.

Rich continues as a Senior Designer in the RPG R&D team and ended up heading the development team on the revised Monster Manual for the 3.5 project, so it all worked out in the end.

Clash of Culture?
By Ed Stark

This is a place where TSR's old style and Wizards' modern perspective ran headlong into each other. Despite objections from virtually all the creative staff involved, TSR followed virtually every other publisher of fantasy art by portraying fantasy characters in "cheesecake" (and "beefcake") illustrations. Trying to get a female warrior wearing anything but a chainmail bikini was sometimes rather difficult.

If the campaign setting didn't dictate that male and female characters should be shown fully clothed and in reasonable outfits, we'd often get these images "because that's what the audience wants."

Wizards, however, supplied a different perspective. Wizards said, "We don't think that, given a choice, that's really what the audience wants, and we're willing to say we don't want that. We want to portray empowered, interesting characters of both genders." Female paladins should wear full armor. Female rogues don't wear miniskirts to adventure in dungeons.

LOOK AND FEEL

Illustrations, maps, and graphics have always played an important role in Dungeons & Dragons, and this role has only increased over time. In the early days the novelty of Dungeons & Dragons was sufficient to carry sales, but over time it became necessary to continually raise the bar with better illustrations and a higher proportion of color art in the core rules books.

With the publication of 3rd edition D&D on the horizon we challenged the art department with the fundamental question of how they would respond to the challenges of the market and raise the bar once again. Frankly, I personally had no idea how we would do this, but thankfully the artists had a great idea—a more realistic portrayal of D&D characters.

Until now D&D art, while great art, didn't really reflect what D&D characters would really look like. D&D art was too "clean." Heroes and heroines were shown with armor and weapons but not the "tools of the trade" that most D&D characters would typically have. The art department proposed a new look for D&D, one in which the characters would be armed realistically. I was immediately sold on the concept when I saw an early draft of the rogue Lidda. Instead being dressed like the traditional thief with just a dagger and a cloak, Lidda had soft leather armor and was armed with thieving tools, a silk rope, a belt with potions, magical jewelry, and so on—just like a female rogue halfling PC would probably be.

The new look drew enthusiastic support from staff and playtesters alike, and the art department, thanks significantly to Todd Lockwood, Sam Wood, and Arnie Swenkel, did a fantastic job defining a look for D&D that was new, yet fit the genre as well.

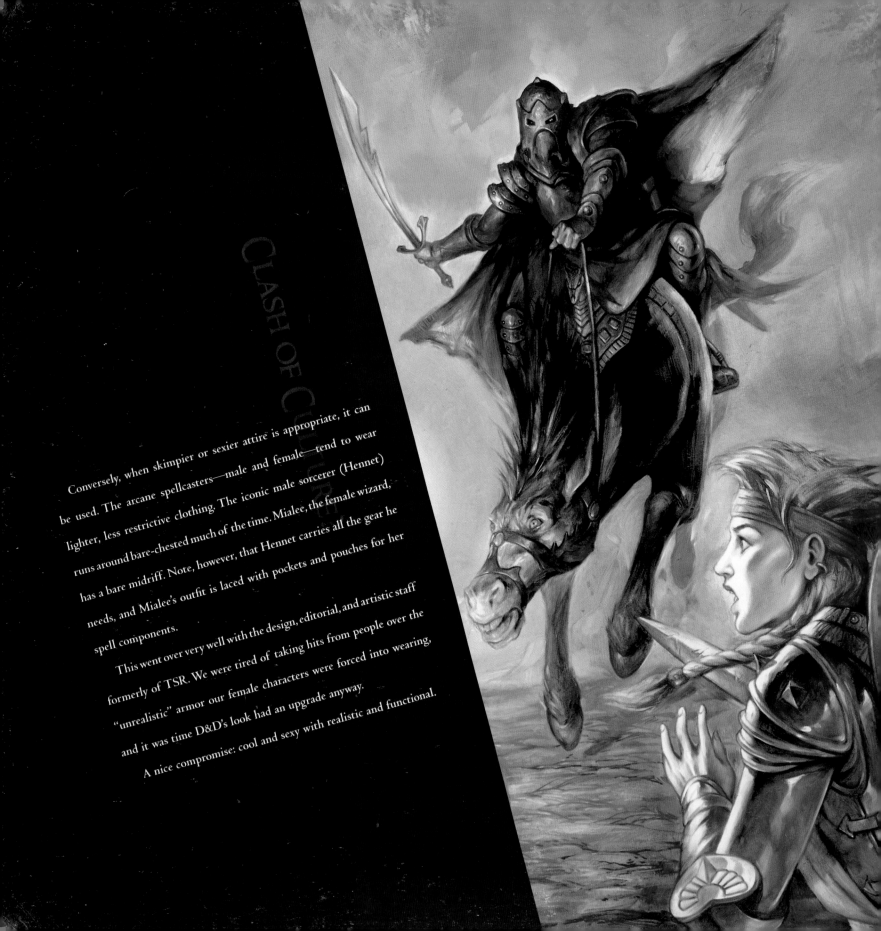

Conversely, when skimpier or sexier attire is appropriate, it can be used. The arcane spellcasters—male and female—tend to wear lighter, less restrictive clothing. The iconic male sorcerer (Hennet) runs around bare-chested much of the time. Mialee, the female wizard, has a bare midriff. Note, however, that Hennet carries all the gear he needs, and Mialee's outfit is laced with pockets and pouches for her spell components.

This went over very well with the design, editorial, and artistic staff formerly of TSR. We were tired of taking hits from people over the "unrealistic" armor our female characters were forced into wearing, and it was time D&D's look had an upgrade anyway.

A nice compromise: cool and sexy with realistic and functional.

While the over all design philosophy could not rightly be left to popular vote, I was a strong advocate of having an extensive list of playtesters involved in the development of 3rd edition. At several points in the development of the system, we released new versions of the rules to the playtesters and solicited their inputs. The work of coordinating so many playtest groups was big enough that the responsibility was assigned to Kim Mohan with the understanding that this would be a major portion of his work responsibility.

In many cases the comments from playtesters were brought into design meetings between Jonathan, Monte, and Skip. It's hard to pinpoint exactly how much influence these comments had, but they were definitely omnipresent. I can recall two specific examples where playtest comments caused a lot of debate.

One of these was with the magic missile spell. Throughout 3rd edition D&D design one of the things we strove for was consistent application of how rules would apply to various magical or natural phenomena. One of these was that every targeted phenomenon would either require a to-hit roll, or a reflex save to dive out of the way. Examples of the first were things like attack rolls or ray spells, whereas examples of the latter were effects that would let you partially get out of the way (like a lightning bolt spell) or dive completely out of the way (like a flaming sphere spell). To keep with this philosophy we changed the magic missile spell from doing 1d4+1 damage per missile, with no to-hit roll or saving throw, to 1d6+1 damage per missile, but with a save to half damage. We figured this was roughly equivalent to the older version of the spell, as it had more damage potential, but if the target saved the damage would be less, basically averaging out.

This change was very unpopular among playtesters though! The outcry against this change was so significant that we decided against the revision and changed the spell back to its original form, in spite of the inconsistency this created between design theory and application.

In another situation we made a conscious decision to go against the preferences of the playtesters—this was the case with the question of whether to use cyclical initiative or re-roll initiative rolls for each round of combat. Traditionally in D&D players would re-roll initiative at the beginning of each round of combat and then declare their actions for the round. Actions would be resolved in order of initiative, modified by the speed of their actions. For 3rd edition we proposed a cyclical initiative system where the initiative roll would be made only once per combat, at the beginning, and would determine the order in which player actions would take place for the rest of that battle. This change was not very popular with playtesters, and the design group was disappointed that this change was not recognized as enough of an improvement to be worthy of a change in the rules. After much debate the designers decided to stay with their decision of a cyclical initiative system because it saves time in a fight. It also makes it simpler to run a game, since there's no need for a pre-declaration of actions but rather a system where each character acts in order and chooses his or her (or its!) action when that character's initiative comes up.

The comments from the playtesters were extremely helpful in developing 3rd edition D&D. In most cases playtest comments helped us find problems we otherwise overlooked or fix problems we didn't think were that bad. In a couple of cases we went against playtest feedback, but in those cases we were conscious of the fact that we were making a risky decision. In such cases we gave the design decision tougher scrutiny through internal debate to make sure it was being made for the greater benefit of the game.

OGL STANDS FOR "ARE YOU INSANE?!" ...OR MAYBE NOT

BY ED STARK

When Ryan Dancey and Peter Adkison explained the d20/OGL license to the creative staff of Wizards of the Coast—particularly those who'd been working on DUNGEONS & DRAGONS for many years—they were not, shall we say, applauded wholeheartedly. Ryan, in many ways, was still an "outsider" brought into handle "the business" while we got on with the important "creative" stuff.

We couldn't understand why the owner of the company and the brand manager of the world's most successful roleplaying game line would want to give away the rules set that made D&D such a success in the first place.

I have to give both Ryan and Peter credit, however. They stuck it out. Ryan came down and talked over the d20/OGL license with us over and over again. He showed us how the OGL and how the d20 license would game would benefit from the OGL and how the d20 license would actually expand our audience.

Peter and Ryan might have gone forward with their plans even if they couldn't convince most of the creative staff they knew what they were doing, but I applaud them, in retrospect, for being so patient and taking the time to explain how the license would work and how it would help D&D grow stronger and more interesting. I just got back from a game store, and I've never seen so much stuff compatible with D&D in my life.

D20 AND THE OPEN GAMING LICENSE

When we released the third edition of Dungeons & Dragons, we also decided to launch the d20 Open Gaming License. The basic idea here was to grant the gaming industry at large a broad, royalty-free license, to publish source material compatible with the Dungeons & Dragons game. This seemed like a crazy idea at the time, and still does to some, but I believe it was an amazingly good decision for Wizards of the Coast.

This concept was largely the brainchild of Ryan Dancey. Ryan is one of those very rare people in the gaming industry who is smart, is good at business, understands the gaming industry, and actually plays games. When I was CEO at Wizards there were a small number of people who I would regularly bounce ideas off of just to see what they'd think, whether the idea had anything to do with their department or not. Ryan and I didn't always agree, but he always got me thinking.

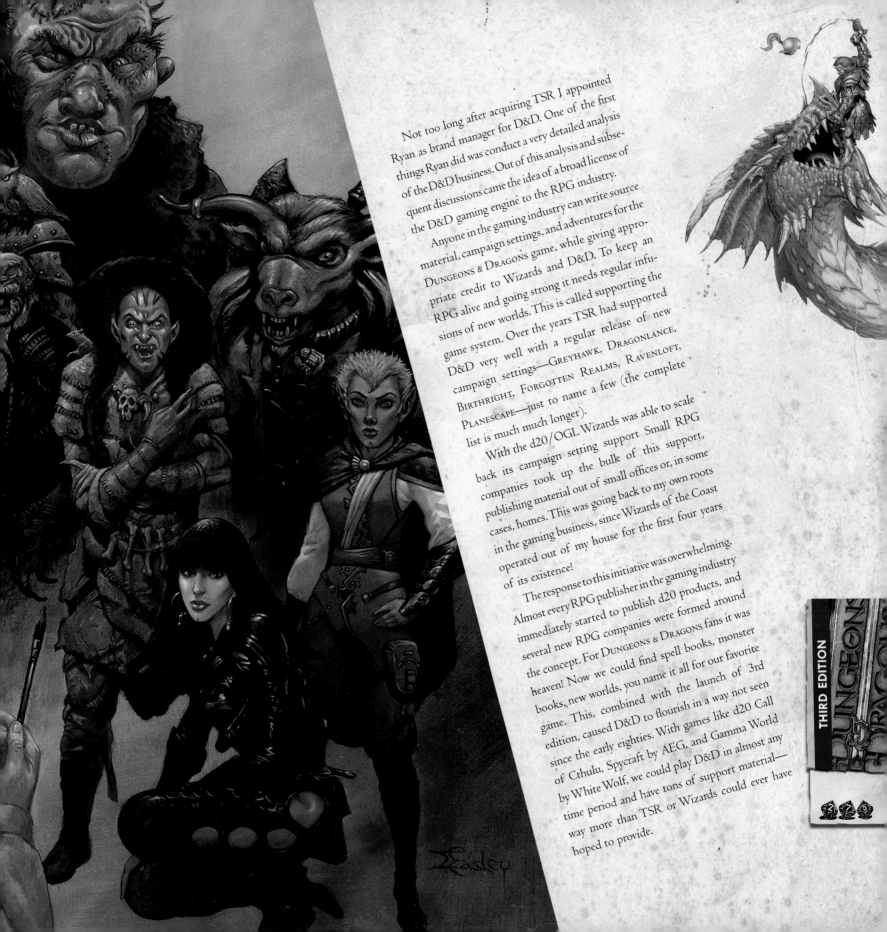

Not too long after acquiring TSR I appointed Ryan as brand manager for D&D. One of the first things Ryan did was conduct a very detailed analysis of the D&D business. Out of this analysis and subsequent discussions came the idea of a broad license of the D&D gaming engine to the RPG industry.

Anyone in the gaming industry can write source material, campaign settings, and adventures for the DUNGEONS & DRAGONS game, while giving appropriate credit to Wizards and D&D. To keep an RPG alive and going strong it needs regular infusions of new worlds. This is called supporting the game system. Over the years TSR had supported D&D very well with a regular release of new campaign settings—GREYHAWK, DRAGONLANCE, BIRTHRIGHT, FORGOTTEN REALMS, RAVENLOFT, PLANESCAPE—just to name a few (the complete list is much much longer).

With the d20/OGL Wizards was able to scale back its campaign setting support. Small RPG companies took up the bulk of this support, publishing material out of small offices or, in some cases, homes. This was going back to my own roots in the gaming business, since Wizards of the Coast operated out of my house for the first four years of its existence!

The response to this initiative was overwhelming. Almost every RPG publisher in the gaming industry immediately started to publish d20 products, and several new RPG companies were formed around the concept. For DUNGEONS & DRAGONS fans it was heaven! Now we could find spell books, monster books, new worlds, you name it all for our favorite game. This, combined with the launch of 3rd edition, caused D&D to flourish in a way not seen since the early eighties. With games like d20 Call of Cthulu, Spycraft by AEG, and Gamma World by White Wolf, we could play D&D in almost any time period and have tons of support material—way more than TSR or Wizards could ever have hoped to provide.

INTO THE
FUTURE
BY ED STARK

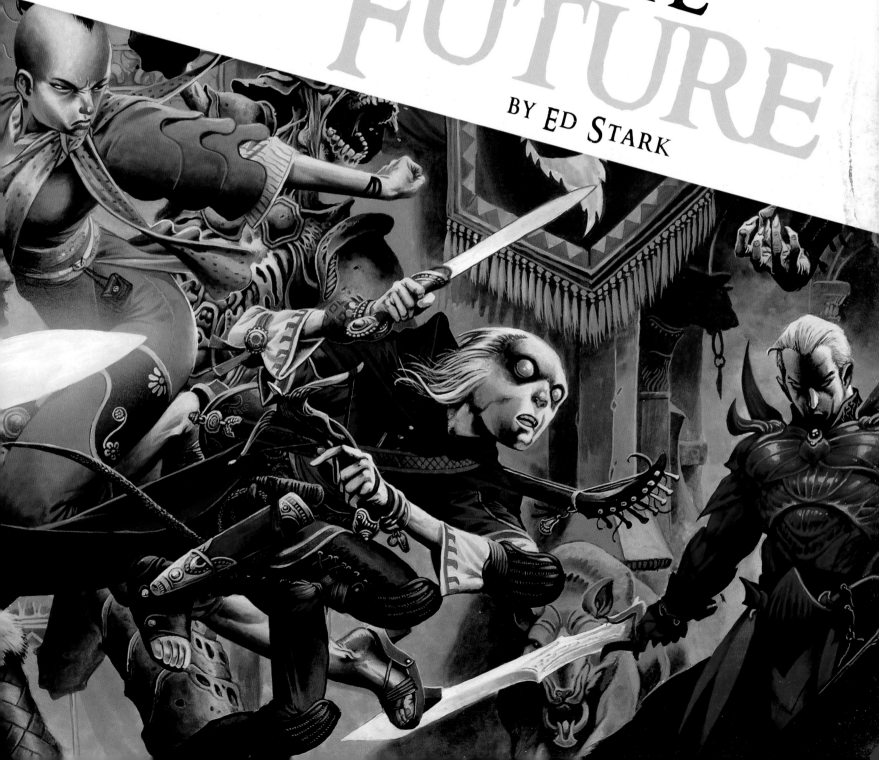

It's a sign of the times these days that when most people hear the words "roleplaying game," they think about something you do on your computer. That's fine, but old die-hards like me remember when the only way to play an RPG was to sit down at a table with your friends, some pretty thick books, and a bunch of funny-shaped dice.

It's to its credit that DUNGEONS & DRAGONS not only established the form and content for the earliest computer games but it continues to thrive in the competitive computer gaming market. Fantasy Roleplaying Games are all over the software stores, but the name recognition and the look, feel, and gameplay of a true D&D game still commands respect.

Back in the old days at TSR, computer games grew up with the company. A game company named SSI published classic D&D games under what became known as the "Gold Box" label. The first of these classics was called Pool of Radiance, and it became one of the most popular computer games of the time.

As TSR got older, D&D computer games got fewer and fewer. TSR itself made a few forays into electronic publishing but with only a modicum of success. Computer game design houses moved fast, and TSR still focused on its paper-and-pencil market.

When Wizards of the Coast acquired TSR, however, it put computer games up a notch or two on the company's radar. There was a game in development called Neverwinter Nights based, in part, on an old MUD operating on America Online. A design house in Edmonton, Canada, called BioWare had been given the task of updating the game and making it more interesting and more exciting to play.

This dovetailed very nicely with Peter Adkison's and Ryan Dancey's plans for D&D. The creative staff at Wizards was hard at work trying to plan out the future of D&D, specifically in regards the third edition of the game. Bill Slavicsek, the director of the RPG department, and Ryan Dancey talked to BioWare's software designers, and the race was on: Could Wizards of the Coast's crack design staff put together enough material, fast enough to satisfy the BioWare game designers, or would we end up with another "D&D computer game" that didn't look at all like D&D?

It was quite a race. I was involved as the Creative Director for D&D and had to work with the design team to make sure they made their milestones. Meanwhile, up north, the BioWare folks had their own deadlines. Months went by without any communication from either side. The BioWare designers had early drafts of the D&D 3rd edition rules, but that was it. Wizards hadn't had much contact with them and didn't until Hasbro purchased Wizards of the Coast and subsequently sold the rights to D&D computer games to Atari.

Then the approvals started rolling in. I received a large design document, hundreds of pages long, showing how BioWare's designers would address the D&D rules. We knew that we'd made great strides in D&D's ruleset to make it more compatible with a computer's capabilities, but we knew things weren't perfect. One look at that document, though, and I hadn't realized how imperfect they were.

Anthony Valterra, Business Manager for D&D at the time, understood a lot about computers I'll never understand, so I got his attention. "This isn't D&D!" I said, showing him the document. That pushed a few alarm bells, and, before I knew it, we were on a plane to Edmonton. Edmonton is nice. There's a huge shopping mall, the city is scenic, and the restaurants are . . . oh, who am I kidding. We were there to work. We had three days and hundreds of notes to go through.

281

We spent the next three days painstakingly (and painfully, for some) going over the NWN design document and playing through the latest build of the game. Amazingly, the BioWare folks remained calm and patient even though many of them were putting in sixty-hour weeks and two guys from America had just come to tell them they'd have to make significant, eleventh-hour changes. Tim Campbell of Atari spent more than a little time worrying about the release dates, but while he and Anthony conferred, I worked with Trent and the designers.

As a result, many changes were made to the NWN final game and many compromises occurred. Not everything that could work as part of a D&D computer game did work that way but, surprisingly, most of it did. As it turned out, the BioWare designers were all big-time D&D fans, and they wanted the game to be as much about D&D as we did.

As a result, Anthony and I left for America severely sleep-deprived but feeling a lot better. When Neverwinter Nights released, we saw the first in what would be a long line of D&D computer games.

Soon after Hasbro acquired Wizards in 2001, the company sold the computer game rights to Dungeons & Dragons to Atari. Neither Wizards nor TSR—nor Hasbro, for that matter—had had much success in the computer game industry. Atari, on the other hand, invented success in the home console market and did pretty well in computer games as well.

Hasbro, Atari, and Wizards of the Coast work together to produce D&D games like Neverwinter Nights, D&D Heroes, and other projects. It's amazing, but sometimes when you get the experts involved, things really can work out. Right now I'm looking forward to a series of wonderful games that will release over the next couple of years and will take D&D to millions of dedicated computer and video gamers.

CREDITS

EDITING: Peter Archer

ART DIRECTION: Matt Adelsperger

GRAPHIC DESIGN: Matt Adelsperger & Brian Fraley

TYPESETTING: Matt Adelsperger, Brian Fraley & Angelika Lokotz

IMAGING: Travis Adams & Jay Sakamoto

DEARCHIVING: Bryn Rector & Neil Shinkle

PRODUCTION ENGINEERING: Randall Crews & Josh Fischer

PREPRESS: Jefferson Dunlap

PROOFREADING: Cortney Marabetta

FRONT COVER ART

Larry Elmore

BACK COVER ART

Jeff Dee, Erol Otus, James Roslof, Dave C. Sutherland III, D.A. Trampier, Tim Truman, Tom Wham

INTERIOR ART

Carlo Arellano, Tom Baxa, Paul Bonner, Brom, Jeff Butler, Clyde Caldwell, Carl Critchlow, Jeff Dee, Jeff Easley, Larry Elmore, Fred Fields, Scott M. Fischer, Dan Frazier, Tim Hildebrandt, Jim Holloway, Daniel R. Horne, Paul Jaquays, Diesel, John & Laura Lakey, Todd Lockwood, Monte Michael Moore, Mark Nelson, William O'Connor, Erik Olsen, Glen Orbik, Erol Otus, Keith Parkinson, Alan Pollack, rk Post, Adam Rex, Wayne Reynolds, Robh Ruppel, James Roslof, Dave Simons, Ellym Sirac, Greg Staples, Matt Stawicki, Jon Sullivan, Dave C. Sutherland III, Justin Sweet, Tony Szczudlo, D.A. Trampier, Tim Truman, Walter Velez, Anthony S. Waters, Tom Wham, Sam Wood, and Mark Zug

PHOTOGRAPHY

Matt Adelsperger, Harold Johnson, & Alex Tinsman

SPECIAL THANKS

Nick Bartoletti, Joe Fernandez, & Angie Lokotz.
Also to Paula Greenfield and CelebritySource
and to Cindi Rice.